CAPTURING ANGELS

Virginia ANDREWS

**SIMON &
SCHUSTER**

London · New York · Sydney · Toronto · New Delhi

A CBS COMPANY

First published as an ebook in the US by Pocket Books, 2012
A division of Simon & Schuster, Inc.
First published in hardback in Great Britain by
Simon & Schuster UK Ltd, 2013
A CBS COMPANY

1 3 5 7 9 10 8 6 4 2

Simon & Schuster UK Ltd
1st Floor
222 Gray's Inn Road
London WC1X 8HB

www.simonandschuster.co.uk

Simon & Schuster Sydney, Australia
Simon & Schuster New Delhi, India

A CIP catalogue record for this book
is available from the British Library

Hardback ISBN: 978-1-47112-863-9
Ebook ISBN: 978-1-47111-344-4

Printed and bound by CPI Group (UK) Ltd, Croydon, CR0 4YY

CAPTURING ANGELS

CAPTURING ANGELS

Virginia Andrews® Books

The Dollanganger Family Series
Flowers in the Attic
Petals on the Wind
If There Be Thorns
Seeds of Yesterday
Garden of Shadows

The Casteel Family Series
Heaven
Dark Angel
Fallen Hearts
Gates of Paradise
Web of Dreams

The Cutler Family Series
Dawn
Secrets of the Morning
Twilight's Child
Midnight Whispers
Darkest Hour

The Landry Family Series
Ruby
Pearl in the Mist
All That Glitters
Hidden Jewel
Tarnished Gold

The Logan Family Series
Melody
Heart Song
Unfinished Symphony
Music of the Night
Olivia

The Orphans Miniseries
Butterfly
Crystal
Brooke
Raven
Runaways (full-length novel)

The Wildflowers Miniseries
Misty
Star
Jade
Cat
Into the Garden (full-length novel)

My Sweet Audrina
(does not belong to a series)

The Hudson Family Series
Rain
Lightning Strikes
Eye of the Storm
The End of the Rainbow

The Shooting Stars Series
Cinnamon
Ice
Rose
Honey
Falling Stars

The De Beers Family Series
Willow
Wicked Forest
Twisted Roots
Into the Woods
Hidden Leaves

The Broken Wings Series
Broken Wings
Midnight Flight

The Gemini Series
Celeste
Black Cat
Child of Darkness

The Shadows Series
April Shadows
Girl in the Shadows

The Early Spring Series
Broken Flower
Scattered Leaves

The Secrets Series
Secrets in the Attic
Secrets in the Shadows

The Delia Series
Delia's Crossing
Delia's Heart
Delia's Gift

The Heavenstone Series
The Heavenstone Secrets
Secret Whispers

The March Family Series
Family Storms
Cloudburst

Daughter of Darkness
Into the Darkness

Prologue

All around me, everything was going on as if nothing was unusual, nothing terrible had happened. People were talking to each other and to sales personnel, announcements were being made periodically about something on sale, and other people were laughing and strolling through the various departments as if for them it was a Sunday walk in the park.

The voice I heard, however, was whispering. It seemed to come from the darkest corner of my mind and slip into my ear.

"She's gone," it said. "Your precious daughter is missing."

I started to turn slowly, pausing at nine o'clock, five o'clock, and three o'clock like some mechanical mannequin in the showcase window of Lesson's Department Store, where I had come to buy my mother-in-law a birthday present. I found myself facing the saleslady, who stood there holding the pair of earrings I had chosen, her face frozen in a confused smile. She had been talking to me, but I hadn't heard a word, nor did I hear anything she was saying now. Her lips moved, but the voice whispering in my ear overpowered anyone or anything else.

"Missing," I heard myself say.

"Pardon?" I heard the saleslady say.

"My daughter, Mary. She's not standing beside me!" I screamed and started to charge to my right, calling for her, not seeing her, and then turning to charge to my left. I glanced back at the saleslady behind the jewelry counter. She was grimacing at me and shaking her head.

Then I started running through the store.

As I ran, I fingered the silver cross John had given me on my birthday last year. It had a diamond at the center. Maybe we never come right out and say it, but we wear religious icons for protection. Mary had one, too, I thought, trying to keep out the troubled thoughts that were streaming out of the darkest corners of my brain behind the whisper. It would protect her. Surely it would protect her. Please let it protect her.

Two security guards came running after me as I went up and down the aisles looking for her.

"Hey, miss, lady, hold on," one called. He had a potbelly that bounced as if he had swallowed a basketball. I thought he would have a heart attack before he reached me. His face was more of a burnt orange than red, and his nostrils enlarged as he snorted oxygen.

The African-American guard who came with him was a good five inches taller and firmly built, with hair the color of charcoal briquettes. He had unusually small ebony eyes. They looked like last-minute facial features substituted for correctly shaped and sized ones that had run out. However, when he spoke, he did have a commanding, assertive voice, one that in most circumstances would give the listener some sense of security and confidence. I was desperately in need of someone to take command. The panic was turning me into a frightened little girl again.

I recall these details so well because at the time, I was looking to them to rescue me from what could potentially be a great family tragedy. I wanted them to be special men, to be like two comic-book heroes, capes and all, swooping in to save the day. There would be flashes of lightning, puffs of smoke, and voilà, my five-year-old daughter, Mary, would be restored to my side. Was I just an ignorant innocent who was blind to all the pain and misery that swirled around us?

"What's going on, ma'am?" the taller one asked. His identification badge read "Tom Miller." "What's wrong? How can we help you?"

"My little girl, Mary. She's gone."

I looked around to emphasize.

"Gone?" the heavy security guard repeated, looking at his partner as if he needed an English translation. His badge read "Burt Wallace."

"She's gone! Missing! She was at my side, and now she's gone. She's only five years old!"

"Maybe she's just wandered off to a different part of the store. Why don't you just relax a moment and let us search the area?" Tom Miller said. He put his hand on mine.

"I've been doing that!" I shouted, even though they were right beside me. His hand flew off mine. "What do you think I've been doing?"

Burt Wallace signaled to a floor manager who was standing just off to the right. He had the palms of his hands pressed against his chest. My running down the aisles and screaming for Mary apparently had turned him to stone. In fact, he was standing so still that for a moment, I thought he was a store mannequin with his mouth shaped in an oval, like an egg. Finally, the lean young man hurried to me.

"What is it?" he asked, and tucked his thin lips into the corners of his mouth, grimacing like someone who was anticipating bad news from his doctor.

"Her daughter is missing, Mr. Mulligan," Tom Miller said. "She's only five."

Just to hear someone repeat it made my heart jump and then plunge.

"Five?"

"Yes, actually a little more than five," I said. To hammer that home, I added, "It's been four and a half months since we celebrated her birthday. We took her out to dinner with both sets of grandparents."

I don't know why I gave him that information, but he nodded as if he had known. I was so afraid of embarrassing myself with tears, which would only make them uncomfortable and hinder them from helping me. I didn't want them to waste an iota of a second comforting me. *Find Mary*, was all I could think.

"Find her!" I ordered. Why were they just standing there?

"Please, stay calm. How long has she been missing?" the manager asked.

"How long? Only minutes," I said, not sure now exactly when I had lost track of Mary.

"Minutes? Okay. Then she can't be far. Let's go over here while they conduct a search."

"I've been searching," I told him. I could feel my jaw tighten, my throat closing.

"They'll make a wider search. It doesn't take long for a child to wander farther away. She might even have gone up a floor," he said.

"No, she wouldn't. No. She would never wander that far away from me. Not my Mary. No," I insisted.

"Okay, okay. Let them look," he said, indicating a chair for me in the women's shoe department.

Reluctantly, I sat with my knees together, my hands nervously twisting on my lap like two separate little animals, trying not to ball them into fists.

"What does she look like?" Tom Miller asked, following us.

I had a picture of Mary in my purse and dug it out quickly.

"Recent?" he asked.

"The picture is four and a half months old. We took it on her birthday," I said.

He looked at the manager, and then he nodded and showed it to Burt Wallace, who was still wiping the sweat off his forehead and cheeks.

"You see," I said, pointing to the picture. "She has a wonderful smile. It was a happy, happy day for her, for all of us, but she's always like that," I knew I was babbling, but I couldn't help it. "You have to understand. This is not just another mother talking about her child. My daughter's very special. She has such a soft, melodic voice, and there's so much wonder in her eyes that she makes everyone and anyone who meets her feel good about themselves. Sick people feel better, and sad, depressed people become hopeful, cheery. People tell me that all the time."

Now they all nodded as if they were large puppets

and someone was pulling their strings simultaneously. I continued my rambling, but I was terrified and couldn't stop.

"No matter what your mood is before you see her, you're smiling when you leave her. She has wonderful energy about her. It's soothing, healing."

The men looked at each other again.

"If your day begins gray and depressing and you meet Mary, it's bright and warm again. People tell me she makes the sound of their own laughter ring in their ears like sleigh bells on Christmas. That's my Mary. She's too sweet to recognize evil, don't you see? You have to understand that. If you don't, you won't . . . I mean . . . you could miss something important and—"

"Okay, okay. Give us a chance to comb the whole first floor. I'm sure we'll find her," Tom Miller said, and then they both began to search.

"Let me get you some water," the manager said. He looked as if he didn't want to be near me, as if he thought my terror might be catching. I shook my head, but he went to get the water anyway.

I was torn between getting up and running through the store again, screaming Mary's name, and just sitting there obediently and waiting. I looked at the entrance not far from me, but I told myself she wouldn't leave the store without me. She just wouldn't. And she would never take the escalator up to a higher floor. She had to be someplace nearby. Maybe she hadn't heard me calling to her.

I smiled to myself the way someone who was humoring me might smile. Maybe I hadn't been shouting as loudly as I thought I had. They'd find her. In just a few moments, they'd bring her back, all smiles. Or maybe she would just appear and explain how she'd had to help someone who was very sad or very sick. Mary wouldn't cry. She would be sorry, but she wouldn't cry. She would know how frightened I was, and she would just try to reassure me. That's why she was so special. What other five-year-old would have that sort of insight?

I debated whether I would tell John later after it was all over. Why make a big deal of it and get my husband all upset? I thought. He hated reprimanding her. Whenever he did, he looked as if he'd be the one to cry. He'd catch me looking at him with a smile on my face, and he'd screw his face back quickly to an expression as stern as he could manage. *No*, I thought. *I'll bawl her out, and that will be enough.*

"You can't go off helping everyone you think needs help," I would tell her. She always tried to comfort another child who was crying or afraid or just tired. It was a wonder to watch how they would calm as if they'd come through a cold rain into the warm sunshine of her smile.

I took a deep breath, closed my eyes, and then looked up when I sensed the manager standing there with a cup of water.

Maybe it's miraculous holy water, I thought. Half-kidding, John would tell me that. *I'll take a sip, and then Mary will appear.* I reached for the glass, thanked him, and drank.

"She's a good girl, a very good girl. She wouldn't do anything to bring pain and worry to anyone, especially to me. That's why this is all so strange."

He nodded, holding that idiotic smile, but I ignored it.

"She enjoys going to church. How many little girls

enjoy that? She loves the choir, the sound of prayers, and the beauty of the church itself. You know Father McDermott, by any chance, the Church of the Sacred Heart?"

He shook his head. "No, sorry."

"He's always fawning over her. Everyone does. You don't have to bribe Mary to do good things. She does things from the heart."

"I'm sure she's just fine," he said, looking more and more uncomfortable, and then his smile faded when he looked up. The two security guards appeared, now accompanied by a third. They shook their heads at him.

"There's no sign of her in the store on the first floor, and we called up to the second," Burt Wallace said. "But no one's seen a little girl alone up there."

"Would she go out of the store?" Tom Miller asked me, nodding toward the closest entrance.

"No, never. I was just telling your manager what a good girl she is. Something's not right. It's not right!"

I stood up. Panic, which had been spinning my heart like a top, suddenly seized it in a tight grip and was squeezing the blood out of it. I felt as if I had just stepped into an icy lake and was quickly sinking. I had to take action before my body became completely numb.

"Mary!" I screamed, turning every which way. Then I started down another aisle. "Mary, where are you?"

The three guards and the manager followed me, and then the manager took my arm to turn me toward him.

"Relax, ma'am. They've covered the floor. She wouldn't be hiding from you as some sort of childish prank, right?"

"Of course not."

"Okay, we're calling the mall's security department right now," he said. "Try to stay calm."

I could see that the customers nearby were beginning to look disturbed. The gathering of a manager and security guards was unnerving. I was sure that the first thing coming to their minds was that it was a bomb scare. Some were already leaving the store.

I shook my head, pulled my arm out of the manager's grasp, and screamed for Mary again and again. To get me to stop, Tom Miller asked me exactly where I was when I realized Mary was gone. I paused and pointed to the jewelry department. The manager left, repeating that he was going to contact the mall security and the police.

"There was no one else shopping in the mall with you, was there? Someone she would go with outside the store?" Tom Miller asked, looking toward the jewelry counter.

"No. Of course not. I would have told you that immediately."

He nodded. "Does she ever do this? Walk off on her own?"

"Never," I said. "I told you what she was like. Weren't you listening to anything I said? She's a very special five-year-old, and she wouldn't dare cause me any worry!"

"Yeah, well, we've seen kids that age doing things like that," Burt Wallace said. "Special or not, they're just kids, remember."

"Not my Mary. You don't understand. She's far beyond any normal five-year-old. She doesn't wander off without telling me where she is going. She's capable of watching over another five-year-old or a younger child, in fact."

He looked skeptical.

"You don't believe me? I'm telling you something's not right!" I emphasized. I think he thought I might pound on his bloated stomach if he even tried to disagree. He stepped back.

"Just take it easy," Tom Miller said. "We'll get to the bottom of it quickly. Not that much time has passed. We can alert the entire mall."

Again, I wondered just how much time had passed. How long had I ignored her?

A few minutes later, the mall security police arrived and asked me to go with them to their office.

"I don't want to leave the store," I said. "She's here; she's got to be here."

"It looks like she's not," the mall policeman said softly. "Let us get to the bottom of it. Please, ma'am. We want to help you."

"Let them help you," the floor manager pleaded.

I knew he wanted me out of his store, out of his life, but no more than I wanted him and all of this out of mine. I looked around helplessly.

"There's nothing more you can do in here," the manager added. "Please, let them help you."

I looked at him so intently that he blanched. Then he looked down. He couldn't face me. *Maybe he knows something*, I thought. Paranoia was crawling all over me.

Something is not right, I thought, and started out of the store.

1

❦

Blue Ribbon

Reluctantly, I followed the mall police to their office. They told me they were contacting the Los Angeles police.

"Why? Can't you find her yourselves? What are you saying?"

"We're working on it, ma'am, but it's a missing person. We have to contact them," the mall security officer said.

Twice while I waited, I felt myself becoming so faint that I thought I would just keel over on the floor. In fact, I began to look so bad and was so dizzy that paramedics were summoned. When they took my blood pressure and saw how high it was and how fast my heart was pounding, they wanted to take me to the hospital emergency room, but I wouldn't leave until the police came and found Mary.

They came in the form of a detective accompanied by a uniformed patrolman. The detective introduced himself as Lieutenant Samuel Abraham. He spoke in a soft, calm manner, which, although it was reassuring, annoyed me, making me feel as if I was being handled. Because of that, I avoided looking at him and looked down at my hands as I threaded my fingers in and out. This was a nervous gesture I'd had all my life.

Lieutenant Abraham asked me to go over everything again, but he wanted me to begin with when I had left our house in Brentwood with Mary. I was certain he could tell from the tone of my voice that I didn't understand the purpose of that.

"Aren't we wasting time?" I asked. "She is missing here, not back in Brentwood."

"Details are so very important to us now," he told me. "The smallest things will help."

He reached out to take my hand and stop my nervous activity. Finally, I looked directly at him for the first time. Although he didn't look much older than I was, he had an air of maturity and competence. It would sound strange to anyone listening, but I suddenly felt like throwing my arms around his neck and lowering my head to his shoulder just so I could feel the strength in him circling my body, comforting me. *I am just a little girl again*, I thought. *I want Daddy*.

He brushed some of his dark brown hair away from his forehead and fixed his hazel eyes on me.

"For example," he continued, "maybe she was wearing something very distinct, unique." He looked at the information the mall police had written on a form. "Besides a blue skirt, light blue blouse, dark blue cardigan, and white and blue loafers with light blue socks," he continued. "Some mothers have their little girls wearing earrings at this age," he added with a quick shrug and a soft smile.

"No, no earrings. She has a blue ribbon around her hair. She wears it like I do," I said, indicating how my light brown hair was brushed back and fell to the base of my neck. "We have the same color hair, and she loves wearing it however I do."

"See?" he said. "That's not on here." He made it sound like a break in the case. "Go on. You left the house. You're married, I gather."

"Yes, of course. I mean . . . yes, we've been married nearly seven years. Mary's our only child. We've been trying to have another for some time now," I added. I didn't know whether that sort of information was necessary, but I was afraid of leaving something out now that he had pointed out the ribbon I had forgotten. "My husband wanted us to wait until Mary was five. He thought it was a good age difference and best for college planning."

Lieutenant Abraham smiled. "Yes, that's probably very wise."

"John researches everything, even down to a new can opener." I paused. "I don't know why I'm telling you these things," I said with frustration. "I feel like I'm babbling nonsense, like a babbling idiot."

He smiled softly again. "It's all right. I understand. Was your husband home when you left with Mary this morning?"

"No, he had left early for an important business trip."

Lieutenant Abraham nodded and looked at the form. "John Clark Jr. He works for Eternal Software?"

"He's their business manager."

"I see. Where did he go for this business trip?"

"San Bernardino."

"Well, that's just a little more than an hour away. Have we tried to reach him yet?" he asked the mall security guard.

"Not yet."

"Okay. I guess we should be doing that," he said, mostly to me. I nodded and searched my purse for one of John's business cards because they had his mobile number on them, too. I realized that avoiding informing John now was a hope that had dissipated like steam.

I handed Lieutenant Abraham the card.

"Thank you. So, you left the house about what time?"

"Nine-thirty."

"And did you stop anywhere before arriving here?"

"No, we came right here. I went directly to the department store. What, do you think I went somewhere else, forgot my daughter, and came here before I realized it?"

"No, no, of course not. Were you holding your daughter's hand the whole time you were at the mall?"

"Of course."

He looked as if he was swallowing a poison pill and then gently said, "At some point, you must have let go."

The words seemed to go into my ears and plunge down my spine, echoing as they descended. Of course I had to have let her go. Of course this was my fault. Snapping at him or anyone else wasn't going to change that fact.

"I'm not sure when I let go of her hand. I can't remember. It just seems so foggy."

"Sure. I understand." He looked at the mall parking ticket. "Your parking ticket has you here at ten forty-five," he said. "That's a little long for how far you had to come if you were coming here directly."

"Maybe it wasn't exactly nine-thirty," I said. "How can

anyone plan on the traffic here?" My voice was becoming shrill again.

"We just want to lock in these details."

He glanced at John's business card as if he had just realized he was holding it.

"Do you want to call him first?" he asked.

I didn't reply. I was sure I would have trouble speaking. I'd probably start to cry so hard that John wouldn't understand a word.

"We could call him for you," he said. "Let me handle that. I know how upset you are."

"Yes, thank you." I released the pent-up hot air in my lungs. I remember thinking, *This man is very sensitive for a policeman. He reminds me more of a kindly male nurse.*

"I imagine you've been here before with your daughter?"

"Yes, many times since it opened. Well, maybe not many, but at least three."

"Did your daughter ask to go anywhere special in the mall when you arrived? Did she want something to eat? Go to a toy store?"

"No."

"So, you came up the escalator from the parking lot and went directly to the department store. Did you go right to the area where you were when you realized she was missing?"

"Yes, yes," I said. These questions felt like death by a thousand cuts. I threw up my hands. "How could someone take my daughter out of a department store? She wouldn't let anyone forcibly take her. She would scream for me. Someone must have seen her," I said, finally feeling the tears flooding into my eyes.

"We've got people interviewing every salesperson in the store. Well," he said, getting up, "let me phone your husband. You want anything—coffee, cold drink, anything—in the meantime?"

I shook my head and dabbed at the tears on my cheeks. Surely, I thought, any moment someone would come in holding Mary's hand. I stared at the door and with all my might willed it to happen.

When Lieutenant Abraham returned, he had two cups of coffee.

"Just in case," he said, handing one to me. "I just put a little milk in it, but here are some sugar packets if you want."

I immediately put them and the coffee on the desk. He sipped his and looked at me more intently. It was as if he was looking in my face for clues about Mary's disappearance. What was he thinking? That I had made all this up, that I didn't even have a daughter? What?

"Your husband didn't pick up, but I left a message."

"If he's in a meeting, he won't have his phone on," I said. "He's adamant about that and not above chastising anyone who does leave his or her phone on in a meeting."

"Gotcha. Just to be sure, I also called his office and left a message with his secretary."

"Okay."

Just to have something to do with my hands, I picked up the cup of coffee and sipped some. It felt as if it was burning my throat even though it was just warm.

He felt his cell phone vibrate, took it out, and rose to take a few steps away from me. He turned and nodded to me to indicate that it was John. Then he walked a few more steps away to talk. A minute or so later, he turned back to me.

"He was just leaving his meeting. Pretty calm guy," he said.

"Oh, yes, that's my John," I said proudly. My whole body was trembling, but I tried to hide it. "Actually, one of the reasons I fell in love with him was his inner strength and stability. There's no one better in a crisis than my John. He thinks first and never lets his emotions run away with him."

"Not bad qualities to have nowadays," Lieutenant Abraham said.

"He's very religious, too. I think that's where he gets his inner strength."

"Oh? How so?"

It didn't take a genius to see that he wanted to keep me talking.

"John never misses a Sunday at church if he can help it. I'm not as devout, but even if I don't go, my daughter does. He's a big football fan, too."

"Oh, Rams?"

"Believe it or not, he's a Giants fan and a Yankees fan."

"That is surprising. Is he from New York?"

"No, but he went to NYU."

"Ah."

"Graduated with honors. He's a strong man. He'll know what to do," I muttered. "John will know what to do."

"That's good. We've got to keep clear minds, keep thinking about everything. Try to picture the scene again," he added as he sat across from me. He leaned forward and focused on me as if he wanted to hypnotize me. For a moment, I actually wondered if that wasn't a police detective's technique. I'd gladly go into a trance if that would solve the problem, I thought. "Go on, please, visualize," he said.

"I'll try," I said.

"Good." He smiled again. "Let's just go over it all again. Sometimes there's a detail we might have missed or overlooked, okay?"

He's good at this, I thought. *He knows what he's doing. I've got to be more cooperative.* I felt a little more relief, a little sense of calmness. I was happy that he was the detective on duty.

"Yes, yes, of course."

"So, you're at the counter. You're talking to the saleslady. Does your daughter ask anything, want anything? Kids get impatient."

"No, she's a very well-behaved little girl. She never pesters. I told them that. She's being homeschooled, but she already knows a great deal more than the average first- or second-grader, especially when it comes to history. John's hobby is ships in bottles, and he only builds famous ones and then explains them. You should see how patiently she sits and listens. So you see, she wouldn't be impatient in the store. My daughter wouldn't run off. The whole idea is ridiculous."

He paused, sipped some more coffee, and then said in a surprisingly casual tone, "The saleslady doesn't recall a little girl standing beside you."

It felt as if he had delivered the famous bombshell in a courtroom during cross-examination of a witness. It took me a moment to gather my wits and respond. I bit down hard on my lower lip, trying to keep my rage from overflowing like volcanic lava.

"She was probably just intent on making the sale," I said in a very controlled but sharp tone. "She had dollar signs in her eyes that were blocking her vision."

He nodded, with a slight smile crossing his lips, and then sipped his coffee, his eyes still fixed on me with an intensity that was beginning to unnerve me. I closed my eyes and thought about what he had said about my letting go of Mary's hand.

Somewhere else in the mall, in malls across the country, on city and village streets, mothers were walking with their little girls. Statistically, as John might say, there were probably thousands, maybe tens of thousands, of those little girls who were the same age as Mary, many even born on the same day. These mothers had their daughters' hands firmly in their grips. Their eyes went everywhere as they walked. We'd all been made so aware of the dangers that lurked around us, especially for our children. As difficult as it was, all of these mothers tried to remain alert, protective, and sensibly frightened, sensibly because fear could be a good thing. It made us safer. We double-locked our doors and put alarms in our homes and in our cars. We installed cameras on the fronts of our homes, and more and more these days, we were installing them in streets and in stores. John always said that we should be more like London, where there were cameras everywhere.

"Cameras," I said aloud when a thought suddenly followed. "Doesn't the store have a security camera? We can see that the saleslady is wrong."

Lieutenant Abraham nodded. "Mall security is checking it out right now," he said. "Now, I'm not jumping to any conclusions here," he continued, "but it's important to cover everything in a case like this, okay? Don't jump to any conclusions from my questions."

"Yes, yes," I said, now feeling more impatient now than frightened.

"Have you noticed any strangers in your neighborhood lately who happened to be watching your house, your family? Have you noticed any stranger, the same stranger, who just happens to be in places you are? Something like that?"

"No."

"You didn't notice anyone lurking near your home?"

"No, of course not. I would have mentioned something like that to my husband immediately, and he certainly would have warned me. We live on a cul-de-sac, so someone loitering would be very obvious."

"Do you usually go shopping alone with your daughter? Any friends go along?"

"Sometimes, yes. I just . . . what difference does that make?"

"I don't know," he said, almost smiling. "I have to be as thorough as I can here. What about other relatives? Anyone you're not getting along with, anyone who is critical of how you bring up your daughter, maybe?"

"No," I said. "Both my husband and I are only children. My parents are retired. My mother had me late in life. They live in Rancho Mirage in a development. My father's addicted to golf," I added. He widened his eyes and smiled, but I wasn't trying to be funny. John repeated it so often that it became attached to any description of my parents whenever anyone asked about them.

"How do you get along with your in-laws?"

"Fine," I said.

"Like tolerable fine or . . ."

"We get along," I said. "I don't understand these questions. This has nothing to do with family. In fact, we're a perfect family."

"Yes, I'm sure," he said. If he was bothered by my attitude, he didn't show it. "I had a case recently, though, where a woman's mother-in-law did something like this to teach her son's wife a lesson. She thought she was too careless with their child. Most missing children are actually family-related abductions."

"Well, that's not us. Neither John nor his mother has ever been critical of the way I take care of our daughter. No one has, especially not my in-laws or parents. If anything, they're always accusing me of doting on her too much."

"Do you have a regular babysitter?"

"Yes. She's a neighbor, actually, Margaret Sullivan. She's a widow in her fifties and like another member of our family now. My husband is very comfortable, as I am, with her watching our daughter. She's a religious woman and often goes with us to our church or with John and Mary when I don't attend."

"No children of her own?"

"No. I think that is another reason she took to Mary so quickly, why she became a member of our family so quickly."

"Why didn't she have any children of her own?"

"She's never been fond of talking about it, but from what she did tell us, her husband couldn't get her pregnant, and Margaret would never agree to try any of the scientific alternatives, nor would she adopt."

He nodded and asked for her address.

"It's the house right next to ours on the right when you face our house," I explained.

"Does she only babysit at your home, or does she take Mary into her own house?"

"Mary feels comfortable in her home, but she babysits in our home only. I have never let Mary sleep in Margaret's house, not that she would have felt uncomfortable doing so. It's just the way I am with her. John usually accuses me of smothering her with attention, which is what makes all of this even more bizarre."

"So, Margaret has never taken your daughter places without you?"

"Why are you asking me all this about Margaret?" I asked, losing my patience. "Margaret is like another grandmother to Mary. She's been there to help nurse her when she's been sick. She's been at every birthday. It's debatable who dotes on my daughter more, me or Margaret."

"Things could have happened around her that she was not aware of. Did she take her somewhere without you recently?"

"No." I shook my head and brought my hands to my face.

"I'm sorry. I don't mean to upset you any more than you already are. I'm just trying to get a full picture," he said, and then turned to the door when a security guard entered the office. I saw him jerk his head to indicate that Lieutenant Abraham should come to him.

"Excuse me a moment," Lieutenant Abraham said, walking over to the guard.

They moved to the side and talked. Then the security guard left, and Lieutenant Abraham returned, walking very slowly, a new and more concerned expression on his face. My heart raced. He knew something more, something significant.

"Was that the man looking at the videotape?" I asked hopefully.

"Yes."

"Well?"

"When you approached the counter in the jewelry department, you didn't have a little girl with you on the videotape," he said.

2

Strangers

Numbness tingled in my fingertips, perhaps because I had my fingers locked so tightly together. I shook my head like someone trying to shake the words she had just heard out of her ears.

"How could I think I had my daughter with me in the store if I didn't?" I asked Lieutenant Abraham.

Actually, I was asking myself, but I looked at him, hoping that he would pluck an answer from his investigative experience. From the expression in his face, I thought he was struggling for one because he really wanted to help me. The pained look in his eyes told me he couldn't explain it, either, however.

"I guess I must have let go of her just outside the entrance and thought she had come in right behind me. She always hangs on to me or stays right beside me, so I just assumed . . ."

He nodded. "Very likely. Obviously, something must have distracted her long enough for the door to close between you. Maybe she didn't even realize you had gone in," he said.

"She knew I was going into the store, though. She

wouldn't just stand out there dumbly. She knows how to open a department-store door and follow her mother in through it."

I could see the point settle firmly in Lieutenant Abraham's mind. Any innocuous reason for Mary's disappearance disappeared as quickly as she had.

"How does your daughter get along with strangers?" he followed.

"Strangers? We don't have any strangers in our life," I replied, not fully understanding.

"No, I mean people she would see on the street or in a store, somewhere when she was with you. Didn't strangers ever try to talk to her?"

"Oh, yes. She's very special, very pretty. People often stop us to remark about her, talk to her."

"Exactly," he said. "What was usually her reaction to that sort of thing?"

"She always responds correctly and with respect."

"Is there any particular sort of person she favors?"

"Particular sort?" I asked. "You mean elderly or young, someone in uniform or not?"

"Yes, exactly," he replied, looking and sounding grateful for my intelligent response.

"No, I don't think so. Except maybe a priest."

"A priest?"

"Anyone in any religious garb."

"Okay. That's helpful." He made some note in his pad.

Another thought occurred to me. "Maybe there's a security guard here with some sort of negative history."

"We'll check that, but they do screen people they hire for security, Mrs. Clark."

"People fall through the cracks. Pedophiles have even

been hired to work in grade schools and preschools."

"Right. Okay. I'll get this picture of Mary duplicated and up all over this place," he said. "We'll also put out an APB and an Amber Alert with a detailed description. We're still interviewing other salespeople in other stores, the parking-lot staff, anyone and everyone who might have seen something."

I nodded. Was I crying, or were my tears falling inside my eyes and raining down over my heart?

"I should get you home, Mrs. Clark," he said. "There's nothing else you can do here. I'll have one of the patrolmen take you."

"No. I can't leave. I can't leave without Mary," I said.

He looked as if he was having trouble swallowing.

"What?" I practically screamed at him.

"I really don't think she's here, Mrs. Clark," he said.

"I can't believe I let that department-store door close between Mary and me," I said. "I can't."

"You were probably rushing in and, as you said, assumed she was right behind you."

"But why wouldn't she just open the door herself and follow me into the store? Someone's definitely taken her. But if someone did that, why didn't she scream?"

"I don't know," he said. "Once that part of the puzzle is solved, it will all be solved."

"I'm sure she expected that I would notice she wasn't with me and rush out looking for her. If I had seen her with someone, some stranger, I would have rescued her. But I didn't notice she was gone in time. What is wrong with me?"

"It won't do any good to blame yourself, Mrs. Clark. Look, we've pretty much covered this place. There's no sign of her here now, or anyone's having seen her, but we will have those pictures up in a few hours. I just made contact with the FBI. I have a good friend in the Bureau's office here, Special Agent David Joseph, and he said he would take personal interest in and control of this situation."

"The FBI," I repeated, the idea driving home how serious it all had become.

"We have to look at the possibility that this kidnapping is to extract money from you, a ransom."

"We live in Brentwood, but we're not ostentatious. We're not anywhere near what would be considered very wealthy people today," I said.

"They might not ask for that much. There's good reason for people like this to go after moderately well-off families. There's less media attention, and they'd believe there would be less police involvement than there would be with a high-profile family. So," he continued, "let's get you home. Dave and his agents will meet us there. They'll get your phones tapped. We'll wait to see what these people have in mind."

He stood up and reached for my hand. I started to rise but felt my whole body tremble and sat again, shaking my head.

"Can you get me some water first? I'll take a pill."

"Sure," he said. He hurried out and came back in with a cup of water.

I opened my purse and found the pill bottle.

"What is that?" he asked when I plucked out a capsule.

"Just a tranquilizer. A mild one," I said.

"You didn't take one before you came here today, did you, Mrs. Clark?"

"No. You shouldn't drive after taking one of these. I'm careful about it."

"How long have you been taking them?"

"A while," I said, and swallowed the pill.

"Might I ask why?"

I shook my head. "I don't feel like going into all that right now."

"Okay, let's get you home. Your husband should be on his way. He was leaving immediately."

I took a deep breath and stood up. Now I did feel as if I would faint. I started to cry, my sobs coming in small, tight gasps that tightened my body and closed my lungs, freezing my arms, my legs. This was really happening. I was going to leave without Mary, get into the car and go home to an empty house, look at her things, smell the scent of her hair, and not hear the sound of her voice. Every part of me said no. It was as if there was a great scream being sounded inside me. My legs wobbled.

Lieutenant Abraham put his arm around me. "Lean on me," he said. "I'll get you home myself."

I closed my eyes and practically let him carry me out of the mall security office. On the street just outside the mall, he helped me into his automobile. He spoke quickly with some patrolman and then got in to drive me home. I lay back, my eyes closed. My pill had put me in a state of limbo, numbness. It was as though I were drifting in some dream. I embraced it.

I was confident that by the time we arrived at my home, I would wake up and find myself sitting in the living room, thumbing through one of my fashion magazines. All that had happened wouldn't even be a bad dream, much less any sort of memory. Mary would appear in the doorway to tell me that John was almost home. It was remarkable how she could sense that, but she was remarkable in so many ways that I had stopped being amazed.

I felt us stop at a traffic light and opened my eyes.

"You okay?" Lieutenant Abraham asked.

I looked at him as if we had never met. Then it all came rushing back at me. I turned and looked back toward the mall. What if I was leaving forever without Mary? I envisioned John and me at the dinner table days, weeks, and months from now without her. During our meal, both of us would avoid looking at Mary's chair. Whenever John would speak, he would sound like someone afraid of silence. No matter how hard he would try, for me, his words would fall like iron pebbles from his lips. He could try everything, talk about his day at work. He could run on and on with descriptions of the stock market and the economy that I was sure would be welcomed on CNBC or Bloomberg. None of it would work.

But he wouldn't be able to stop talking, and for that matter, neither would I. At these once-precious dinners, now without Mary, we would become two people housed together in some prison cell who spoke different languages but needed the sound of their voices to keep their sanity.

Afterward, I would welcome the kitchen cleanup. I would avoid using the dishwasher. Scrubbing and drying pots, pans, plates, glasses, cups, and silverware would feel like penance. In fact, all of my housework would become an act of contrition. Not to mention how deeply dependent I would become on pills to get me through the day. Too often, that was already happening.

I thought that John might not blame me for losing my focus, failing to pay attention to Mary, and instead concentrating on material gifts with such intensity that I didn't see my little girl led off and out of our lives that dreadful day, but I would always blame myself. I would always carry the cross down my own Via Dolorosa and dream of myself crucified in our backyard, moaning, "Why hast thou forsaken me?"

I sat up in Lieutenant Abraham's car. "I'm so frightened," I said.

He nodded and drove faster.

"Somehow, you read about these things in the papers or see them on television but never feel vulnerable, never think it can happen to you," I said.

"I know."

"Will I get her back?"

"I'm on it. Special Agent Dave Joseph will be on it. We'll get her back," he said firmly.

I closed my eyes and leaned back again.

I'll be home soon—home—and John will be home soon, too. Surely he'll know exactly what to do. I couldn't wait to get home now.

We had a two-story, three-bedroom Tudor house on Westgate in that area of Brentwood that seemed more like city suburbs than city. Although Brentwood had more than its share of celebrities from Hollywood and well-known businesspeople living there, its national infamy had come with the O. J. Simpson case. Everyone we knew and everyone we met who learned that we lived in Brentwood always managed to ask how close we were to the murders. John hated that.

But there was no denying that we lived in a rather

upscale community. Even the smaller houses and condos in Brentwood had drifted into the sea sailed by millionaires. Of course, every resident's initial cost depended on when his home was built and sold. John said there were old homeowners sitting on millions in capital gains. There was a rapidly diminishing number of building lots and square feet still available, which kept the prices up.

John wasn't a very wealthy man when we first met. He had a good salary, but his parents had signed over some significant stock assets to him. Some of them poured out significant additional income, and some he sold at an opportune time. In fact, he had doubled his portfolio before we were married.

When my parents learned that John and I were getting serious, they were pleased, because it was easy to see that he was very intelligent when it came to financial planning. After all, this was his career, his life's work and interest. A girl's parents are almost more interested in their future son-in-law's economic prospects than they are in his personality, even his passion for their daughter.

Here was this man, John Clark, handsome to the point where he could be compared with movie stars or classic statues and paintings, who also had a stability most parents fantasized about when it came to a daughter's future. Why shouldn't my father and mother gush over him to the point where I would be embarrassed? While we were dating, I was always making excuses for them, and John was always understanding.

"If and when I'm like your father, I'll think along the same lines, especially if I have a daughter," he said.

"But you won't behave like he does when your daughter brings home a boyfriend you approve of."

He just gave me that knowing, self-confident smile and gently jerked his head to the left, a small gesture that made me smile, too. When you first find yourself falling in love with someone, you are so tuned in to his or her every gesture. I loved the way John poured my glass of wine at dinner, for example. He would never reach over to do it but would first take my glass, pour the wine, whirl it in the glass, and then hand it to me. Little things like that made me feel special. I couldn't help lavishing compliments on him, subtly or otherwise. Rather than thank me, he would kiss me, almost like a royal stamp of approval. But our relationship was far from one-sided.

John never picked me up for a date without telling me how beautiful I looked. They weren't simply appropriate comments or words of praise that one of my girlfriends could call "good come-ons." I knew he was sincere because of what he appreciated. He was truly impressed with my attention to style, to choosing clothes that flattered my figure and favoring colors that heightened the beauty of my complexion and my eyes, a shade of blue he swore he had never seen. Those sorts of things were important to him, and he would no sooner be attracted to a ravishing, sexy beauty who paid no attention to them than he would to a female ape.

"I love the fact that you know yourself so well and know that less is often more," he told me, referring to how I wore my makeup, how much jewelry I put on, or how I styled my hair. It was important to him to be comfortable with a woman. As trite as it might sound, I knew he really believed it when he said we were a good fit.

Besides looking good together, we could have intelligent

conversations. I knew enough about economics, the stock market, and business to understand the things he said and add substantively to the discussion myself. I never tried to be someone I wasn't or put on airs, and neither did John. Whatever hesitation, walls, and guarded language a man and a woman have when they first meet was diminished with every subsequent date John and I had, until we were naked and exposed, every fear, quirk, and dream revealed.

Trust has to come before love. Maybe that was why John didn't believe in the "at first sight" concept. "You can be immediately attracted to someone sexually, but love requires an investment and a risk," he said. "Once you confess it, you're out there hanging, hoping you have not misjudged the person you hope loves you, too."

I knew he was more religious than I was, but he was never obsessive about it when he was with me. I think it was simply part of his faith to believe that whatever he believed, eventually I would, too, and to the same extent and intensity. We had disagreements about it, but he was always tolerant during those early days.

Of course, my parents just loved that he was a religious man, even though they weren't very religious. They went to church on holidays and for funerals and weddings, but in my father's mind, giving up his golf on a Sunday was more of a cardinal sin. John made no argument. He was about as accepting a man as I could ever imagine. I know that was because of his confidence that what he believed was right. He didn't have to convince anyone.

"I'd be just as comfortable in a room full of atheists," he once said. "No matter what they profess, they live in doubt. I don't."

In a social world where young men were increasingly

superficial and openly arrogant, John Clark was a dream come true. I could see the envy in the eyes of my girlfriends whenever they saw us together. Every one of them surely asked herself what I had that she didn't, why I had found a man like John and she couldn't. When I complained about this once to John and told him how I couldn't stand the jealousy I saw in my so-called good friends, he thought a moment and said, "The only people who really feel happy for you are people who already have what they want, people who are comfortable being who they are. Seek those out to be your close friends. Acquaintances are fine, but think of them as just what they are—temporary, disposable imitations of real friends and pools of green envy."

How could I not fall in love with John Clark and want to spend my life with such a man, a man who could give away wisdom as easily as one of those people hired to stand on street corners could hand out advertisements?

Before we were married, John had already gone after the Tudor house we would own. He loved the cul-de-sac, the clean, quiet neighborhood. The first time he showed it to me, I did think it looked like an illustration torn out of a children's fable, with its white picket fence, immaculate front walk, hedges, and bright green lawn. No one had a great deal of acreage in Brentwood, but the house had a good-sized lot with a row of lemon, orange, and grapefruit trees in the backyard. It was easy to imagine us as a family there, our children laughing and squealing with a feeling of complete security. There would be no drive-by shootings, no inner-city terrors. Fences were designed more for appearance than for safety. It would always be safe to walk at night.

John knew the real estate agent handling it, and he knew just how to bargain for it, because the owner was in some distress. The day after we bought it, its value was already up twenty percent. Anyone hearing all of this wouldn't have to wonder why I thought that every day, every month, every year of John's and my life together would be filled with success and perfection.

Of course, it wasn't that way. It isn't that way for anyone. Lately, I was having more and more trouble navigating the sea of perfection on which John had placed our marriage. Ironically, it was his mother who had suggested my therapist. She had a good friend whose daughter used him. She relented with, "If you young people today need such things, at least you can seek the best."

The pills he prescribed were meant to bring me to an even keel so our sessions could be therapeutically successful. I had kept this from Lieutenant Abraham because I feared that he would think this was all my fault, that my psychological and emotional problems were the culprits. I was afraid that in his mind, it would be a convenient way to explain what had happened and he wouldn't be as vigorous in his pursuit of discovering whatever had happened to Mary.

Of course, I couldn't escape from my own thoughts and questions. Was this turmoil I had been experiencing the reason I had neglected her, hadn't noticed she was gone? If so, it was even more my fault. I knew that the first question out of John's mouth when we were alone would be, "Did you take one of your pills before you went to the mall?"

Would he believe me if I told him no?

Would I believe myself?

3

Ringing

Lieutenant Abraham's FBI friend was waiting at the house with a team to tap our phones and run the sting operation and retrieval of Mary in the event that ransom was indeed the purpose for her abduction. Although he was as tall and as stocky as I'd imagined an FBI agent to be, David Joseph had a soft, almost feminine face, with eyelashes most women would die for. He had thin lips and a light complexion, almost tissue-white, emphasized more because of his carrot top and the freckles on the crests of his cheeks. I thought he had a comforting smile and imagined he was successful in his work because of how quickly he might put a nervous mother especially at ease.

He introduced me to his two accompanying agents. Agent Frommer was a much tougher-looking, dark-haired man, with lines etched so deeply in his chiseled face that they looked almost like scars. The other associate, a female agent, looked older than both of them, but Tracey Dickinson had no gray in her closely cropped mahogany-brown hair. Her smile was more like the flash on a camera, but I wasn't looking for sympathy, only competence.

When I went to open the front door so they could enter with their equipment, the reality of my returning without Mary struck me like a severe blow to the back of my neck. I moaned, gasped, and would have sunk to the walkway if Lieutenant Abraham hadn't shot forward to wrap his arms around my waist. I leaned against him, my eyes closed.

"Easy," he whispered. He gently took the key from my hand and gave it to Agent Joseph. "Let's get you inside and lying down."

I regained some of my composure, but I really didn't feel my legs. He was holding me up until we turned into the living room and he guided me to the sofa. Tracey Dickinson rushed forward to place a pillow against the side so I could lie back.

"I'll get you a glass of water," Lieutenant Abraham said, and went to find the kitchen.

The FBI agents began to set up their equipment while David Joseph explained what they hoped to accomplish.

"If this is a ransom grab, we'd expect the call to come soon," he said. "They usually do by now, especially when they've taken a girl as young as your daughter."

Lieutenant Abraham returned with a glass of water. I sat up to drink. He fixed his eyes intently on me, looking as if he was ready to lunge forward should I suddenly become unsteady.

"But what if it's not for ransom?" I asked.

"Rest assured, we're out there in every way we can be. Every airport and exit into Mexico and Canada—all have copies of your daughter's picture and description."

"But what if they didn't take her for that? What if . . ."

"Take it easy, Mrs. Clark," Lieutenant Abraham said

softly. "David's team will cover all bases. Would you rather I helped you up to your bedroom for now? Maybe you should . . ."

"Until her husband arrives, we'll need her near the phone," David Joseph said.

"I'm okay. I'll be fine," I said.

I lowered myself back onto the pillow. My left arm grazed the rich cherry-wood side table, and one of the books John had been reading on the changing American economy slipped off. Lieutenant Abraham moved quickly to pick it up and place it back on the table.

Our eyes met again, and if I needed any reminder about what he and the others were doing there, his look provided it. There was more than just professional concern and duty in his look. He seemed to be in real emotional pain for me.

"Thank you," I said.

"A car is pulling into the driveway," Agent Frommer said. "Going into the garage."

"John. Thank God," I said, sitting up.

"He must've been flying over the Ten Freeway," David Joseph told Lieutenant Abraham.

He glanced at me. "Can't blame him for that," he said.

John entered the house through the kitchen and came hurrying into the living room. He paused for a moment and then moved quickly to my side. He knelt to hug me and held me firmly.

It was then that all my pent-up tears broke through whatever emotional dam I had constructed. My body shook so hard I could see his shoulders shaking, too.

"Easy, easy," he whispered. "I'm here. Trust in God," he added.

I held my breath, and he released me, guided me back onto the pillow, and stood. Lieutenant Abraham introduced everyone. John shook hands and then sat at the other end of the sofa, listening as Lieutenant Abraham summed up what had happened and what had been done so far.

He looked at me and smiled. "She's been holding up like a real soldier," Lieutenant Abraham said.

John turned to me. He reached for my hand. "I think you should go upstairs and rest for a while, Grace."

"No, they need me."

"I'm here now," he said. He turned to the agents. "She's been a little fragile as it is."

"No, I'm all right. Maybe there is something else I can do or remember."

"You're close to a nervous breakdown, Grace," John said softly. "That won't do any of us any good. I'm sure you won't remember anything more right now. You were questioned for hours, weren't you? The stress is enormous. These people know what I mean." He looked up at the agents and Lieutenant Abraham. No one spoke, but they were all looking at me. "What we need is for you to regain your strength so you can really be of help, okay? C'mon," he said, standing. He reached down for me, but I didn't move.

The phone rang, and everyone froze.

"We're set," Agent Frommer said.

"Okay, Mr. Clark. Pick it up. Don't lose your temper or anything. Listen to what they say, and do your best to keep them talking."

John nodded and lifted the receiver. "Hello," he said as casually as ever. He listened for a moment and then looked at everyone and shook his head. "She's been fighting a bad cold. She's taking a nap. I'll let her know you called. What? I was at a meeting that ended early," he said with obvious annoyance. "I'll tell her you called," he said again, his voice colder, sharper. Then he just hung up.

"Your friend Netty Goldstein," he said. "I wish she'd get into e-mail. The woman hangs on to a phone conversation with the desperation of someone drowning in silence," he told David Joseph, who forced a smile.

"We should call our parents, John. We can use one of our cell phones and keep the lines open."

"No," he said. "There'll be plenty of time to get everyone into this."

"But they'll hear about it because of the alerts, won't they?" I looked to Lieutenant Abraham.

"They could, yes. Or someone who knows them could hear and call them." He looked at John. "When you call them is your decision entirely, of course."

"We'll deal with that soon," John said. "Maybe there'll be a quicker resolution than we think." He nodded toward the equipment. "What's your success rate with this sort of thing, if it is this sort of thing?" John asked.

"Oh, not bad, really."

"Seventy, eighty percent?"

"Something like that," Agent Joseph said. "I'm not much of a numbers cruncher."

"What about Margaret?" I asked. I couldn't imagine our neighbor and babysitter not noticing that something was happening, despite how discreet the FBI was.

"She hasn't called, and I don't want to call her, either, just yet. The whole neighborhood will go into heart failure, especially people like the Masons and the Thomases who have young children, too, as soon as the news spreads, so you can just imagine what's going to occur when Margaret finds out."

"But what did you tell your people at work when you were called away from your meeting?" I asked.

He looked at the others and then at me as if I had revealed some fault of his. "I didn't tell anyone anything, Grace. What good would that have done?"

I nodded. "They'll know soon, too, I'm sure."

"Yes, soon," John said, looking away.

"Your husband's done the right thing by holding back as long as possible, Mrs. Clark. We don't want anyone dropping in to commiserate with you just yet," Agent Joseph explained in softly modulated tones. It was as if they all saw that the air around me was crackling. "It's better if we give whoever calls the sense that he or she could get away with it, get something and return your daughter unharmed."

"Isn't it on the television news yet?" I asked.

"Not yet. We're holding back on that for a few hours."

"Too much media coverage right away might spook them," Agent Dickinson followed. She wore no makeup and was quite stocky. My imagination whipped around, and I thought maybe she was wearing a bulletproof vest. Maybe the taking of our daughter was simply the first act in this assault on our family, our perfect little family. Some other form of attack was pending. Agent Dickinson looked like someone expecting it. If a female agent had been sent to help comfort me, she would be a failure, I thought.

"You think whoever took Mary is watching our house right now?"

"They could be, yes," she replied. "On and off. No one is standing out there, of course."

I looked at Lieutenant Abraham for some confirmation. Maybe because he was first on the scene or maybe because he really was a compassionate man first and a policeman second, I found comfort in the way he looked at me and spoke to me. Right now, I felt as if I had to have everything confirmed and agreed to by him. He closed his eyes gently and nodded in support of what Agent Dickinson had said.

"She must be so frightened," I said, my lips quivering, my throat closing.

John turned back to me sharply. "You should be upstairs. It's better you stay upstairs right now, Grace. Listen to me."

"I don't want to be alone," I said mournfully.

"I've got to remain here with them," he replied, looking at the FBI agents. "I've got to answer the phone, and this has to be done as perfectly as possible so we don't mess it up if it happens. You just heard that."

"I'll help you back up to your room if you'd like," Lieutenant Abraham said. He nodded at the others. "They're really running this thing now. It's their bailiwick. The FBI has far more experience with this, and take it from me, they're good at it."

I looked at John.

"Go on, Grace. Do as he suggests," he said. "We'll call you if something happens."

I rose, feeling so helpless. Wasn't there anything I could do, anything I could add, think of? Lieutenant

Abraham walked alongside me but didn't reach for my arm or my hand. I started up the stairway and paused.

"You okay?"

"Yes," I said, turning to look down at him. "I was just thinking that Mary would be waking from her nap by now. Do you think they let her take a nap?"

He hesitated and then seemed to decide to go for it. "People who do this often sedate the children. It's actually more humane."

I nodded and continued up, pushing away the follow-up question: What if they gave her too much sedation? They could be amateurs. I knew he wanted to mitigate my worrying, and I didn't want him to feel bad about telling me what really might be happening, or he wouldn't be honest about anything else.

I paused again at Mary's bedroom doorway. He looked in, too.

"Mind?" he asked. I shook my head, and he entered the room.

"Very nice room," he said. He looked at the shelves of stuffed animals neatly arranged. "Quite a collection."

"Everyone who knows her has known to give her something like that for her birthday."

"Yes. Has anyone given her a lot more than others? I don't mean any relatives, grandparents."

"No," I said. "I mean, some of those are more expensive than others, but . . . well, Margaret Sullivan has more to do with her, so she always gives Mary something nice." I paused, studying him for a moment. "You're still thinking that someone we know, someone who knows us well, might have done this?"

He looked as if he regretted having spoken. Maybe it

was the tone in my voice that gave him the impression that I was on the verge of being explosive, that the smallest, seemingly most inconsequential thing could get me screaming.

"Tell me what you really think, please. I'm okay. Why did you ask that question?" I insisted.

"Every case is different in some way. I had a case where a supposedly good friend of the mother's had an unnatural attraction to the child. She had lost her own in an accident. It was more complicated than I'm making it seem."

"There's no one like that in our lives," I said.

"I'm sure there isn't. You look like the kind of mother who would sense danger if it was that close by," he added with a smile. It brought no comfort.

"I didn't today. I didn't take any pills before we left for the mall," I emphasized. "Maybe I take them more than I led you to believe, but I didn't take them this morning. I swear."

"I believe you. You were distracted in some other way. None of us is that perfect."

"But when it comes to Mary, I am. She's with me so much. It's as if they never cut the umbilical cord. How could this happen?"

"It happens. Stop beating on yourself. It doesn't help anyone at this point."

I shook my head and bit down on my lower lip. I wanted to punish myself somehow.

He leaned toward me like someone about to reveal a big secret. "I was in an automobile accident last week. Oh, not that serious an accident, but it was a little bit more than a fender bender. The point is, it was my fault.

A young woman on roller skates wearing short-shorts caught my attention, distracted me just long enough. It was quite embarrassing, especially for someone in law enforcement. I felt like a doctor who smokes, is overweight, or something."

I smiled. Of anyone involved with Mary's disappearance so far, Lieutenant Abraham seemed to be the easiest person to talk to. I wondered how long he had been a detective. I didn't think he was rough and edgy enough to battle very violent and evil people. For a few moments, at least, thinking about him took my mind off what was happening.

"Are you married or seeing someone?"

"No, I'm not married and not seeing anyone at the moment. I'm not exactly brilliant when it comes to my romantic relationships. Most of the women I've dated look for the nearest exit when they see my . . . . let's say my enthusiasm for my work. I don't blame them. A woman should feel she's first in a man's priorities. Besides," he continued, walking toward Mary's closet and then turning to me, "when I fall in love, I want it to be of biblical proportions."

Now I was really smiling. "What does that mean?"

He shrugged. "I once read somewhere that a man said to the woman he loved, 'Oh do not die, for I shall hate all women so when thou art gone.'"

"I love that quote."

"You've heard it? I don't know where it's from. One of my school buddies gave it to me to use in pursuit of someone once."

"John Donne's poem 'A Fever.' An overly dramatic high school boyfriend wrote it to me on a get-well card when I had the flu. I was impressed but too sick to care."

He smiled and held his gaze on me, then opened the closet to look at Mary's things.

"Everything's so neat, organized, just like those stuffed animals. I don't think most kids are this neat, are they?"

"No, but that's our Mary. She's just like her father when it comes to caring for her things and being efficient. Believe me, I'm not the one she takes after. John is usually fixing what I mess up."

I looked at Mary's bed, and his gaze followed.

"She makes her own bed. John took great pains to show her how to do it properly, and she's very proud of how she does it and the fact that he gives her his stamp of approval."

"Remarkable," Lieutenant Abraham said. "She does much better than I do."

Suddenly, the idea of talking about her in her room was too overwhelming. My whole face started to quiver. My body felt as if it were liquefying. I would melt and splatter on Mary's pink carpet. His eyes widened, and he rushed to me and embraced me. The vision I'd had when I first met him in the mall returned. I welcomed his arms around me and lowered my head to his shoulders. My sobs were more like hiccups.

"I'm sorry," I said, pulling back a little.

"Your husband is right. Better get you lying down. You did take a pill, and with the tension tearing at you . . . ," he said in almost a whisper.

I nodded, took a deep breath, backed away, and went to the master bedroom. He followed to the door and stood there for a moment as if he thought it wouldn't be proper to enter.

"How about a fresh glass of water?" he asked, looking at the glass on my side table.

I nodded, and he came in, took the glass, and started out.

"You can draw the water from the sink in our bathroom," I told him.

He went quickly into the en suite bathroom to get my water. He handed me the glass, and I sipped some and then put it on the side table.

"I'll let you try to sleep," he said.

"Don't leave yet."

He paused.

"I just need to hear another voice, think of something else, or I'll go crazy."

"Sure." He looked at me and then around the bedroom, nodding. "This is a very nice room. I like your taste in furniture, décor. More like a home in New England. Are you from the East originally?"

"No, but I've always liked the décors you find more in the Northeast. John does, too."

"It's amazing how everyone tends to buy the same things out here. Naturally, I've visited many homes in L.A. Sometimes I couldn't tell one from the other and had to remind myself where I was and whom I was seeing, what case, what victim. I won't forget this," he added, still looking at our curtains, our armoire, and the matching secretary desk in the corner. He went to it and saw how the desk opened when the drawer was pulled out. "Beautiful piece."

"Thank you."

I sat back against my pillows. He glanced at me but then shifted his eyes to the oil painting John had bought last year at an auction.

"This looks like somewhere on the East Coast," he said. "Maybe Cape Cod?"

"Yes, Provincetown. We spent our honeymoon there. John bought me the painting."

"Oh, yes, I've heard of it. I've never been, but I've heard it's very nice."

"We went way out on the dunes. You feel like you're in some desert. Great fun," I said, remembering. My lips began to tremble again. I took a deep breath and said, "We were going to take Mary there one summer."

"You will," he said.

I held on to his gaze, to his confidence. "No matter what you say, I can't believe I lost track of her and didn't realize she wasn't with me when I entered that store. What kind of people could just swoop down on us like that? On me? That much time couldn't have gone by. It doesn't make sense. Can't you help me understand?"

"We don't want to conjecture about it yet. Right now, all the possibilities exist. It could very well be a crime of opportunity for any of these possibilities, as well as someone who was—"

"Was what?"

"Watching and waiting because they had chosen your family, your daughter," he said.

"For any one of those horrible possibilities? What do you think, really think? Don't worry about my complaining that you guessed incorrectly later. I don't care how experienced the FBI people are with this sort of thing. There are too many variables. I'm right, right?"

He was silent for a moment. "We should really wait to see what happens here. It's still early, and—"

"I want your opinion," I said firmly.

"Right now, I think the second possibility is more likely," he said. "Someone was probably following you and waiting for the opportunity."

"And I gave it to him."

"Or her," he said.

I looked up sharply. I was sure there were women who were jealous of me, jealous of our family. Was someone I knew capable of such an act? Maybe someone's maid? I felt like a shopper on Black Friday, zipping through a store and looking for bargains as I searched every possible memory of every acquaintance.

We heard the phone ring. I widened my eyes and tried to listen. To me, it seemed like at least ten minutes before we heard any sounds, but I'm sure it was less.

"Did something happen?"

"I'll check and come right back," Lieutenant Abraham said.

I think I held my breath almost as long as he was gone. I started to get up again when I heard his footsteps on the stairway.

"Your in-laws," he said instantly upon entering. "They were asking you all to dinner tomorrow night."

"Did John tell them finally?"

"No," he said.

"He's making a mistake. Everyone will be angry about it."

"Maybe you should try to get some sleep," he added. "It could be a very long night."

"Are you leaving?"

"I did get a call about something else, and this is really in the hands of the FBI now, but I will check back."

"What if they never call? How long do we wait before we give up?"

"This investigation has just begun. Don't think the worst things."

He closed his hand to show me to keep myself together and then turned to leave.

"Lieutenant Abraham?"

He paused.

"If you're right and it is the second possibility, what do we do?"

"Agent Joseph will go into that with you both. You'll have to rake your memory, try to think of someone, places you were where you saw the same people, perhaps, and things like that. Eventually, something will come to mind, some clue. You'll see."

"That's why you asked me similar questions at the mall? You already were considering a premeditated kidnapping, weren't you?"

"I like to be thorough. This still could be anything. Too early for any conclusions."

"I was always with her. I mean, even if she played with someone else's daughter at her home, I was there, too. She's never even slept at my in-laws' home without us, or my parents' house, for that matter. I don't understand. There weren't opportunities for someone outside of our family other than Margaret Sullivan to get that familiar with her. I mean, she's hardly had much time, much of a life, experience with people, with—"

"Don't do this yet," he said, stepping back in. "Let's wait to see if they call for a ransom." He looked at his watch. "Tell you what. I'll return around nine. Get some rest."

He smiled, and I thought that there was more than just polite warmth in his smile. Immediately, I hated myself for having any other thought than thoughts pertaining to Mary, especially thoughts about another man's warmth and good looks.

It felt almost sinful, and for a moment, I thought, *If I'm sinful, God won't let her come back to us.*

See, Grace, I told myself, *this is your fault. Almost any which way you look at it, it will always be your fault.*

I wanted to burst out and tell John that his God was not that hard to understand after all.

4

The Blame

I did try to sleep again when he left, but all I could do was doze off for a few minutes and then wake sharply to listen for anything. Close to five, John came up to tell me that he was sending out for some food.

"Has Margaret come over?"

I was sure the first thing on her mind when she found out would be to get us some food, prepare something.

"No, not yet, but you should eat something, Grace. You haven't eaten since breakfast."

"I can't imagine swallowing anything."

"Keep telling yourself you have to be strong. I'll let you know when the food arrives."

"Why haven't they called, John? If they want a ransom, why wouldn't they call?"

He shook his head. I always felt a small panic when John was unable to answer even the most insignificant questions.

"What do they say downstairs?"

"They say we should be patient, and this delay is not unusual. They say the more they make us wait, keep us on pins and needles, the more cooperative we'll be. It makes sense."

"What if it's one of those other possibilities? Someone hoping to sell her in Mexico or . . ." I could almost answer for him. I knew what he would say.

"We'll cross that bridge when we come to it."

"If there is a bridge," I muttered, mostly to myself. He was already out the door anyway.

Later, I ate some vegetable rice soup and a quarter of a ham and cheese sandwich, only because John stood over me and repeated that if something happened to me or to him right now, our situation would become even more dire. Of course, he was right. John was usually right about everything, because he took so much time to think things out. Maybe it was part of his nature, or perhaps it came from his education and his training, but he wouldn't be above researching what was the best new can opener for us to buy. Most of his leisure reading involved periodicals that focused on consumer research and investments.

We had already determined that I wouldn't continue homeschooling Mary, especially after I became pregnant again. John had focused on what school was going to be right for her. He had arranged for our visits to the possibilities and had spoken with board members, the teachers, and other fathers of children who already attended the various institutions, and I would have to agree that he had come away with more insight for us to share. I always thought he would push Mary toward a parochial school, but despite his religious devotion, he subscribed to the belief that diversity was essential.

"But you attended a parochial grade school," I reminded him.

"I was never happy about that, and when I entered a nonparochial junior and senior high school, I felt I was at a disadvantage," he said. He had also made it clear many times in discussions with friends and with me that he was an advocate of separation of church and state.

One wouldn't think so if one saw how firmly John held to his religious convictions, but I would have to say that he never looked down on anyone else for his or her religious beliefs. In his way of thinking, anyone who had any spirituality was fine. "We all arrive at the same place from different roads," he would say. He practiced what he preached. Our friends were diverse. Sometimes our parties looked like UN receptions.

Now that I look back on it all, I realize that John was a complicated man in so many ways. Someone who settled on a first impression of him would almost always be wrong. I know the tendency was to think of him as rigid and narrow, but he was capable of sudden bursts of acceptance and compassionate understanding, too. I told myself many times that I had to have seen great good in him to have fallen in love with him.

Of course, most of these conclusions came from my therapy sessions. At times, I did feel as if I was unwrapping myself. Every relationship is a journey. Some go all the way, and some just veer off to the right or the left and end. I felt I was at some crossroads or another when I began my therapy. Sometimes I thought I should feel guilty for having any unhappiness in such a marriage, and sometimes I thought, how could I not?

After I had eaten what I could, I went downstairs again. It was a little after eight by now. From the sight of the dishes and the boxes, I thought our three FBI agents had eaten well. Whatever party atmosphere they'd had for a while died a quick death at the sight of me again. Agent Dickinson started to clean up as if she were an errant teenager who had thrown a forbidden party and been caught by her parents. She barely looked at me.

It was pitch-dark outside by now, of course. Our street lights were on, but because we were on a cul-de-sac, there was no traffic. It was strange how this comfortable part of the world, the city, suddenly looked so ominous. Beautiful evergreen and eucalyptus trees lined the street, but right now, they looked haunting. Pockets of shadows seemed to contain unseen, never-thought-of dangers, and every parked car in my imagination contained evil people. The time that had gone by had hardened me. Maybe I was just numb, but I wasn't trembling, and the pills I had taken were receding like some hazy tide that had washed over me.

"They took her before eleven," I said, pointing to our miniature grandfather clock on the fireplace mantel. "Approximately, that is, and it's after eight. That's nine hours. Why, if they wanted money, wouldn't they call by now? Haven't they waited enough to be satisfied that we're frantic and eager to please them? It has to be happening for another reason."

"We've had some cases where they haven't called for days," Agent Joseph said, opening up every possibility for me. "Desperate parents are willing to do almost anything by then."

"I would," I said.

I was more angry than frightened now, or maybe my fear was so hot that it burned anger into me, branded me with red rage. It was on the tip of my tongue to say, "Everyone, just leave. We'll do whatever they want, get

Mary back, and tell you about it later. Then you can play cops and robbers."

I looked at John. He was staring at me as if he could read my thoughts and was afraid that I might just say them aloud. Whatever he saw in me, however, convinced him that it was time to bring family into the situation.

"We'll call our parents now," he declared with that iron firmness he could evince. Anyone hearing him would know there was no appealing any decision John made. It was as final as death. He looked at Agent Joseph. "We need our family."

Agent Joseph nodded. "Sure," he said.

"Come into my office, Grace," John told me, and led me out of the living room. "Your parents are farther away. Do you want to wait until morning?"

"No," I said.

"Okay. Then I'll call them first."

He went behind his desk. I sat on the leather settee to the right and watched him tap their number on his speed dial. Calling our parents and informing them drove everything deeper home. When something like this happens to someone, he or she continually pushes the reality back. It's like watching a television show with your favorite character. No matter how exciting and nerve-wracking the threat to him or her is, in the back of your mind, you know the character will survive. Otherwise, there would be no show the following week.

There could very well be no show with Mary in it ever again, I thought.

John offered me the receiver, but I shook my head. I didn't think I could speak to either of my parents right now. If I tried, I would only burst into tears.

"Mom, it's John," he said when my mother answered. My father usually made her answer the phone. He had owned and operated a very successful limousine company and had to be on the phone so much that he despised it.

When John began, there was no hesitation in his voice, no girding of the loins first, no taking a deep breath, nothing but looking the reality in the face. He'd have everyone be the same, have the same self-control, if he could.

"I'm afraid I have some bad news to tell you both. Mary was abducted today at the mall. . . . Abducted," he repeated. I'm sure she had said something like "What are you talking about?"

He looked at me as he continued. "She was with Grace at a department store in one of the malls. They got separated accidentally, and during that brief time, someone must have talked Mary into going with them or tempted her far enough away to force her."

He looked at me, and again I shook my head. Just hearing John tell it like that turned me to stone. I really didn't want to talk to my mother on the phone and have to explain to her what I couldn't explain to anyone else, including myself. No matter what I said or how she reacted, I was sure I would feel her blaming me. My throat ached almost as much as my heart did without my hearing her voice right now.

"Yes, that's what I'm saying. Apparently, their separation was long enough for whomever to disappear with her before Grace realized what was happening. No, she's still missing. By now, it's reaching the news sources. There's an Amber Alert. That's why we decided to call you. We don't want you to hear it from some strangers. The FBI are here now, and we're waiting for what may be a ransom demand," he continued, "but it's been some time, and no call has come through."

He listened and then said, "She's been taking some of her regular sedation. She's naturally overwrought. Well . . . that's up to you now. Come whenever you are able. We'll keep you up to date and call the moment there's something new. No, I haven't called them yet. You were the first."

He put his hand over the mouthpiece and mouthed, "She's crying."

I nodded and looked away. Tears were coming into my eyes. I had thought that I had run out of them or at least my daily allotment. I know John wanted me on that phone to help calm her down, but right now, I couldn't be of help to anyone.

"We've all got to be strong now, Mom," John said. "Yes, yes, we know, but we've got to hold together and work as best we can with the police. That, and pray," he added, looking directly at me.

He listened, then finally took a deep breath and said, "No, don't call. Every time this phone rings, we hold our breath. Just come when you can, and tell Dad whenever you come to drive carefully. We don't need to add anything else to the situation." He hung up.

"They're coming now?" I asked.

"Maybe. It's a little over two hours, and she said your father's night vision is not that great. But I have the feeling your mother will push him. Maybe you should see about the guest room," he said. Then he picked up the phone to call his parents. They lived in Sherman Oaks, so they could be here in a little more than a half hour. I was sure they would.

"I'll check the room and get some tea and coffee set up in the dining room," I said, rising. "I've got to keep busy, and once they arrive, we want to keep all of them out of the FBI's way."

I don't know why I felt I had to justify doing something other than sitting and waiting with the FBI agents, but I did.

I paused in the doorway and turned back to him. "Do you think we should call Margaret, too?"

"No. Just family for now," he said.

"She's become like family," I reminded him. "And she'll hear about it like everyone else very soon, like you said."

"Just real family for now," he emphasized.

"But one of the detectives is sure to interview her soon, don't you think?"

"Of course, but let's wait until that occurs," he said, and then called his parents.

When his father answered the phone, John began the same way he had with my mother. It was almost as if he was reading from a text the FBI had provided.

"Dad. I'm afraid I've got some bad news to tell you both."

I left quickly. Hearing it again was like replaying the pain I had just endured. I could imagine my mother screaming for my father, his look of astonishment, their hugging, and then, as John suggested, their most likely getting themselves together for the trip here.

I was still in the kitchen when Lieutenant Abraham returned. I heard Agent Joseph greet him and say, "You can tell you're a bachelor. Who else would be able to stay on a job even when he was basically relieved? Only someone without a love life," he added for the two others.

The sound of laughter seemed as grating in my ear as fingernails on a chalkboard. I actually cringed. I quickly carried a tray of cups and saucers into the dining room and returned to the kitchen to prepare the teapot. My father favored an herbal tea at night. Like my mother, John's parents drank decaffeinated coffee. I took out some biscuits.

Thinking about small details like this seemed cold and foolish, but I was doing everything I could to avoid envisioning Mary standing beside me or sitting quietly at the kitchen table, waiting for John to come in from work or after working on his ships in the bottles. She had such terrific patience for a girl her age. I had no doubt that my friends with children were jealous of how well behaved she was in comparison with their own. This house, this family, did float on a pool of green envy, I thought.

Neither John nor I was the kind of parent who constantly bragged about our child, or about anything concerning our life, for that matter. In some respects, I had become like John, infected with his quiet confidence. He always said, "We don't have to talk about it. We do it. People who tell you how perfect their lives are suggest to me that they're full of insecurity. They need you to say yes or tell them how much you envy them."

It made sense to me. So much of what John said made sense to me. Living with him was truly a continual educational experience. I knew I should feel more grateful than I did, and maybe that was what had driven me to seek therapy, but even now, even after my sessions and medication, I was thinking there was something more, something we were missing. It hung out there like the forbidden fruit in the Garden of Eden, waiting for me to pluck it and be driven out of what I thought was paradise.

When I heard the front doorbell, I looked out, surprised that John's parents had gotten here so quickly, but it wasn't his parents. It was two other FBI agents to relieve Frommer and Dickinson. Agent Joseph was apparently around-the-clock. I went into the living room and was introduced to two young men, Agent Breck and Agent Little. Both Frommer and Dickinson wished us luck before they left. I understood that they would return in the morning.

I gazed around the living room. The agents would be sleeping on and off in there, I thought.

"I'll go get some pillows and blankets."

"Not necessary," Agent Joseph said. "We're fine. Lieutenant Abraham has a question for you both," he added.

John was standing with his arms folded. He nodded and sat on the longer settee, indicating that I should sit beside him.

Lieutenant Abraham glanced at Agent Joseph and stepped toward us. "I had some time between things," he began, "so I returned to the mall to speak with their security people. I'm just looking for something different, something out of the day-to-day, so to speak."

"Then you're still on this?" John asked quickly.

"Well, they're in charge, but I'm doing what I can to assist."

"So?"

It had been just as long a day for him as it had been

for me, I thought, and he hadn't been able to get through hours of it by taking tranquilizers and sleeping. His impatience and irritability were understandable. I could see everyone thought that, especially Lieutenant Abraham.

"Well, this is going to sound like a dumb question, maybe, but did—I mean, does your daughter still believe in Santa Claus?"

"Santa Claus? C'mon," John said. "What does that have to do with any of this now?"

"No, I'm serious. It's early in the holiday season. I don't know of any stores that have already set up their Santas in the children's departments or whatever. In another week or so, yes, but . . ."

"What's your point?"

"Well, there was someone dressed as Santa in the mall today at the time your wife and daughter were there, but as far as we know, no store in the mall had a Santa."

No one spoke.

John stared at him a moment. "Of course she believes in Santa Claus," he said. "But we don't threaten her with statements like 'If you don't behave, Santa will fly by the house' or anything like that. I don't call home and pretend to be Santa to ask if she's been a very good girl. But we have presents around our tree, the stockings hanging on the fireplace mantel. Neither of us is like Maureen O'Hara in *Miracle on Thirty-fourth Street*. We both tell her Santa's coming." He smiled and looked at me. "Sometimes I don't know if she is humoring us or we're humoring her. Grace?"

"She believes in Santa," I said. "And I haven't done anything to dissuade her. I think there's plenty of time to destroy childhood faith and illusions."

Lieutenant Abraham smiled. "Well, as I said, I don't know if it means anything yet. I have the mall security people on it."

"But you should add that no one yet recalls seeing a little girl walk off through the mall with Santa Claus," Agent Joseph added. He was obviously determined not to give us any false hope.

Lieutenant Abraham nodded but hung on to his theory. "That's true, but I didn't get to speak to many people about it. I'm going to return to the mall tomorrow about the same time and reinterview some people, including the parking-lot staff."

"Tomorrow?" I said. Hearing it said was like the sound of a bell marking someone's passing.

Everyone paused to look at me. My face revealed my thoughts. *This will still be going on tomorrow?* It was as if the world had suddenly stopped turning. We were just playing a game of false hope. All the equipment, the trained agents, the Amber Alert, information at airports and entry points, none of it was moving us closer to an answer, bringing Mary back tonight.

When the doorbell sounded, I nearly jumped out of my skin, but it was a welcome interruption, John's parents. They came bursting in, his mother embracing me, his father grim, shaking John's hand and then hugging me. John's father always hugged or kissed me quickly, as if he was afraid he would be caught doing something untoward. He had been in the banking business, an investment broker. John's mother had been a bank teller, which was how they had met. She had stopped working when she became pregnant with John and had never gone back, whereas my mother had worked with my father in their business until he sold out and retired.

"Has anything new happened?" his mother immediately asked John. She was normally a perfectly put-together woman when she stepped out of her house, but I could see that she had barely taken time to brush her bluish-gray hair or put on much makeup. Both of John's parents were about five feet ten inches tall and, from what I could tell, they took good care of their figures.

"No, Mom. We're still waiting. Grace's set up some coffee in the dining room. It's better we stay out of everyone's way."

She nodded, reached for my hand, and walked with me to the dining room.

As if we were both teenagers sharing a secret, in a voice barely above a whisper, she leaned toward me and said, "Tell me how this all happened. You weren't on any of your medication, were you?"

John heard her. "I told you. Mary was abducted in the mall. I didn't say anything about Grace's medication. She doesn't take pills and drive with her daughter in her car," he said sharply.

She turned back to him. "I didn't mean—"

"We need to pray together and not rake over the details right now," he said firmly. "It's like tearing scabs off of fresh wounds."

His mother nodded and reached for his hand, too. With our heads bowed, we all entered the dining room, John's father trailing behind. In moments, I knew, it would take on the aura of a private chapel. We all faced the crucifix on the wall, but to me, Jesus looked deaf and blind. *Does he really hear the prayers of the rich who would have a harder time entering heaven than a camel would have passing through the eye of a needle?* I thought, but I prayed just as loudly. I would do anything to get Mary back.

My parents were far more emotional when they arrived. My mother looked as if she had been crying for most of the trip, and when she embraced me, she held on tightly until my father gently urged her back so he could also embrace me and kiss me. Unlike John's parents, my parents looked their age and also looked as if they enjoyed their food. Both sets of parents immediately began to comfort each other more than us. Fortunately, my parents were very tired, and after a good hour or so of talk seasoned with frequent sobbing and then curses and rage, my mother agreed to go to sleep. My father tended to her. John's parents stayed at our house until nearly one and then left. Except for a call John received from a friend at work who was checking to see if he was all right since he had left work so early and hadn't called in, the phone didn't ring all evening.

Now that it was late, a cemetery stillness had come over our home. Lights were dimmed. Darkness seemed to crawl in under the doors, seeping in and around me like black smoke. I drifted in and out and finally, after John's prodding, took another pill and went to sleep.

The moment I woke up, I asked John if there had been any calls. He was already up, dressed, and brushing his hair in the bathroom.

"No," he said without turning to me. He finished his hair and stepped out. "As soon as you're up and about, they want to meet with us."

"Has something happened to her? It had nothing to do with any ransom, did it? Did they find her?"

"No, Grace. I would have woken you if anything like that had occurred. Take a shower and get dressed," he said. He didn't look tired and overwrought now. I didn't know why it should, but it irked me. His strength and self-control were something I had come to despise. I had brought that up in therapy often, but it was especially true right now in light of my fragile hold on sanity. I knew I should be grateful to have someone this strong to lean on and depend on, but it had a different effect on me. My therapist agreed. It made me feel weaker, less competent, in fact worthless, especially now, when I was needed the most.

"I'll be right there," I told him, getting out of bed.

"Good," he said. He stepped forward and embraced me, but it was his father's sort of embrace, quick and with little warmth.

He does blame me, I thought. *Despite his faith and belief that God knows and controls all things, he blames me.* He would never say it, however. At that moment, I wished he would. That seemed to me to be more natural—even, ironically, more loving. I was no Abraham ready to sacrifice his Isaac, and deep down inside him, he was no Abraham, either, I thought or maybe hoped. But I knew in my heart that if this continued and was never resolved, I'd be the only one in the family who hated God.

5

Waiting and Praying

My parents had gotten up way ahead of both of us. My mother had sent my father out to buy some groceries. When I descended the stairs, I discovered that she had already prepared some breakfast for everyone, one of her elaborate breakfasts with a choice of omelets, bacon, and sausages. I knew she was trying to be helpful, but I also knew she was showing me that work would hold us together. "Keep busy" was the message in her eyes. John's parents arrived, and his mother pitched in, too. When I refused to eat much, John's mother, as John had done, pointed out that this was not the time to get sick. Of course, my mother agreed. I ate mechanically, but I ate. It was as hard to swallow as it would be with a serious sore throat. All the while, I couldn't take my eyes off Mary's chair. No one dared sit in her place. It was as if they all could see her spirit still there.

Mom had prepared breakfast for the FBI agents, too, but they ate in a different room. I quickly understood that the morning meeting we were to have with them was when the second phase of the investigation would really begin. It was tantamount to assuming that there would be no ransom call, no hope of a quick return. Although Agent Joseph assured me that kidnappers looking for ransom could and did call after twenty-four hours, I could sense that he was leaning toward the same theory that Lieutenant Abraham seemed to have developed immediately, maybe out of some better police instinct.

Whoever had taken Mary wasn't interested in money—at least, not money from us. It was very possible that someone had taken her not for the money that they could gain but simply because they wanted her. If I was to believe this, which every part of me fought, I would have to believe that my precious little daughter was in the hands of a very disturbed individual. The damage on her emotionally or physically could be everlasting.

I sensed that whatever made a woman a mother, that essential part of her that only other mothers could understand, was in great distress within me. It was as if we had two hearts, one for the woman in us and one for the mother, and the mother's heart was crumbling with every passing, horrible moment that Mary was not in my arms again.

The agents' questions began. Many were similar to the ones Lieutenant Abraham had asked me at the mall, but I answered as quickly and as accurately as I could. A question about my medication was raised, but this time, as he had with his mother, John assured them that I wouldn't have taken anything before I drove somewhere, especially with our daughter in the car.

Our parents were present for all of it. To me, they all looked like observers watching some reality show, probably trying desperately to believe that this wasn't really happening to us. Occasionally, my mother added to something I said, but nothing she said seemed to make any difference, and she could see that John wasn't happy about any interruptions.

Earlier, John had called his boss to tell him what had happened. The story was public now anyway. The FBI had put Mary's picture in the newspapers and on television and had released the details of the abduction. John asked that no one at his office call to see what was going on, but it was clear that what had happened would spread quickly, probably even before people saw the newspapers and television. The husband of one of my friends, Sandra Johnson, worked with John. I was sure that by now, he had called his wife and she was phoning my other girlfriends with the terrible news.

I could almost feel the web being woven around our home, our little world of friends outside closing in with their expressions of sympathy and hope, their offers to help in any way, and, finally, their mournful, fatalistic expression of defeat and never-ending sorrow.

Sometimes during the questioning that Agent Joseph and his team conducted, I began to feel like someone on a witness chair in court. I knew they were only trying to work through possibilities, demanding more exact answers about places we often went to, especially places I had gone with Mary. They wanted to know the names of as many people we had visited as possible. Often, they came back to me to ask about anyone who had come to our door to sell something, to preach something. I found the interrogation and gathering of information exhausting but welcomed any opportunity that kept me from crying. Talking seemed to be the only way right then. That and keeping busy in the kitchen with my mother and my mother-in-law.

Later, I learned that the FBI agents finally had gone over to Margaret Sullivan's to speak with her. We were told that she was so overwrought that she said she couldn't come right over to comfort and be with us. She told them she would make some food to bring over later. Flowers and baskets of fruit with messages of support and hope began to arrive almost every passing hour after the news became more widespread. It really began to feel like a wake.

Lieutenant Abraham called Agent Joseph late in the morning to say that he had not been able to make anything of the Santa Claus who had been seen in the mall. The few who remembered him during the possible time of Mary's abduction clearly remembered him being alone. In fact, from what he could tell, the man wearing the Santa costume hadn't even stopped in any store. None of the security personnel recalled anyone in a Santa Claus outfit driving in or out. It was as if his going through the mall was like taking a shortcut to somewhere. The whole thing hung out there like an anomaly no one could explain satisfactorily, perhaps as bizarre as the sighting of a possible flying saucer.

The remainder of the day went by without any call for ransom and with no new information. It was truly as if Mary had just disappeared from where she had stood outside the department store. As far as we knew, there hadn't even been any credible possible sighting reports generated by the posting of her picture. Of course, the FBI agents kept assuring me that there would be, and that they would spend as much time as necessary chasing them down.

Margaret Sullivan finally came over just before dinner with one of her delicious pot roasts. She was a sixty-four-year-old woman with remarkably thick and rich red hair with just some slight graying at the roots. She kept her hair wrapped in a tight bun because she hated the idea of cutting it. Margaret was only an inch or so taller than I was, but she looked much taller because of how svelte she kept herself and, according to John, because she had perfect posture, giving her a strikingly stately appearance. That and her youthful emerald-green eyes and soft habitual smile won her admiring looks almost anywhere she went. People were always trying to introduce her to a rich widower, but she was too content with her widow's life. Her husband had left her very comfortable. She enjoyed not having to compromise anything in order to find a new companion.

I knew she used babysitting Mary as her top excuse for turning down dinner invitations or other dates that men and would-be matchmakers proposed, but I also knew she really loved Mary, saw her as special, and enjoyed being with her.

When we all had first met, I thought John and Margaret wouldn't get along and that he wouldn't approve of her as a babysitter for Mary. Margaret was much more rigid when it came to her political beliefs. He liked to tell her that she was just to the right of Attila the Hun, but she was unflappable, and I think in the end, he respected her more for her self-confidence and the certainty with which she held her opinions. He always admired men or women who were like that, because he was, too.

The other thing that guaranteed her a seat at our

table was her religious beliefs. She believed everything that John believed but was even more confident, if that was possible, that God had a role in anything and everything that happened on his prize creation, earth. John was willing to describe some of the biblical stories as metaphors, but Margaret was not. She was, as he would call her, a strict constitutionalist. She refused to accept evolution in any form, creative or not. She believed that Satan walked the earth and that the world was a constant battleground between God's army and his. She could be quite vivid about it.

When I asked her why God would permit that if he could control everything, she replied that God wanted man, meaning man and woman, constantly tested.

Well, I thought this evening, we were certainly being tested.

Margaret was the fourth child of five and surely had been a beautiful woman when she was in her late teens and twenties. She had been working as an assistant hotel manager in Ireland when her husband set eyes on her. He had come to Dublin on business, and from the way she described their whirlwind romance, he wouldn't leave without her. She was fond of calling her husband and herself soul mates.

Now she cried with us, she comforted us, and she led us all in prayer. It wasn't a prayer that ended with what I wanted, "Please, dear God, return Mary to us," but instead, "Please, dear God, help us to understand."

John looked satisfied. I was too exhausted to complain about anything. My parents decided to go home to get more of their things and return, but John talked them into staying there.

"Come back in a few days," he said. "You'll only wear yourselves out with the traveling, and that won't be good for anyone. Of course, we'll call you with any news whenever we hear it."

Reluctantly, my mother agreed after my father agreed with John and especially after Margaret promised them that she would look after us, get all the groceries and other things we needed, and prepare all the meals, at least over the next few days. John's mother looked very tired, too, even more tired than my mom. She seemed to have aged overnight, or, I thought, I was just seeing more of her without her detailed makeup preparations and attention to her clothes and hair. In the end, everyone was grateful to Margaret. They left and said they would call in the morning and be close by if and when we needed them.

When it looked certain that we were going into late-night hours with still no phone call from someone asking for ransom, Margaret suggested that I try to get some sleep.

"Go on, dear," she said. "I'll sit with John until he wants to go to sleep. If you exhaust yourself with worry, you'll be as useful as a lighthouse on a bog. I'm used to being up late, as you know."

That was true. She seemed to need only a few hours of sleep a night to function, and as she often said, she was fond of watching old movies late into the night.

"Like with most people my age and older, television has become a close companion, you know. I fall asleep to it during the wee hours. Sometimes I turn down the sound and bathe in the light as if it were a heavenly glow sent to comfort souls like me," she told me.

She hugged and kissed me, and I retreated to the bedroom. I didn't need to take any more pills. I was struggling to keep my eyes open as it was. Despite my determination to stay alert and think only of Mary, I literally passed out. I didn't even dream that night, and when morning came, and I could sense that nothing was different, I struggled to get up to start another day of defeat and loss.

In fact, the next three days seemed to take months. So much of what happened, what we did, what we said, felt exactly the same. It was like treading water, as if I was caught in some horrific version of the movie *Groundhog Day*. People who eventually leave Southern California or never settle there use the sameness in the weather as a reason. There's not enough difference between summer, fall, and spring especially. When I looked outside now, it was truly as if the exact same cloud was in the exact same spot in the sky. There was no change in temperature, and even the breeze lifted the leaves on tree branches just the way it had the previous day.

The effect of all of this déjà vu was to deaden my reactions. I stopped jumping into the sea of hope whenever the phone rang or someone came to the door. I barely looked up or shifted my dead gaze. I ate and slept in spurts. Margaret was always there prodding me to do this or that. I wouldn't have changed my clothes if it weren't for her, nor would I have brushed my hair or put on any lipstick. She even ran my bath. She took over looking after the house, and just as she had promised my parents and John's, she handled our shopping needs.

When I asked her how she could have such energy at such a tragic time, she paused and told me stories about family tragedies back in Ireland, stories she had never related. As I listened, I was even more astounded by her strength and demeanor. She had seen little cousins killed, husbands of relatives killed, in riots and terrorist bombings during Northern Ireland's worst days. Her mother had lost a sister in a factory accident that was preventable. Yet she spoke without any bitterness. She would rage against no one. I didn't have to ask; she would say it was all part of God's mysterious ways.

Once, when John fell into a darker mood during those first few days of Mary's abduction, he told me that we don't die quickly even if we have heart attacks, are shot, or are killed in a car or plane accident.

"We die a little more with every defeat, every sorrow in our lives, until God decides we've suffered enough," he said.

After having heard more about Margaret's life, it didn't surprise me that she agreed. This was why, to most people who believed in what John and Margaret believed in, death was not an end but a beginning. I knew he was trying to tell me that if Mary was dead, her suffering was over and her eternal life had begun.

As he spoke, it occurred to me that people like John and Margaret who said these things were saying them to help themselves believe them, even more than they were trying to get you to accept them. It reinforced them, strengthened them, and diminished their own skepticism. They were the ones who were truly looking for comfort. If I accepted it, if any listener accepted it, people like John and Margaret were satisfied more with themselves than with whomever they were talking to.

I said nothing to either of them, maybe because I was

too bitter and was afraid of how whatever I said would sound. But the truth was that I had come to believe that God had only a vague interest in mankind now. We were just an experiment that had gone wrong. He was working on another planet. We were solely responsible for everything: climate change, wars, all violent acts against others, and our own personal destinies. Prayers and the vows we made were just good intentions or therapy.

The truth was, I craved anger and hate now. I wanted to turn them into weapons that would defeat my sorrow. I longed for vengeance and welcomed dreams in which I was able to get it, to inflict pain and sorrow on whoever had done this terrible deed to us.

Even though I said nothing, I knew John sensed my rage. I think my silence brought more pain to John than his faith brought to me. He did his best to ignore it. Maybe it was because of this more than anything else that he began to permit visitors after the third day. The FBI kept a tap on our phones, but they were no longer at the house. Finally, John decided to return to work. He couldn't stand staring at the walls and waiting for the phone to ring, and then, when it did, and it was a friend of mine or even one of our parents, he would be short and snap back at them.

"I'll go out of my mind here," he said. "I'll be close enough to come back quickly if you need me."

I just nodded. It was as if neither of us was there anymore anyway, I thought.

Of course, John was told to report any calls he might receive at work, and both of us were told to keep our cell phones charged and on all day and night.

Occasionally, Agent Joseph dropped in to ask another

question about a place where I had been with Mary or someone we had met or knew. He was always interested to see if something else had come to mind, some other person, detail, anything I had forgotten. He was very sincere and always apologized for seeming to be too annoying. Of course, I told him he couldn't ever be too annoying.

I had yet to see Lieutenant Abraham again and asked Agent Joseph about him, adding that I assumed that because it was an FBI case, Lieutenant Abraham was off it. He confirmed that.

"They have a full plate with other things every day," he said, "but he did a great initial investigation of this case. The law-enforcement agencies are straining with their workloads and budgets just like every other agency, not that telling you that makes it any easier."

When she heard this, Franny Hastings, one of my girlfriends, suggested that we consider hiring a private detective. I asked John about it, but he thought it was a waste of money.

"No private detective is going to have the facilities and capabilities of the FBI," he said. "We have to be careful. People prey on people like us."

The only thing he would agree to was an interview with a reporter from John Walsh's *America's Most Wanted* television show. John Walsh had suffered the tragedy I woke up fearing and anticipating daily. His and his wife's six-year-old son, Adam, had been abducted and murdered.

When they aired our interview and showed Mary's pictures, I nearly fainted. John held my right hand, and Margaret held my left the whole time. As soon as it ended, John said, "That's it. No more of that."

Margaret agreed and had story after story describing how people in some turmoil or other were exploited. She had heard many of these sorrowful tales at the senior center where she volunteered three times a week.

"Satan's predators are out there," she added.

When I used to hear her say things like that, I would just nod and sometimes even smile. If it made her comfortable and secure to believe in the world she envisioned, fine. She was amusing, almost like a character out of a Dickens novel. Even John would shake his head and laugh at some of the things she had said, but now her view of things and her remarks annoyed me. I snapped back at her a few times, telling her I didn't want to hear about any of God's plans. I didn't want to hear any excuses for horrible things. I just wanted my daughter back. She was quiet, but she kept what was becoming that annoying damned soft smile of understanding. It was as if I had to be humored for mourning my daughter's disappearance.

Finally, I told John to ask her politely not to come over so much. He looked at me oddly and suggested that if I didn't want to go to church and seek solace, I might need more therapy, maybe even some stronger medication. I didn't get upset. I knew that there were many reasons for him to suggest it. I no longer rose in the morning when he did. I spent the entire day in a nightgown or pajamas, and I rarely stepped outside. In fact, almost immediately after Mary's disappearance, I started losing weight and paid little attention to my coiffure, my complexion, or my clothes. My vanity table began to look neglected, jars left open, eyebrow pencils scattered, and used cotton pads left in trays. Even the mirror had an unwashed haze.

Few of my friends revealed that they noticed my dreary appearance, because they all expected it, I imagined. John tried his best to ignore it, except any time I didn't look clean enough because I had failed to wipe off a smudge on my cheek or at the corner of my lips. When he reached out to wipe it off, I anticipated that he was going to touch me lovingly, but instead, he held up his hand to show me the stained tip of his finger. I half expected him to wipe it on his forehead, like ashes on Ash Wednesday. That was how bad things were becoming between us.

Most days, I sat by the phone, waiting and praying. When it rang, I lifted the receiver so quickly that anyone calling knew I was hovering over it. I could hear the regret in their voices. They always apologized for bothering me, and after a while, friends stopped calling on a daily or even weekly basis.

"You're eating very little when we're not hovering over you and forcing you to eat," John said. "And if Margaret doesn't bring over something for dinner, you don't prepare anything. Right? Am I right? I usually have to order in or bring something home on my way back from work. And look at the house," he added, turning in a half-circle with his hands held out. "I don't have to ask you if you're overdoing your medication."

"I'm not," I said, tears burning my eyes. "I don't want to be asleep or out of it in case something . . . happens."

"You don't want to be out of it? Where do you think you've been?"

He didn't have to elaborate. I hadn't vacuumed or dusted for days. I never made our bed or even changed the linen. There were dirty dishes everywhere, even cups and plates in the living room.

Ever since I had stopped working, I had cared for our home and resisted having maid service. My little Mary would try to help and actually had begun to be a real help. She had learned how to polish furniture, worked the hand vacuum to do some of the cushions, and was meticulous when she washed windows. She had even come up with the idea to use a Q-tip to do the corners of the windows, where it was difficult to get at them with just a cloth.

Now I found that if I started to do anything that Mary had helped me do, I couldn't continue. I would envision her beside me, her face full of determination and seriousness, as if folding clothes after we took them out of the dryer was brain surgery. Occasionally, she would blow some air between her lips to move some strands of hair away from her eyes. My hands would tremble when I pictured her and realized she wasn't there; she might never be there again. No, John didn't have to tell me how bad things had become. He didn't have to point to anything. I knew that when Margaret wasn't pitching in, everything was quite a mess.

"You don't want Margaret here all the time. Okay. But we'll need a maid now."

"I can't help being depressed, John. It would be unnatural for me to be otherwise, in fact."

"No, of course not, and I'm depressed, too, but I can't live in a pigpen, and neither can you, Grace. I'm embarrassed even to have the FBI stop by."

"Okay, okay," I said, just to stop his badgering. "Hire the maid for once a week."

"I'll do that." He paused. I could see that he didn't want to say what he was going to say next. He hated it, but he couldn't avoid it. "Perhaps you should return to therapy. Maybe there's some other medication . . ."

"That won't bring her back. There's no drug to cure this pain," I said.

"No, but maybe it will help keep you somewhat stable until we . . . until we know what's what."

He surprised me by putting a card on the table. It had the name of another therapist, someone who specialized in my sort of problem, and her phone number. I didn't touch it. I just looked at it as if touching it might burn my fingers.

"It might be better if you worked with a woman this time. I asked our doctor about it, and he recommended her," he said, and left it at that.

Eventually, I picked up the card and put it in one of the kitchen drawers. I knew it was probably a good idea, but I was afraid of any new medication, afraid of anyone being able to talk me into any sort of acceptance.

I learned that John had spoken to my parents and his own about it. Both my mother and my mother-in-law followed up, urging me to do as he had suggested. My mother basically had ignored my previous therapy, and I already knew my mother-in-law's feelings about it, but both were ready to go along with anything that would make even the slightest change in me and in all our lives.

They all visited as much as they could, my mother and John's mother sharing the responsibilities for our dinners when they came, but no matter how much everyone tried, family gatherings were more like wakes. Once the basic questions about the investigation were asked and answered, Mary's name became forbidden. Any reference to her would bring a heavy and deep series of moments during which my mother's eyes would tear up. She would quickly rise and leave the room. John's mother would join her, and then our fathers would follow John into his office to have quiet men's conversations about the abduction, what the police had done, and what else they could do. Everyone was whispering to keep me from hearing what they said about Mary. They had all become afraid that I would simply implode right before their eyes.

Of course, John insisted on our going to church every Sunday. In his mind, it was even more important for us to do that now. We had to show God that we had not turned from him. John muttered something like that every Sunday morning. Margaret often came with us in our car. I went along, moving like a robot, dressed in a mechanical manner, and avoided speaking to people as much as I could by keeping my head down, my shawl wrapped tightly around my face.

The first time we attended after Mary's abduction, Father McDermott revealed our tragedy to the congregation. All faces turned our way, even of those who already knew. Special prayers were offered. To me, each and every expression of condolence and sympathy was another needle in my heart. Finally, after two months, I refused to attend another Sunday service.

"No matter what's preached or said, I feel as if I'm attending a funeral," I said.

John simply said, "All right."

I thought he was thinking or feeling something similar about it, but he would never admit it. He went alone or with Margaret. When he returned, he didn't mention anything Father McDermott or any other church member had said about Mary. He knew that if he did, I might cover my ears with my hands and scream. All he did do was talk about the therapist again, especially since now I couldn't even attend church services.

Since the football season had ended, on Sundays he would simply retire to his workshop and begin another ship-in-a-bottle project. Rather than ridicule it, I began to realize that the meticulous work was his way of keeping his sanity. I actually became envious and wished I had developed a compulsive thing for puzzles or needlework, anything that would put my brain on pause and keep the echo of Mary's voice and the ghost of her face out of my heart for a few hours, at least.

However, once, when I passed the doorway of his workshop, I caught him staring at the place on the floor where Mary would sit and patiently wait for him to acknowledge her, ask one of her questions, or just stare up at him in wonder at how he could manipulate tiny things with his big fingers and turn them into beautiful and precious old ships. His face softened. He looked close to tears, but then, either sensing me standing there or realizing his weak moment, he turned quickly back to his work and hunched his shoulders so that he looked like a bird of prey feasting on something it had just killed.

I would never say that John returned to the way he had been before Mary's abduction, but he was much stronger, and he could function at almost the same levels of competency at work that he was so well known for having. On the other hand, I thought that for me, time didn't heal; it hardened over wounds and tragedies so that they were not right in my face all the time. That was about all the relief I could enjoy, and I still wasn't willing to find any more with a new, perhaps more sympathetic professional therapist.

However, I realized that the hardness was beginning to change who I was, who I had been. The complete failure of the FBI to produce even a single hopeful lead began the massacre of all my faith and hope about anything and everything. I often wondered during those five months how anyone was able to cope with me, even my husband, John, the unflappable constant gardener of eternal promises.

Couples who lose a child through accident or illness often have trouble with their marriages. It wasn't too dramatic to say that our love for each other had been crippled. Since Mary's disappearance, romance between us had become a kite well launched into the wind but one that had broken free of the string that anchored it to any earthly hold. It was carried off and disappearing in the clouds or the darker sky closing off the twilight. The feeling was palpable. What could either of us do to change it?

I longed for him to come home because he was unable to work. I needed him to rage and be almost as hysterical as I was.

When would we both break down and cry in each other's arms?

Perhaps worst of all, when would he stop pretending that our lives would ever be the same? Everything we were doing now was really more like window dressing. Although he did his best to hide it, he didn't have the heart for any distractions except his hobby.

As much as I feared it, I couldn't help but wonder when I would give up all hope.

When would we accept that Mary was gone, buried under distance and time?

When would John and I accept that she was dead to us and we were left without even a grave to visit, a place to put flowers and shed tears?

6

❧

Falling

During this long, dreary, and hopeless passage of time, days had a way of surprising me with how quickly they turned into night. Most things that were happening surprised me. I realized that whether I was on medication or not, I was living like someone constantly drugged, jolted by the ringing of the phone, the bonging of our miniature grandfather clock, or the buzzer on the stove telling me something I had put in was ready to come out. When I looked at myself in the mirror, I saw emptiness in my eyes and felt as if my soul had vacated. It had gone on to find another vessel to inhabit. A shell had been left behind. Whether I lived or died was gradually becoming beside the point. The only thing that gave my heart any reason to keep beating was that word policemen used: *yet*. *Nothing is new yet*. I lived and breathed *yet*.

Eventually, even though I refused to accept the fact that Mary might never be returned, I tried to get back to being the perfect little housewife, cooking and baking again, cleaning the house well enough to dismiss the maid, and I even went out with John to an occasional dinner. I tried, but I couldn't do it well enough to satisfy anyone, much less myself. I think I could actually feel my skin crust over, my eyes darken and turn steely, and my voice deepen. I was with people again, but I rarely laughed and never started a conversation. My answers were almost always monosyllabic. I suppose to others, I resembled someone who had just been released from a mental clinic. Some even thought that I had taken John's advice and secretly been in some therapy. More thought that I was on some medication.

It was impossible not to see the difference in the way my girlfriends and other people spoke to me, even the way they touched me. It was as if they thought I was now composed of thin china. Press yourself against me too hard, embrace me too tightly, even kiss my cheek a split second too long, and I would shatter before your eyes. Everything that was said to me was said more softly than it was said to anyone else, and certain words had become blasphemous, such as *missing, gone, lost,* even just the word *daughter.* How guilty my girlfriends with children looked when they talked about them. No matter how I smiled or what I said, they seemed to want to swallow back their words, unring every bell sounding motherly joy.

There was only one possibility that gave them any escape from the heavy layer of tension hovering over us. Would John and I have another child?

As soon as two months after Mary's abduction, I had no doubt that John wanted us to have another child. It was, after all, what we had planned to do since Mary had turned five, but now there seemed to be a new urgency about it. Whenever he turned to me in bed and began to make love, I wasn't receptive, but he pushed on and in as if he was a doctor carrying out a treatment that he knew was unpleasant but necessary. Although he never came right out and said it, I could hear him thinking it. *If God wanted our Mary or had planned another destiny for her, he would not deny us another beautiful child, perhaps the boy we want.*

But if God wouldn't deny us, my body apparently would. I still didn't get pregnant. Maybe, as trivial as the analogy might seem, I was like someone who had fallen off her bike and suffered injuries that were so bad she couldn't see herself riding that bike anymore.

I was sure that my closer girlfriends thought my not getting pregnant was by choice. Without hearing me say it, they knew I wasn't looking to have another child to replace Mary. Especially those with young children themselves knew I couldn't live with the possibility that I would never set eyes on her again. No one openly said or did anything to reveal her belief that I wouldn't. Ostensibly, at least, they kept Mary at the forefront. Whenever I met any one of them, her eyes were always full of the question: *Anything new?* I realized that it was almost as painful for them to ask as it was for me to answer. They weren't anticipating anything more than a shake of my head or a simple "Not yet."

Yet was the key word again. It implied that an answer was coming, was out there waiting to be pulled in like some fish. It was only a matter of time. Eventually, factors would come together in that magical way that brought a smile to an angler. He knew that all his hours of patience and determination were going to pay off when he felt the pull on his line and saw his sinker bobbing.

How could I live any other way but barren? After all, how would I hold the hand of my new child, boy or girl, whenever I left the house? Would I squeeze his or her hand so tightly that he or she would scream? Would I hover over my new child as if I were his or her shadow? Would I give the child a chance to breathe? Would I become terrified if a stranger merely looked our way or, God forbid, tried to talk to him or to her? I could see myself screaming bloody murder if a stranger tried to touch my new child.

And when John took our new child somewhere without me, would I sit trembling until they returned? Would I make it impossible for John to enjoy this child, especially if we had a son and he wanted to take him to football or baseball games or just someplace to play?

And what about the guilt I would feel for loving my new child? Would it be as if I had buried Mary? Would every kiss I gave my new baby be the acceptance of our loss of Mary? Would thinking that way prevent me from loving my new child as much as he or she needed to be loved, and would that make for new and difficult social and psychological problems for all of us? Would I hate filling Mary's chair at the dinner table with my new child, redoing her room for him or her, and buying him or her new clothes? Could I let a new daughter wear Mary's clothes?

How does a mother who's lost her child live with these questions and go on to make her marriage live?

Months after my coming out, as John liked to refer to it, my now private mourning over the loss of our daughter was temporarily overtaken by the death of his mother. I was surprised to learn that she had been treated for a leak in a heart valve during the past eighteen months. Her doctors had just been considering a valve replacement when she simply didn't wake up one morning. Even John hadn't known the full extent of it and how serious it had come to be.

However, I wasn't all that surprised at being surprised. Keeping things from one another that other families might share was John's family's MO. (Yes, I was beginning to think in police terms now and use their jargon. After all, there was still an APB out on Mary, and I had begun to read as much as I could about child abductions, combing through police reports and newspaper stories as if I expected to learn that one important detail that would solve our tragedy.)

Not sharing bad news or problems among themselves was a family value for John's parents and him. Some people kept their illnesses secret because they didn't want to be constantly reminded of them through the sympathetic looks they would get or the questions about themselves they would be constantly asked. But I always felt it was more a question of self-pride and even embarrassment for the Clarks. It occurred to me that maybe they were more like Puritans, people who believed that we were punished on earth for the things we did on earth. If you had a serious illness, God was getting back at you for some serious sin. Maybe they believed, contrary to what I believed or what other people thought, that they wouldn't receive sympathy when people heard about their misfortune but would receive suspicion and derision instead.

It was ideas like these that battered the fortress of my own faith. More and more, I was viewing not only our religion but all religion as more of an obstacle to good feelings about yourself and also to good relations with others. Either we were born with original sin discoloring our souls, as John and Margaret believed, or we were weak and very susceptible to it. How imperfect we were, and how often our religions reminded us. I wasn't coming to these conclusions because God let my little girl be taken from me. I was coming to these conclusions because religion was trying to tell me that it was all right. There was a greater destiny awaiting us. Get over it. Go back to church.

By now, my bitterness was spilling over. John was beginning to keep his distance, stepping back like someone who was afraid of being scalded. For nearly eight months, even with John keeping close track of my periods, I failed to get pregnant. I wondered if our failure to produce another child was damaging his faith and if that could only be my fault.

One night, after one of our usual almost rehearsed dinners, I sat back and stared at him so coldly he had to say, "What?"

"I was just wondering if you believe God is punishing us for something that I might have done."

"Why would you think that?"

"He can't be rewarding us by taking away our little girl," I said.

"We've been through this, Grace. We are to God what ants are to man. Just like ants can't understand us, we can't understand God's decisions."

"Good," I said dryly. "I was worried I was doomed to go to hell because someone abducted our daughter."

He folded his napkin neatly. Whenever he became annoyed with me—or with anyone, for that matter—John closed himself up and directed his attention and energy to something he could do meticulously. I laughed to myself, thinking he might have made a great brain surgeon if he could be kept angry at the time of surgery.

"Do you have any interest in our going on holiday this year?" he asked.

"Provincetown, maybe?" I said sarcastically, thinking of our honeymoon and our plans to take Mary to the dunes.

He looked at me with a lightning flash of anger in his eyes.

"I think it was a mistake for you to avoid this new therapist. In fact, I think you should consider it even more seriously now."

"I'll wait for God to tell me," I said.

"If you listen, you can hear Him telling you now," he replied, and rose to leave the table and go to his ships in a bottle.

Maybe that is where he has put me now, I thought, *in one of his bottles. With his meticulous efforts, he's taken me apart and put me together in a tiny way so he can lock me up under glass and put me on a shelf.*

How do I get out?

I tried not to think about it. For the next few days, we were like two shadows moving around the house. Back-to-back we slept. The house that we had once loved and cherished like a garden growing love and hope was closing in on me. All of the rooms began to look smaller, with furniture crowding more and more space. Clocks ticked louder, water gushed out of our faucets instead of streaming, and lights were blinding. Whenever I saw Margaret coming to the front door and ringing the doorbell, I didn't answer. Later, when she called to see why, I pretended I had been asleep.

"You should get out more," she said. "Fresh air will do you some good. Do you want to go shopping with me?"

"No. I don't need anything right now. Thanks for calling, Margaret," I said, and hung up before she could string along some other sentences to keep me talking.

In fact, I went through a torturous debate whenever the phone did ring. *Should I answer? Do I hope it's some miraculous news, and when I discover immediately that the call has nothing to do with Mary, do I continue to hold on to the receiver? Do I speak?*

Margaret's mention of shopping reminded me that I had yet to return to the mall where Mary was abducted.

A number of times, I set out to do so, harboring the hope that I would see something, remember something, that would lead to her safe return, but every time I started out for it, I turned around because I would start to tremble and cry.

How many times had I dreamed of returning and finding her myself? I told myself I should have gone back that first night. In my dreams, I always heard her voice and turned to see her come running to me, her arms out, her face full of joy. I covered that face in kisses, embraced her, and lifted her.

"Where were you?"

"Just over there looking at something pretty," she would say, and point off to the right, but off to the right everything was in darkness.

That didn't matter. She was back in my arms, and I was taking her home. She was hungry and eager to help me prepare dinner. Daddy was going to be proud of her. There would be choruses of laughter around our table. The glow would return. Every minute would be more precious than the previous one. Once again, our home would be a womb of contentment giving birth to happiness beyond compare. Our windows would brighten as if they were filled with hundreds of candles building a fortress of light to stave off the darkness. Our neighbors would once again look upon us with reverence and envy.

John's rendition of the Twenty-third Psalm would resonate and echo into the homes beside ours, giving hope and faith away generously. "The Lord is my shepherd . . ." Later, we would tuck Mary into bed, join her in evening prayers, and then find ourselves settling comfortably into our own beds to sleep and greet a new day.

My dream was my prayer now. I couldn't ask God for anything in church. I had exhausted the words, the promises, like Hemingway's old man in *The Old Man and the Sea*, who vowed he would say all the Hail Marys if only God would let him have his big fish.

"You cannot bargain with God," John would tell me. "God can't be made to owe you anything. He's not a storekeeper who will give you what you ask for if you just pay Him the price. That's why these people who attend church services only when they feel like it or only on holidays are even more despised than those who don't attend at all. You can't give God five days a year and expect something in return, a little good fortune, a little health and happiness. It doesn't work that way."

He quoted more scripture, tried to read passages to me from the Bible or relate some words of religious wisdom that Father McDermott had offered. In fact, it seemed to me that the more time that passed since Mary's abduction, the more religious John became. It was almost as if he wanted to show me more than he wanted to show his God how strong his faith was.

I stopped mentioning the subject entirely.

Finally, one morning, I rose when John did, and after he had left for work, I decided I would return to the mall and even to the department store and the very place I had stood when I had first realized that Mary wasn't beside me. I even located the very clothes I had worn that day and put them on. I struggled to remember every detail about what Mary and I had done before we had left to go shopping, and I repeated each and every action I could recall. Then I got into my car and started away. Looking into my rearview mirror, I saw that Margaret had just come out of her house. She looked after me and stood there until I had made the turn and left our street.

Maybe I should have taken her along, I thought. Maybe I could have used her strength. Besides, it wasn't right to keep rejecting her kindness. She had cried with us and prayed with us, and she knew, as we did, that Mary's birthday was approaching.

Yes, I would have benefited from her company. I could feel the trembling in my hands as I clutched the steering wheel. When I came to that cross street where I had turned away every time before, I slowed, and then, holding my breath, I jerked into the turning lane, nearly cutting off another vehicle. The driver let me know it with a blaring of his horn as he shot past me.

"Sorry," I whispered, "but you'll just have to endure it." I kept driving.

It was eerie, but I was able to park in the exact same spot in the underground garage. I sat with the engine off, practically hyperventilating. Finally, I got out and made my way to the escalator. When I reached the store level, I felt as if I had truly come up from the dark depth of the nightmare I was living and could breathe clean, fresh air. Maybe if I did this, I would suddenly be brought back to that very day, and I wouldn't lose Mary after all. Everything since would have been a nightmare destroyed by the morning sun.

I turned toward the department store just the way I had turned that fateful day. Retracing my steps as precisely as I could, I reached the entrance and tried to recall how it was possible that I had not realized that Mary was lingering too long behind me and had not entered the store right alongside me. Where had I let go of her hand? I must have taken it when we were on the escalator. I had to have let go immediately afterward.

I stared at the door. People walked past me, some gazing oddly at me because I was just standing there staring at the entrance. A stout older woman, not watching where she was going, knocked into me. She started to apologize and then, maybe because of something she saw in my face, just walked away. Even people coming out almost paused when they looked at me. I must have appeared quite terrified. *Why did I come here?* I asked myself, and I had started to turn away when I heard someone say, "Mrs. Clark?"

I turned to see Lieutenant Abraham coming toward me on my left. He was carrying a bag filled with a purchase he had made at a men's clothing store. I stared at him so long that he paused and said, "Lieutenant Abraham. Sam Abraham."

"Yes," I said. "Sorry. Of course, I know who you are. I was just . . . shocked to hear anyone say my name."

He nodded, holding his smile. "You okay?" he asked.

I shook my head. He lost his smile and stepped closer. Then he looked from me to the department-store entrance and back to me.

"Why are you standing here like this? Were you in the store? Did you just come out?"

"No. I wanted to go in, but I just reached this point and couldn't go any farther," I said. "This is the first time I've returned to this mall. I was hoping . . . I don't know what I was hoping."

"Oh." He thought a moment. "How about we get a cup of coffee?" He nodded at the café three stores down on our right. "Maybe if you just sit for a while."

I started to say no and then looked at him. Did he have something to tell me? Was the FBI trying to get hold of me that very moment? I shuddered, struggling to speak.

"They haven't found her or found any clues or—"

"No, nothing I know about. I've kept myself informed on the case," he said. "C'mon." He put his arm on mine. "Let's have a cup of coffee."

I nodded and let him lead me to the café. We took a table in the far right corner and both ordered lattes.

He pointed to his bag. "I desperately needed some new shirts. When it comes to buying things for myself, I'm the world's best procrastinator."

"I can't imagine when I would even think of something new for myself," I said.

He nodded. "I wish I could have remained full-time on your daughter's disappearance, but once the FBI took over, I had trouble defending more time."

"They have been a great disappointment," I said.

"When you hear it's the FBI, you think of super detectives or something."

"Well, they're pretty good most of the time. They do a lot. I know local police are supposed to resent them coming in and taking control, as if we were inexperienced or incompetent, but they do bring a great deal to the table." He leaned toward me. "Don't tell any L.A. cop I said that."

I smiled. Seeing him there was somewhat shocking, but it didn't bring the sort of dread I could have associating anything or anyone with that dreadful day.

"I understand what you're saying, but they're still a disappointment to me."

"To themselves as much as to you, I'm sure. They don't like drawing a complete zero."

"I doubt their disappointment could be as much as mine," I said, sipping some coffee. "Nothing came of that Santa Claus thing?"

"I've gone over and over that." He drank some of his coffee and looked at me like someone who had something else to say.

"What?"

"It's a wild theory. It presupposes so much."

"What?"

"Santa is quite a distraction for any little boy or girl your daughter's age. Kids are comfortable around Santa. I mean, we hope every parent warns her children about strangers these days, but you don't hear of anyone warning them against Santa."

"So?"

He hesitated and then leaned toward me again. I felt as if I were falling into his eyes.

"So, what if even though this guy didn't take your daughter's hand and lead her away, he was responsible for it? I mean deliberately so. What if he was meant to appear and then someone else told your daughter that Santa wanted to speak to her or Santa was leading her back to you? It's a hard thing for a kid to turn down."

"Sort of a decoy?"

"Yes, exactly," he said. "He took her mind off you and whoever was able to get her to go along. It's crazy to even think of it, I know. Some might call it fantasy police work."

"Why?"

"It's too premeditated," he said. "It presupposes that someone expected that there would be an opportunity. That is, if it was indeed your Mary they were after and no one else. Of course, they might have just been waiting for an opportunity with any child who fit the bill."

"I see," I said with some disappointment dripping from my lips.

He shrugged. "That's how you get sometimes when you're in my line of work and run up against walls and more walls. You start to envision what a more intelligent thief or killer or—"

"Kidnapper?"

"Or kidnapper might come up with. I'm afraid it would lead us nowhere."

I stared at him for a moment. The memory of the softness in his eyes, his compassion, and what I felt was extra-special care when he had first come to see about Mary at the mall began to return.

"Did you try the idea out on your friend at the FBI, Agent Joseph?"

"I mentioned it. I can't blame him for putting it on some back burner or in some file."

"Suppose you had charge of the investigation, though. What would you have done with the idea?"

"This is wrong," he suddenly said, sitting back. "I shouldn't be doing this. I'm sorry."

"What's wrong?"

"Suggesting wild ideas to a woman who is obviously desperate. I'm sorry," he repeated. "I had no business doing it."

"Why did you do it, then?"

He started to shake his head.

"No, tell me."

"It was quite a surprise seeing you here just now. I haven't forgotten you. I mean, your pain and your suffering."

"Do you always take such a personal interest in the victims of crimes you investigate?" I asked.

I locked my eyes on his.

"No," he admitted. "I don't."

"Well, I don't mean to sound so aggressive. I do appreciate it."

He nodded, sipped some more coffee, and looked away. I found myself studying him. He wasn't as handsome as John. Few men were, but there was something more attractive about the lines in his face, something manlier about him. He looked tough, hard, competitive, but he could soften and be tender, too, I thought.

He turned back to me, and we just looked at each other, neither knowing what else to say.

Then he smiled. "How are things otherwise?"

"Well, my girlfriends treat me as if I'm a time bomb. My parents can't visit or call without crying. I'm practically shriveling up at home, and then, to top it off, my mother-in-law passed away unexpectedly recently."

"Oh? I'm sorry."

"Yes. I don't know how to say this without it sounding unfeeling, but it was only a short period when I wasn't thinking about Mary, and I was glad when it was over, the wake, the funeral, the burial and period of mourning, so I could get back to agonizing over Mary's abduction. I didn't dislike my mother-in-law, but John returned to work rather quickly, so I felt I had permission to put the sadness involving his mother to bed."

"How's his father?"

"He's started playing golf and is so into it that I'm not sure he even knows his wife died." I paused. "That was a mean thing to say. I shouldn't have."

Sam Abraham smiled. "I remember when you told me your father was addicted to golf."

"John says there are a lot of widows with husbands who fell deeper in love with golf. My mother might agree."

Sam Abraham nodded. "So, things are okay with you and your husband? I'm sorry," he added immediately. "That's out of order."

"I'm sure you know from experience what often happens when a couple suffers a similar tragedy. They often take it out on each other. Right?"

He nodded.

"John wanted me to go into therapy again. He even located a new therapist, a female who supposedly specializes in my problem and was recommended by our doctor, so that I could get new medication."

"You never did?"

"No. Maybe I should have, but it just seemed like . . ."

"Like what?" he asked. I could see that he was genuinely interested and not asking questions just to pass the time and get this unexpected meeting ended.

"Like accepting. Do you understand? Can you understand? I want to keep on suffering. It keeps hope alive for me. Drugs, therapists, friends with good intentions, vacations, anything that would mitigate that, seem too much like giving up on Mary."

"I never heard it put that way, but I do understand. In a funny way, I admire your courage or, rather, your willingness to continue in full-blown suffering and pain."

"Well, you're the first to do that," I said, sipping my coffee.

"It's also quite understandable for someone to want to go the other way. Don't misunderstand me."

"Right." There was another one of those pregnant pauses between us, both of us struggling to find something else meaningful to say or ask. I nodded at the bag containing his purchases.

"I guess you're still a bachelor, shopping for yourself."

"Yes, I'm almost hopeless when it comes to romance and marriage."

"That devotion to your work?"

"You remember." He smiled appreciatively. "Yes."

"My husband has a more traditional devotion, to his church, his God."

"His God? Not your God, too?"

"We're not getting the same messages from the Bible these days."

"I'm sorry," he said.

I laughed.

"What's so funny?"

"As I said, John thinks I need therapy. Sitting here with you and telling you these things feels like therapy. I don't mind it, either."

"Hey. Sometimes all you need in this world is a good listener, a sincere listener, not necessarily a professional."

"Yes," I said. We stared at each other a moment, and I finished my coffee.

"Do you want to try again?"

"Pardon?"

"Going into that store? I'll walk in there with you."

"I don't know."

"I think you should," he said. "I think you need to do that." He reached out and touched my hand. "I'll be right beside you."

I thought for a moment and then nodded. He paid for our coffees, and we both rose.

"Don't forget your bag," I told him. He looked as if he was going to do just that.

"Thanks."

He took my arm, and we started out of the café. I knew I was moving, but from my neck down, my body seemed to grow numb. It seemed to disappear. I slowed down, nearly stopping completely.

"It's all right," he said. "It's just a department store."

"Yes."

"You'll see."

I nodded but leaned heavily on him. He sensed it and

put his arm around my waist. I imagined that to other people, it might have looked as if he was carrying me into the store.

He reached out to open the door and looked at me.

Without any prodding, he said, "I'm sure your daughter is still alive."

7

Lifeline

The store wasn't as busy as it would be during a holiday period, but there was enough going on to give me the feeling that I'd had back in November. The same saleslady was behind the jewelry counter. I didn't see the same floor manager or either of the two security guards. For a few moments, I just stood there fighting to regain my composure.

Sam Abraham sensed it. "You all right?"

"Yes," I said, and he stepped back.

I stood there thinking for a few moments. Now that I was long past the hysteria of the moment, it all seemed clearer. I experienced a gradual focusing that helped me better understand what actually had happened. The women's jewelry counter was directly across from the entrance. A mere dozen steps would take me there, and I had been moving very quickly. I had been in one of those *Let's get it over with* states of mind. My purchase was more like fulfilling an obligation. I had a gift list to fulfill, but except for the gifts I bought Mary, John, and Margaret Sullivan, everything else was more like a chore.

My clearer vision of the store itself was accompanied

by a clearer memory of what had transpired. I nodded and whispered, "Yes."

"What?" Sam Abraham asked.

"I was thinking this before, but now I'm positive. I let go of her hand as soon as we came up the escalator," I told him. "She was pulling to get free. Mary liked to feel more grown up and independent. I realize exactly when I let go now."

"I see. So, it's possible that someone or something distracted her from there to the entrance of the department store."

"And I didn't realize it until I was already at the counter and finally looked down to see what she was doing."

"Makes more sense. What was confusing to all of us was how quickly someone snatched her outside the entrance. According to what you're saying now, there was more time for the abductors to act."

"And the reason people here didn't see her with me?"

"Exactly. Let's go back out there," he said, and led me out to the escalators.

I didn't know what he expected to find, but he studied the area with an intensity that caused my heart to beat quickly again. For the first time, I felt as if Mary's abduction really was being investigated. He turned and looked at the corridors of the mall and then at the escalators again. I saw him nod in agreement with his own thoughts.

"What?" I asked.

He held up his hand for my patience and turned around to look back down the escalator.

"Well, what if our Santa came along just at this place

in the mall? It's possible he came up the escalator right before you and Mary did and stood just off to the side to wait for the two of you to appear."

"You mean, you think he was waiting for us in the parking garage below?"

"Something like that, yes. So, he comes up first. Some people see him, but that's why not many see him and certainly why no one in any store remembers him."

"But whoever he was, he would have to know I was coming here, right? This would have to be a well-planned-out abduction."

"Maybe. As I said in the café, maybe he wasn't out to get Mary per se. Maybe he was out to get any little girl, or I should say he and whoever was working with him. It could be that she just happened unfortunately to be the little girl of choice at this particular moment, a girl who presented them with the opportunity."

"So, she was the victim of a random kidnapping?"

"Not random, exactly. This mall, places like this, are where people like that hunt for prey. There are more things distracting parents and many things distracting children. It's a matter of where the best opportunities are."

"People who sell children in Mexico?"

"No one ignored that possibility, and I don't want to ignore it now, of course, but remember that your daughter's photo and information went to border crossings and even to law enforcement in Mexico, for what that's worth."

"I see. So, if that happened, you're not optimistic that we'd get her back." I shook off the pessimism and returned to what he was saying. "Santa spots us, sees Mary. Then what?"

"Well, as you said, you come up and turn toward the department store. He steps away from a storefront nearby and approaches the moment you let go of Mary. She's fascinated with the sight of him, so she lingers behind, and as you said, you didn't notice that she was not beside you until you were in the store. He reaches out for her hand or . . . no," he said, shaking his head and letting the air out of his conjecture. "That's not enough. There has to be something more," he added as if he was a producer listening to a writer pitch him a story.

"What are you thinking? What more?"

"I'm thinking she has to go down the escalator after him. If he takes her hand and pulls her or scoops her up, she would probably cry out, and you would hear."

"Go after him on her own?" I shook my head, sinking back into disappointment with his theory. "She wouldn't do that. She wouldn't leave me, and I would have realized all that. I wasn't on any medication," I said.

He nodded. "I know. You're right. That leaves a hole here, but boy, if it happened that way, no one would recall seeing a little girl with Santa Claus and . . ."

I looked down the escalator toward the parking-lot entrances. "And she'd be down there and swept away very quickly while I was entering the store and going to the counter."

He looked at me. "Yes, exactly. That's why it seemed as if she had literally disappeared. A lot of time was wasted while the security guards ran around the department store and then later, when they and the mall security were searching the mall. The parking-lot staff is all at the exit gates and informed about Mary, but by the time our Santa approaches the gates, he's out of the costume. That's why no one at the gates recalls a Santa Claus, but that's also why there has to be at least two involved. He couldn't drive and keep her subdued."

Just hearing the word *subdued* revived every nightmare scenario I had envisioned these past nine months. I was sure that for a moment, my heart stopped beating, and then it began to race. I felt very dizzy. I must have wobbled, because he put his arm around my waist again. I closed my eyes, lowered my head to his shoulder, and took a deep breath.

"I'm okay," I said.

He still held on to me. "No, you're not. You're still very fragile. We shouldn't be doing this."

"I didn't think it would get to me like this. I thought I had turned to stone. My skin feels like dry bread crust, totally unfeeling."

"That's a description of being fragile," he said. He shook his head. "Really, I shouldn't be doing this with you, especially here."

"Of course you should, and I appreciate it very much," I said.

He let go of me but held his arm out in case he had to embrace me again.

"I'm okay. Really."

He nodded and glanced at his watch. "I'm on duty in two hours. There's an extortion case I'm on and two possible vehicular manslaughters we're investigating."

He saw the letdown in my face. I wanted to go on for the remainder of the day and into the night if we had to. I didn't want to let go of these hopeful moments. Just for a while, I had felt alive again.

"But don't worry. I promise I'll find time for this," he said.

I looked at the escalator. What had we really discovered? The scenario he theorized made no sense to me. Yes, we had separated, but I just couldn't believe I wouldn't have noticed her not beside me for so long. But maybe I just refused to believe it.

"Find time for what?" I asked. "What else can you do?"

"Well, people don't usually have Santa Claus outfits in their closets. I'll get someone to check the costume rentals around the time of her abduction. That might lead us to someone with a record of these sorts of crimes. Perhaps David Joseph will get his people on it."

"I just can't believe she would be that distracted by someone in a Santa Claus outfit."

He shrugged. "That's what we have to do, though, look at things that seem impossible."

"It happened in November. There'll be lots of rentals, I bet."

"Yeah, but maybe not that early. It's a start," he said.

He was trying, I thought. What good was it for me to be skeptical?

"Maybe I can help," I offered. "There must be dozens of retail costume places in this part of the city."

"Might not even be in this city, but this is the sort of nitty-gritty work we do. Don't you know that detectives used to be known as flatfoots?"

"Yes, I know."

"Well, that's why."

"But there must be something I can do, even if it's just on a computer."

"I'll let you know. Let me see what I can do first. I want to give that hole in the theory more thought."

I didn't believe he would really devote much more time to this. He had met me and felt some obligation for the moment, but after we parted, reality would set back in. John was right. We had to prevent ourselves from grasping at our own wishful thinking. We had to plant our feet on hard, firm ground and not listen to any promises, whether they came from the FBI or anyone else.

"With all you have on your plate? When will you have any time for this?" I asked, my voice dripping with disappointment.

He shrugged. "Who needs to eat and sleep? Those things are for sissies or FBI agents."

I found another smile that was able to push through my sadness and depression. I was sure that it popped on my face like a bubble on the surface of a dark gray pond. The tension and anger relaxed their grip on me.

"Thank you, Detective Abraham."

"I think you can call me Sam by now," he said.

"And you should call me Grace."

"Right." He looked at the escalator. "I can take this one down," he said. "My car isn't far from this parking-garage approach."

"Me, too. I have nothing more to do here."

"Okay."

He let me go ahead of him. At the bottom, we had to go in opposite directions. He hesitated. I saw the debate raging in his mind.

"What?"

"If you want, we can meet again. I'm off at four tomorrow."

"Back here?" I grimaced.

"You know Woody's Tavern on the corner of Santa Monica and Floral?"

"No, but I'll get to know it," I said, and he laughed.

"I'll meet you there, and we'll noodle this some more. I'll see about investigating the Santa costume rental tonight. Do you think you should bring your husband along? I mean . . ."

"Not yet," I said. "John is the sort of man who would not like to devote time to—how did you refer to it?—fantasy police work. He doesn't deal with theories, just facts . . . and numbers."

"Just facts and numbers? How come he's so religious, then? Facts contradict faith more often than not, don't they? I'm sorry, that's out of line again."

I smiled. "No, it's a good question, but I'm sure if I asked him, John would quote Walt Whitman."

"Oh." He tugged his ear like Humphrey Bogart did in so many of his films. "My Walt Whitman is a little rusty, as you know my John Donne is, too."

"'Do I contradict myself? Very well then, I contradict myself. I am large. I contain multitudes.'"

He smiled. "Serves me right for not paying attention in literature classes in high school. Okay, see you tomorrow at four at Woody's," he said.

I started away. When I was almost to my car, I turned and looked back. He was still there, watching after me.

Would John worry about me half as much? I wondered, then immediately regretted it. The thought was unfair. John and I fell in love and married, but I knew from the start that we were different people. He had his way of mourning, and I had mine. I shouldn't be so critical. I told myself that once you suffered what I'd suffered through, your tolerance for others and your generosity shriveled up. I hated that happening. The truth was, I no longer liked myself. Would I ever again?

Mary wasn't the only one abducted that day, I realized as I got into my car. I was, too. I was trying to find myself almost as much as I was trying to find her. Maybe someday soon, we would come home together.

Driving away from the mall now was almost as painful as it was when I left without Mary nearly nine months ago. I felt the same pain in my heart, the same empty feeling in my stomach, and I was sobbing silently, with my throat aching almost as much. I kept my gaze forward and quickly turned into traffic to head home. As I drove, I thought about Sam Abraham's question about involving John in this new investigation. Did I give Sam an honest answer? I had to ask myself what the real reason was for me to leave John out.

When he came home from work, I was very tempted to tell him what I had done, whom I had met, and what we had planned, but I didn't. Before Mary's disappearance, John would always ask me what I had done during the day. He didn't ask like a husband checking up on his wife; he asked like someone really interested. Sometimes I had something interesting to tell him about a place I had taken Mary and especially her reaction to things we had seen or some conversation I'd had with a friend. Before he sat down to watch television or read or retreated to his room to work on his ships in bottles, he was still, as I liked to call it, in this world, the world in which Mary's reactions, the things she had said and done, were just as interesting and exciting to him as they were to me. So many times, he and I had laughed together over something she had done or said. Sharing these delightful things your child does really brings a man and a woman closer.

Thinking this made me realize just how much of the conversation between a wife and a husband was taken up with their child or children. Everything—their clothes, their health, their observations about people and places, things you liked and did and things they dreamed—filled up hours and hours of dialogue between you. Losing those topics left a gaping hole in that wonderful and magical bond that tied you together as one. Suddenly, at least in our marriage, we were selfish again.

After all, what else did we have now but ourselves? That meant we were tossed into the pool of childless couples, couples who either had chosen not to have children or had been divorced and remarried and had less to do with their own children. There was no longer any mutual sacrifice. Everything a wife and her husband did for each other was counted. Without realizing it, they were competing. They were more like two partners, with each vying to get more out of the business deal between them than the other.

John and I had friends like this. Some of these people kept separate bank accounts and talked about his or her money. Did they have a marriage or a corporation? To me, it seemed as though they were more critical of what each other had done for their union than the couples who had children. Yes, there were mothers who demanded that fathers do more, and there were fathers who did and fathers who didn't, and that led to some tension, but in the end, they both worried themselves sick when their children were in trouble. They reached for each other to comfort each other and do whatever they had to do, make any sacrifice they had to make, to help their children. The big joke was still out there: Little children, little problems; big children, big problems. But regardless, Mom and Dad were always there to bail them out. They might complain about it, but they would do it.

What would really happen to us if we didn't get Mary back and I didn't get pregnant again? After having a child like Mary, could I just put aside all the motherly instincts and needs within me and become one of those wives in a childless marriage? Could I shift into another mode and be more self-centered? Was it too late for someone like me to care only about herself?

I was so lost in these thoughts that I said barely a word at dinner. John was used to my deep silences now, but he also was keen enough to recognize something different. After a few minutes, I suddenly realized that he had said something significant, but it had gone by me too quickly for me to reach out and pull it back.

"What?" was all I could think to say.

"You didn't hear a word I said, did you?" he asked.

"I was . . . no, I didn't," I admitted.

"Margaret told me you went somewhere today. Where did you go?" he asked.

"When did you see Margaret?"

"She was just pulling into her driveway when I came home. Don't change the subject. Where did you go?"

I sucked in my breath and thought that maybe I should tell him everything. Maybe it was important to see how he would react.

"I finally went to the mall where Mary was abducted," I said.

"You mean, you haven't been since?"

His question floored me for a moment. How could he be so oblivious to that fact? How could he not realize how traumatic it would be for me?

"No."

"Oh," he said, sounding very surprised.

"You didn't know that?"

"No. I know there were other stores there that you favored," he said with a nonchalance that was annoying. "I just thought that some of your girlfriends and you went shopping there or had lunch there."

"No, no one has dared suggest it."

"Dared? Why wouldn't they suggest going to a mall? Not everyone in that mall can be blamed for what happened, Grace." He ate a little and then shrugged. "Matter of fact, I was there two weeks ago for a lunch meeting. We met at Limoncello's."

"And it didn't bother you?"

"It's just a place. It's not a murder scene."

"We hope."

"Nothing violent happened to her there."

"Seizing her, wrenching her from our lives, was not violent?"

"You know what I mean. Don't hound every word I say, Grace. I miss her as much as you do."

"Okay, John. I'm sorry. What did you say that I didn't hear?"

"I said I had gone to see a doctor about our failure to conceive another child."

"Oh?"

"There's nothing wrong with me, no reason for it not to happen as far as I'm concerned."

I shrugged. "And there's nothing wrong with me physically, either. I guess it's God's choice," I said, and began to clean off the table.

"Maybe God wants to be sure we both have love in our hearts, enough love for another child," he said.

I lost it. I slammed a dish to the floor, and it shattered in a dozen pieces. He barely winced. He wiped his mouth and stood up.

"You had no call to do that, Grace. You want to bring God into the conversation, fine, but then don't be surprised at what I might say."

I put my hands on my hips and looked at him. It occurred to me at that moment that John didn't look all that different from the way he had looked the day before Mary was abducted. There were no new lines in his face, no deeper lines, nothing to show his inner agony. I knew I looked as if I had aged years for every month that had gone by. My look of sweet childhood innocence and joie de vivre was gone, while he looked as cool and as handsome as ever. Was it wrong for me to hate him for that? Why should it surprise me? He was always able to remain stable and calm in the face of trouble or tragedy. Originally, it was one of the reasons I was drawn to him, his inner strength.

"Why, John? Do you believe you hear God? Are you special in His eyes? How can you be so special to Him if something like this has happened to us, to you as well as to me?"

"I'm not saying I'm a prophet or anything like that, Grace. I'm just a religious person, and my religion tells me that God can see into your heart. I'm sorry. I didn't mean to upset you," he added, and then began to pick up the pieces of the plate very carefully. I started to kneel down to help, but he put his hand on my arm. "No. I'll do this. Go rest," he said. "Calm yourself. Go on."

I went into the living room and sat looking out the window that faced the front of the house and the street. As if she could have heard what went on in our kitchen, Margaret suddenly appeared on our sidewalk, approaching our front door. She was carrying something. I waited until I heard the doorbell.

"Who's that?" John called from the kitchen.

"Margaret. I'll get it," I said, and rose as slowly as someone twice my age.

"Hello, Grace," Margaret said. "I brought you a freshly baked apple pie." She uncovered it to show me. "I hope I'm not too late for your dessert."

I stared at the pie. She knew that John and Mary liked her pies, especially her apple one. I could take it or leave it, but what also occurred to me was how much we lived on a schedule. Our neighbor knew when we ate, when we slept, and when we rose in the morning. There might as well not be any walls between our houses.

"No, you're not too late," I said. I took the pie. "Thank you, Margaret."

"My pleasure. I saw you run off today. You know I hate to ask. I know the pain it brings, but was it anything to do with Mary?"

I stared at her for a moment. I hadn't said anything about Sam Abraham to John yet, so I wasn't going to say anything to her. I just shook my head.

"What's that?" we heard John ask as he came up

behind me.

"Just an apple pie made from scratch," Margaret told him.

"Well, thank you, Margaret. Just in time. Care to join us for some coffee and a piece of your own pie?"

She looked at me first. "No, I've got to get back to my oven, John. I made some brownies for the seniors at the center."

"You're just an angel bringing joy everywhere," John told her.

"Whatever the good Lord wants me to do," she replied.

"I guess I'm the only one He doesn't talk to these days," I said. I handed John the pie and walked back to the living room. I sat again just as John closed the door.

"That was really unnecessary, Grace. The woman is just trying to be helpful and caring," he said, standing in the living-room doorway and holding Margaret's pie. I didn't respond. "You really have to see someone. I insist now."

"Insist?"

"Yes, Grace, for both our sakes. You need to start new therapy. I'm going to talk to that new therapist Dr. Bloom suggested for you and see about scheduling something."

"Do what you want," I said.

"I want," he replied as he walked back to the kitchen. "At this point, it should be something *you* want."

Maybe he's right, I thought. *Maybe I should return to therapy.*

I stared out the window. Margaret turned as she left our walkway and looked back at me. She looked so sad and concerned. In fact, she looked as if she was the one who needed someone to bring her pies and compassion, not me.

Maybe John was right.

Maybe I was being selfish with my pain.

It was time to share it and accept that others could appreciate what it meant, too, even if that felt as if I was letting go of Mary a little more. What else could I do now? I was lost at sea.

The only hope I had left was the lifeline Sam Abraham was tossing in my direction.

Whether it would lead to anything or not, I wanted to grasp it as tightly as I could and never let go.

8

In the Dark

Sam Abraham waved from a booth in the rear the moment I entered Woody's. It looked like a London pub with its brass and wood. There was a long bar across from a mirror the length of it, but there were also round dark walnut tables spread evenly throughout the establishment. A set of faux-leather and dark wood booths were all in the back, where the lighting was a bit more subdued. There was the aroma of something delicious being prepared in the kitchen.

Four young men in sport jackets, ties loosened, were at the bar and turned to look at me. The bartender was a curly-gray-haired man with a face that had the kind of deeply etched lines that people would rationalize as giving him more character. There was a waitress sitting on the farthest stool at the bar. I saw no other woman in the tavern. Two older men were at a table on my right, and three men who looked a bit older were at another table down from them. One of the men had a golden retriever sprawled at his feet. Everyone stopped talking for a moment to look at me.

I waved back at Sam and started toward him. He rose

when I reached the booth and reached for my hand. He wasn't shaking it so much as guiding me into the booth and not letting go until I started to sit.

"What is this, a men's club or something?"

"No," he said, laughing. "Time of day. It'll fill up in about an hour or so with couples. Would you like something hard or soft to drink?"

"Soft. Just a mineral water, thank you."

He signaled the waitress and sat across from me.

"That does look more inviting," I said, nodding at his drink.

"It's a Cosmopolitan. The guys at the station ridicule my choice of beverage. They say real men don't drink Cosmopolitans."

The waitress approached. "What'll it be, Sam?" she asked him with her eyes on me.

"A mineral water," he told her.

"No, I changed my mind. I'll have what he's having," I said, and Sam smiled.

He waited for the waitress to leave and then leaned forward. For the first time, I noticed that he had a small scar just under his left eye.

"I don't have much to report, except I had a nice surprise when David Joseph agreed to use his manpower to investigate costume rentals. I'll have to tell you," he added quickly, "that doesn't mean he's bought into my theory about the abduction the way I described it to you yesterday. The best I could get from him was 'That's possible. It might lead to something. We'll look into it.'"

"At this point, I guess I have to grateful for anything," I said.

He stared at me a moment, his gaze intense. He

didn't look critical as much as he looked concerned. I actually brushed back my hair and then wondered if I had forgotten to put on lipstick.

"You look tired today," he said, sitting back.

"It's difficult not to. I don't sleep well, but I didn't sleep well especially last night."

"I hope that wasn't because of what I put you through yesterday."

"No, it was more about what I put myself through by returning to the scene of the crime."

He asked, "Did you tell your husband about the things I said, and did that create some problems at home?"

Before I could respond, the waitress brought my drink.

"Would you like something with it? They have great appetizers here," Sam said.

"No, no, this is fine." I took a sip and smiled. "I remember drinking these when I was in college. My girlfriends thought I was pretending to be sophisticated. My mother actually introduced me to them. My parents were more liberal-minded back then. They thought it was proper to permit their daughter to imbibe, but mainly at home. My mother was quite the little Bohemian in her day, and my father was no slouch when it came to causes about which he felt strongly."

"And now?"

I shrugged. "Reformed liberals are like reformed smokers, their biggest critics."

He laughed and then nodded to the waitress, who had stood by waiting and listening, apparently fascinated with what I was saying. She smiled at him and left us.

"I guess I was rambling a bit there."

"No, no," he said, and then obviously had a sudden

thought. "You're not on any medication that prohibits alcoholic beverages, are you? I suppose I should have asked you that first."

"Not yet," I said, and drank some more. "But that looms in my near future, so maybe I should enjoy this while I still can. John is pushing the new-therapist idea with possibly a new prescription."

"Oh," he said, without indicating agreement or disagreement with the idea.

I looked around the tavern again. There were some framed prints of idyllic country scenes on the walls and interesting sconces. "It's a very nice little place," I said. "From the waitress's reaction, I guess you're a regular here, huh?"

"Home away from home thing. I'm not much of a cook. In fact, the last thing I recall making for myself was a peanut butter and jelly sandwich, and I didn't do all that great a job of that. Too messy."

"My husband can cook and bake well when he wants to. Like with everything else he does, he's a perfectionist." I knew the way I said "perfectionist" made it sound like a profanity.

"Getting back to my first question, did you tell your husband anything about our meeting yesterday?"

"No."

"Was that because of the way I categorized it back at the mall? Fantasy police work?"

"Sort of," I said. I sipped some more and added, "As I said, he's now insisting I have more therapy. I didn't want to give him more reason."

Sam nodded and sipped his own drink. "To be honest, I would have thought you were continuing to have it. It would be understandable in your situation, of course, and maybe very necessary."

"I'm sure it is. I'm not the easiest person to live with these days, and that includes how I treat my friends and our closest neighbor, Margaret Sullivan, who's an honorary member of the family."

"And your babysitter, right?"

"Yes. You remember. I'm impressed."

"I'll confess that I spent a few hours going through the FBI file last night in between things."

"Between things? You really don't sleep."

He laughed and watched me finish my drink. He was still nursing his. "I don't think I should ask if you want another," he said.

"I do."

"Then at least have something to eat with it." He signaled the waitress. "You'll like the spanakopita. It's a Greek pastry with spinach and feta cheese."

"I know what it is."

"I'm sure you do. They make their own here. Woody's wife, that is. She's half Greek and half English. She does a great shepherd's pie, too."

"Shepherd's pie? The moment I walked in, I thought this place reminded me of an English pub."

"As I said, my home away from home," he said. "How about the spanakopita?"

"Fine," I said.

He ordered a platter for us and another Cosmopolitan for each of us, too.

"All right," he said when the waitress left us again. "David's doing another favor for me. He's getting me the scan they ran on other abductions in the state that involved children around Mary's age. I'll have the results tomorrow."

"So, they already looked into that idea about it being a random kidnapping?"

"Sure."

"Why didn't they ever say anything about it, especially when they left hunkering down at our house?"

"In the beginning, they were focusing too hard on this being a personal thing, someone deliberately after your daughter. Once they got off that, they put the case in their computers and ran out some similar MOs. They have other agents in other parts of the state and even around the country looking into these, but so far, nothing's come up concerning your Mary. At least, the way I see it."

"You mean, there was no abduction of a girl around Mary's age that possibly involved someone in a Santa costume?"

"No."

"But if they were serial kidnappers, they would use a Santa costume only during the holidays, right?"

"Yes."

"But they might have done it somewhere else around the same time."

"Exactly. And there's been nothing similar reported about any of the other abductions during that period. That's why David Joseph wasn't that excited about my theory. He recalled how it had turned out to be a dead end when I first looked into it." He twirled the little bit left in his glass. "Speaking of that, I remember your husband wasn't terribly keen on talking about Mary's belief in Santa and that sort of thing."

"He just doesn't know what Mary's dreams and illusions are. Sometimes John has trouble talking to children, his own child included. He isn't in any way cruel to her, nothing like that. He's somewhat oblivious, focusing on other things. He has this hobby. He gets lost in it for hours sometimes. He puts ships in bottles. That and watching football are his biggest distractions from his work. He reads a great deal, too."

"Not things you can share so much with kids Mary's age, I guess."

"He did try to turn Mary into a football fan, but she wasn't as enthusiastic as he would have liked."

"A football fan? She's a little girl and just a little more than five, right?"

"Now going on seven," I said. "I think her recent birthday was the darkest day of my life. John and I hardly said a word to each other all that day, and I couldn't eat a thing. I took a sleeping pill in the afternoon and then another in the evening, but I woke up in the middle of the night in a sweat, trembling, and spent the rest of the night in Mary's little bed, curled up in a fetal position. John didn't wake me before he left for work, but he knew I was in there."

"Damn," Sam said. "I'm so sorry for the pain you're going through."

"Thank you."

"Getting back to Santa Claus . . . how much of a big deal was made of him in your home? I hate to dwell on it, but . . ."

"As John told you, I don't think we did anything more than any other family does for their small children. Nothing unusual was said about Santa, by us or by

Margaret. As far as I know, that is. I mean, Mary asked the same sorts of questions other children might, maybe even more serious questions. She's an extraordinary child."

"What sorts of serious questions?"

"How old he really is, how he can read so many letters, how he can deliver all the presents in one night. Stuff like that."

"Interesting. A child like that might be more apt to pay attention to someone in a Santa costume, like why was he there and not working on his preparations for Christmas or whatever."

"Yes, I can believe she would wonder and even ask him."

"Precocious?"

"Yes, very, but she's John's daughter, too. I'm not surprised."

"You sound both proud and angry about that," he said.

"I have no idea what I sound like anymore. I feel like something is rotting inside me."

"I understand. Tell me more about her."

"Like what?"

"Anything special, unusual, something someone else might notice."

"You mean, something that would attract a pervert or a serial child kidnapper?"

He shrugged.

"You saw her pictures, right?"

"Remarkably beautiful, yes. Almost unreal. That smile, the glow in her face."

I smiled through the tears that were forming. "Some people think she is a little angel."

"I'll bet."

"No, I mean literally."

"Pardon?"

"They say they see a glow around her sometimes, and then there was that incident with Molly Middleton's child, Bradley."

"What incident?"

"I call it an incident. Bradley's mother calls it a miracle. Bradley is a seven-year-old who suffered from acute lymphoblastic leukemia. At the time, he was being treated with chemo and radiation, but we all heard that he wasn't doing well. John says children have an eighty-five-percent survival rate with that form of the disease. It looked like Bradley Middleton was falling into the fifteen percent."

"And?"

"This is ridiculous, of course."

"I'm interested. Please go on."

"Molly visited me one Saturday. She brought Bradley along, and he spent most of the time with Mary. Kids who are two, three, even four years older than her don't seem to feel it's beneath them to talk and be with Mary. Anyway, the following week, we heard that Bradley was suddenly reacting to treatment dramatically. As far as I know, he's now in the eighty-five percent."

"And some people attribute that to the time he spent with your Mary?"

"Those who know, thanks to Molly's big mouth."

He sat back. The waitress brought our platter of spanakopita. I reached for one. They were hot, but I used a napkin.

"What did your husband have to say about all that?"

"Why?"

"Well, with his religious beliefs and all. Did he get upset about it?"

"No. Actually, we didn't talk that much about it. John just shook his head. He did say that desperate people are more susceptible to miracles."

"More susceptible to miracles? What does that mean?"

I shrugged. "That they'll grab on to anything that gives them hope. He hates that the church at one time sold holy relics, and he has no interest in going anywhere like Lourdes. He and Margaret have little arguments about it sometimes. She says God works in mysterious ways and could work through someone on occasion. He didn't disagree with that, but then again, he would never criticize Margaret Sullivan because of her religious beliefs."

"Have you ever told this story to David or his people?" Sam asked.

"What story? What would I tell them? It's a bit fantastic, isn't it? And how can that have an impact on any investigation?"

"So, you don't hold the same beliefs that your husband and your friend Margaret hold, that God works mysteriously and could do something miraculous through a child?"

"It seems a stretch for me. John and I have had some heavy theological discussions from time to time. He enjoys that sort of thing. He's actually very tolerant when it comes to what other people believe. It's almost as if . . ."

"As if what?"

"He knows he's right and can afford to be tolerant. Most of the time, that irks me," I admitted.

Sam smiled. He took a spanakopita, and I took another

and held it up.

"These are good. You were right," I said. I leaned back after sipping some of my second Cosmopolitan. "This is actually the first time I've enjoyed eating and drinking anywhere, even home. Thank you."

He looked embarrassed and sipped his drink. "I'd like to talk to Mrs. Middleton," he suddenly said.

"What? Why? You can't be thinking Molly had something to do with Mary's abduction, can you?"

"No. At least, not deliberately."

"What are you thinking, then?"

"You know how a good writer or a good artist doesn't like anyone reading or looking at his unfinished work? Well, a good detective doesn't like to express his ideas until he's got something to go on. I made that mistake yesterday talking about Santa Claus."

"And I thought I was the paranoid one," I said.

"If you don't have some paranoia, you can't be a good detective," Sam said. He took a small pad out of his jacket pocket and flipped it open. "What's her address? Do you have her telephone number handy?"

"Really?"

"Dead serious," he said.

I took out my cell phone and went to the contacts list to read him Molly's address and number.

"Good," he said, closing his pad.

"Maybe I should phone her first," I said. "She'd probably call me instantly after seeing or speaking to you anyway."

"I'd rather you didn't."

"Why?"

"We detectives have more success speaking to people

when they have no time to prepare. Not that I'm saying she has anything to hide," he quickly added. "Look," he continued when he saw the disturbed expression on my face, "in most cases, people aren't aware of clues. They don't realize what they have seen or heard and how something could be beneficial. When they're guarded, worried about saying the right things, they'll skip stuff. It's only natural."

I nodded. "I don't know what's natural and what's not anymore," I muttered. "Including myself."

"Let me tell you something, Grace. Despite how hard you are on yourself, you're holding up pretty good under the circumstances."

"Is that what you think?"

"Yes."

"And I thought you were a good detective," I said, and he laughed.

"Are you originally from here?" he asked.

There was always a moment in a conversation with someone you didn't know all that well when you felt the mood change, become more relaxed. The way you had measured how you spoke, what you said, even how you looked, seemed to slip away. You were no longer afraid of being too revealing, too honest. That moment came then with Sam Abraham. *Maybe*, I thought, *it's the vodka in the Cosmopolitan*.

"You mean California? Yes. I grew up in Woodland Hills. The only time I left the state was to go to college in Oregon, Willamette University. I majored in English, but I resisted going into teaching and never got my MA. My father found me a good job. I was well on my way to becoming the manager of a software retail outlet when

I met John." I paused. I knew he was expecting to hear more. "I'm afraid I don't have a terribly interesting story."

"Depends who's listening," Sam said.

"Yes. I have to keep reminding myself that I am speaking to an L.A. detective. Did you always want to be in law enforcement?"

"Yeah, I guess. My father was a state CID investigator in Pennsylvania. My older brother married and moved to Texas, where he became a county sheriff. I started there thanks to him, but I wanted to do more, so I attended the University of Phoenix and got an associate's degree in criminal justice. Then, with my brother's connections, I found a position in L.A."

"What brought you to Southern California?"

"I wanted to be sure I didn't have to buy snow tires," he said.

I laughed, feeling more and more lightheaded. "So, really, why are you still a bachelor?" I asked.

He studied his glass for a moment, twirling it by the stem, and then smiled. "I never married, but I did live with someone for nearly five years. She got tired of my schedule, our lifestyle, I guess, and found someone who fit her goals better. Talk about being a good detective, I had no idea she was seeing someone. One day, she was gone, and it all came crashing down."

"I would say a woman who was ignored to the extent you probably ignored her had some justification for, as the British say, 'doing a runner.'"

He laughed. Then he looked serious. "Maybe I just wasn't as committed to her as I thought I was. We all fool ourselves as much as or even more than we fool others sometimes."

"Yes," I said. We just looked at each other, neither knowing what else to say. "Another pregnant pause," I said.

He smiled. "I hope it doesn't take nine months for either of us to say something."

I glanced at my watch.

"It's getting there. You all right to drive?" he asked me.

I looked at what remained of my second Cosmopolitan. "The sad thing is, I enjoyed these, but I don't feel a thing, no buzz, nothing. Sometimes you want to, or need to," I said.

He signaled the waitress. More people were coming in now, and many were couples.

"Check, please, Toni," he said.

"You were right about this place filling up," I said, looking around.

"Yeah, I'd stay, but I feel like Italian tonight. I'll call you," he said when the waitress brought the check.

I stood up. "Thank you," I said.

He looked up at me. "I hope someday I'll have really earned that."

I started away. I headed to my car in the parking lot next door. When I reached the car, I saw that he was coming into the lot, too, walking quickly to catch up.

"You sure you're all right to drive? Those Cosmopolitans can sneak up on you."

"I'm fine." I didn't get into the car, and he didn't move toward his.

"You have to hurry home, I guess."

"Not tonight. My husband has a dinner meeting in Anaheim."

"Really?" He looked toward the street and then

turned back to me. "I'd be happy to buy you dinner at my favorite little Italian restaurant, Favola, on Third Street in Santa Monica. Maybe you've heard of it. Wait," he said before I could even think to respond. "That's out of line. I'll be accused of taking advantage of you. I know better. Sorry."

I smiled. "No one could ever take advantage of me as much as whoever abducted my daughter has. Everything else is insignificant."

"I understand. I'll call you tomorrow," he said, and headed for his car.

He didn't look back. I got into my car and started for home.

There hadn't been that many times since Mary's abduction when I had returned to an empty house. That is not to say that the house didn't feel empty otherwise. As I was driving back, however, I envisioned the darkness, not just in the house but also what I felt had settled around it. Southern California had a justifiable reputation for sunny days. Months could easily go by without one day with a totally overcast sky, but no matter how much sunshine there was, I still felt as if I were now living within a brooding and bruised cloud that had snuggled around every corner and hovered over every window.

It wasn't just the darkness and the way the emptiness in my heart seemed to spread throughout my body, sometimes making me feel more like a ghost, that made my return to our house so undesirable. Although I would never go so far as to say that John had recuperated from our great loss, I would say he was coping very well. As far as I could tell, he didn't see or hear the same demons. He was able to embrace his work and tie it around himself like some medieval suit of armor. I was sure he was giving his company far more these days simply because he hated leaving his work and heading home. I couldn't blame him. In fact, most of the time, I envied him.

But I had given up a professional work life for Mary, and now I didn't have Mary. I didn't want to go back to work. I was positive that I wouldn't be able to give any employer my full attention or effort and that before long I would probably be let go anyway. To John's credit, he never encouraged this. He did his best to get me out of the house for social occasions, but I had come to the point where I couldn't put on the act and recite the lines required. The effort to make some sort of semblance of a normal life right now was too exhausting.

On the other hand, as I drove toward home, I didn't feel like curling up into a ball and locking myself away, either. There was still life in me, feminine life. Every time I thought about doing something that could be fun for me, I was overwhelmed with guilt. How could I laugh, smile, enjoy anything, while Mary was still in the hands of a kidnapper?

The moments of pleasure I had just experienced with Sam Abraham were easy to tolerate and justify because, after all, I was meeting with the one man right now who might be able to do something about Mary's abduction. At least he cared and wanted to try harder. How could it be sinful, selfish of me, to want to be with him?

The rationale was enough.

I pressed my foot on the brake pedal and pulled to the

side of the road. For a long moment, I sat there arguing with myself, and then, almost motivated more by anger than anything else, I wrenched the steering wheel around and did a U-turn, angering some drivers. They let me know it, of course. Road rage was almost part of being a Californian, especially a citizen of Los Angeles. It was practically a driving requirement. I imagined it being part of the drivers' road test: "Show me how you would let a bad driver know he was a bad driver: Give him the bird, scream, lay on your horn, or pass him and deliberately slow down?" There were dozens of ways to show your anger when you were in a car. You felt invulnerable surrounded by all that metal and having that engine power. Maybe that was why people didn't mind the long commutes. They felt safe.

When would I ever really feel safe again?

I didn't think I would go all the way when I made the U-turn. I expected the more sensible and cautious part of me to fight its way back to the forefront and have me put on the brakes, but, determined to keep it down, I whipped around streets, accelerated on yellow lights to get through intersections, and pulled up to Favola's valet parking.

I was shocked that I had gotten there so fast. For a few long moments, I just sat in the car, confusing the parking attendant, but then I lunged out and took the ticket from him, practically taking his fingers along with it. He looked a little frightened. My quick smile didn't relax him that much, either, but I wasn't concerned with his feelings at the moment.

I went to the restaurant's entrance, took a deep breath, and stepped in.

It took a few seconds for me to locate Sam and for him to realize that I was there.

Maybe I was making a mistake, but the look on his face told me I wouldn't be disappointed.

9

Inches Apart

"I'm not in the mood to prepare my own dinner," I said, standing before him at his table. "I hate cooking for only one person, even if it's me. Maybe especially if it's me."

He continued smiling, looking both surprised and amused. Then, as if he realized he wasn't dreaming, he shot up and came around to pull out a chair for me.

"Perfect. I haven't ordered anything yet. You're in for a treat, believe me," he said when he sat again. "This is really like eating in someone's home. They make their own pasta daily, and Mrs. Carnesi, the owner and chef, creates her own special marinara sauce from an old family recipe."

"Are you part owner of this place, too?"

He laughed. "With how much I eat here, I think so. If you like meatballs, theirs are very special, so light, or if you want a great angel-hair pasta with shrimp and—"

"Why don't you just order for me?" I said. "If you go through the menu like that, I'll become ravenous and eat the table."

He laughed again. "Okay." He signaled to a waitress. "You fine with a good Chianti Classico?"

"Yes, I'd like that. Another one of John's hobbies is wine. With him, it's a science. He knows what the weather was like for the vineyard during the year that's on the bottle and therefore how good the grape crop was."

Sam shrugged. "I don't do any research. I just know what I like."

"That's fine. I've come to the conclusion that depending on your instinct is better than depending on your intelligence, no matter what Darwin wrote," I said.

He gave the waitress our order and then talked about other wines he liked. When she brought the Chianti back and opened it, he asked her to pour it first into my glass so I could be the one to taste and test it.

"Perfect," I said. It was. She poured us each a glass.

He passed me some garlic bread. "Homemade, too," he said. "Go on. Try it," he urged when I hesitated.

"Hanging around with you, I'll regain all the weight I lost very quickly. Even the vanity mirror in my bedroom has gone on strike."

He laughed and shook his head. "You're fine the way you are," he said. "Don't gain or lose a pound."

I know I blushed. I hadn't felt that soft surge of heat come up from my neck into my cheeks for so long that it seemed like the first time.

"Thank you. It's been quite a while since a man, including my own husband, has complimented me on my appearance. I had forgotten just how important that is for a woman. In my way of thinking, men can go months, even years, without any compliments about their looks, but take a woman for granted, and you risk being beheaded."

"It's a miracle I haven't been, I suppose. To be

absolutely honest, I'm not that good at giving women compliments."

"Don't underestimate yourself. You're not too bad."

Now he blushed. "Maybe I'm just too . . ."

"Afraid of committing yourself to an opinion? I used to be," I added before he could admit to it.

"Well, I don't know if it's exactly that, although I guess I'm always looking for some confirmation. I look for clues everywhere before I make a decision, even in the grocery store when I go shopping. You know, like when was this meat really put out, or why is this soup behind the other? I probably spend twice as much time in the supermarket as any other bachelor."

"How old are you, Sam?"

"Thirty-three, a year older than you. Sorry, I read that file, remember?"

"There are probably facts in it that I don't even know about myself," I said.

"Probably. It's FBI."

"Then you have an unfair advantage. What I know about you can fit on an index card." I sipped the wine and tasted the bread with a little olive oil.

"She gets that olive oil from a cousin in Tuscany," he said.

I nodded. "Very good. I wish I was a better cook. Margaret Sullivan is a very good cook and baker, too. She's terrific with pies, makes her own crust, and I've yet to have a better Irish soda bread. My mother isn't much of a cook, so I didn't grow up learning little delicious things in the kitchen. You know the joke about women like me?"

"What's for dinner tonight, dear, reservations?"

"That's it. I mean, I'm not a terrible cook. John would rather eat at home, so I work hard on it, but lately . . . nothing I do around the house is any good."

"It will be," he said with a confidence that brightened me.

The waitress served us two caprese salads.

"Don't say it," I warned. "This mozzarella cheese is homemade."

"Close to it. This time, it's a nephew on her husband's side, who happens also to be a terrific cook."

"You know, now that I think of it, every Italian man I know, even John's business associates, can cook and does so."

"Half the time in *The Godfather* and on *The Sopranos*, they're eating or cooking," Sam said. He poured me some more wine.

I looked at the glass and stopped chewing as if my whole body had gone on pause. I had been at warp speed with glib talk to keep my nervousness as well hidden as possible. Suddenly, all the words came back up like some indigestible food and drink.

Mary's little face flashed before me.

"You okay?" he asked.

"How can they be so good at this, Sam?" I asked, not looking at him. So that there would be no doubt that I wasn't talking about our food and Italians, I added, "How can they just sweep her up and not leave a solid clue behind?" I swung my gaze on him like someone moving a flashlight.

"I know what you mean. It's what makes me believe now that this is not a single personal event," he said. "Not in the sense we were thinking in the beginning. Whoever has done this is professional, or let's say very experienced. I'm confident that Mary's not their first. I just have to put together the how and why. I should have never left the case, even with the FBI on it," he added. "I don't usually get personally involved with the victims of crimes I'm investigating. I mean, I learn enough about them to help with the investigation of course, but . . ."

"I understand," I said. "We got to you."

"You got to me. I mean, I felt sorry for everyone in your family, of course, but a mother is special."

He kept his gaze on me a moment longer and then drank some of his own wine.

We ate in silence for a while. I realized there was music on. It was just loud enough to float above the cacophony of other sounds behind us, the chatter and the laughter and dishes being served. A surge of guilt tried to take over, but I fought it back. If I didn't get back into the world, I wouldn't be of any assistance in solving Mary's abduction, I told myself. Was that just rationalizing, or was I right?

"Pavarotti?"

"None other," Sam replied. "I like that you can actually hear the music in this restaurant. In most places, it's just a dull background."

"Italian and French food especially are better enjoyed with music. We have this friend, Asher Roberts, who admits to being a Francophile. He spends his entire summer in Beaulieu-sur-Mer on the Riviera and never misses an opportunity to tell us how poorly Americans dine, rushing their meals and not savoring the flavors, the wine, the moment."

"He's not wrong. From what I can see, most people

gobble everything in front of a television set. You could serve them mush, and they wouldn't know it. I'm guilty of doing that often myself."

"Not John," I said. "He won't bring up the French to make his point. He isn't crazy about traveling. Foreign places put him at a disadvantage because he doesn't speak anything but English, but he likes to make dinner an event. As we eat, he catches me up on his business work. I don't think I'm a good audience anymore."

"So, he's stuck to the same routine despite . . ."

"Yes. John believes that is how we'll have the strength to go on."

"Maybe he's right," Sam said.

The waitress brought our main dishes.

"It smells wonderful," I said, inhaling the garlic.

We ate in silence for a few moments.

"It is very good," I told him. "You're like what truck drivers are to the best roadside eateries, I imagine. My father always says to follow the truck driver wherever he turns off, and you'll have good food on the road."

"Most cops and law-enforcement people aren't as concerned about food as I am," he said. "I wouldn't necessarily follow any of them off the road or to any place in the city."

I paused. Every time I started to feel good or enjoy something, the reason I was really there came rushing back.

"Do you think they're feeding her well, keeping her healthy?"

"It would make no sense for them to take her and do otherwise, whatever their purpose."

"Their purpose," I repeated. The food got stuck in

my throat. I reached for the glass of water quickly and followed it up with some wine. "Are you thinking more about Mexico, Sam?"

"We can't rule it out, especially with our proximity to the border, but my instincts are telling me otherwise."

"Why? What are they telling you?"

"I can't give you an answer that would make any sense to you yet. It's just a feeling, a feeling that comes with the territory, the experience."

"You think she might still be somewhere in this city?"

"I don't know, Grace. Let's be careful about what we imagine. Let me see what else I can do first," he said. It sounded more like a plea.

I nodded, certain that whatever glow I had brought back into my face was quickly disappearing.

"I hope I haven't done the wrong thing by raising your hopes," he said.

"No, no. Trust me, I'll never say or feel that." I played with my food and then took another forkful. *Coming here was a mistake*, I told myself. *I can't do this. I can't let myself enjoy a moment.*

As if he could hear my thoughts, he reached across the table and took my left hand into his. He held it and smiled. "You've got to find the strength, either by doing what your husband does or wants you to do or . . ."

"Or what?"

"Some other way," he said. I looked at his hand holding mine, and he let go.

"I'll never stop hating myself for what happened," I said.

"That's so wrong. They're predators. They pounce. You couldn't carry her around all the time. People get distracted, not out of selfishness or something, at least not you," he said.

"You're so sure of that?"

"I told you, police experience instincts," he said, smiling.

I drank some more wine, ate as much as I could, and then sat back to look at other people. Some nodded and smiled at me. One woman who looked about my age appeared to be celebrating something. I could see it in the glow in her face and the way the man across from her was smiling, too. They kept toasting with their glasses of wine. She looked as if she wanted to share her happiness with anyone who would glance at her, but I couldn't smile back.

How ironic life is, I thought. No one a few feet away from us had any idea of what anguish and misery I was in. The laughter, the good food, and the music were so out of place for me, and yet I yearned for it so much.

"Would you like to try a dessert? They have homemade tiramisu. Coffee, espresso?"

"No, I've had enough," I said. "Thank you."

He nodded to the waitress. "Just the check, please, Sonya," he said.

"Everything all right?" she asked, looking at my plate. I had eaten as much as I could, but they gave a big portion, and I was leaving almost half.

"It was wonderful," I said. "I just can't eat as much as other people, especially Italians in movies."

Sam laughed. It occurred to me that a man's laughter was something I really missed. Neither John nor my father or father in law did much more than smile occasionally in my presence now. It was as if they believed

I would hate them for not soaking in my misery. I certainly couldn't blame them if that was so. How could I be other than I was? Your child, especially for a mother, is always part of you. I felt amputated, crippled, as if part of my very soul was gone. I certainly didn't enjoy being this way or want it to continue, but how could I distract myself with any pleasure and not feel that I was giving up on my little girl?

"Let me pay half of that," I said when the waitress brought the bill. "I invited myself."

"No way," Sam said. "Besides, it's now an expense."

I knew he meant that to be funny or make me feel better, but it didn't settle on my ears that way. His soft smile dissipated like smoke in the wind.

"I didn't mean that the way it sounded," he said when my expression changed.

"I know. But I'd rather speak to you than to a therapist, so maybe it does fit the category of an expense."

The waitress took his credit card.

"Not to me. It fits the category of pleasure," he said.

"Me, too, but a guilty pleasure."

"You can't think like that, Grace. You need to live, be strong. It will matter in the fight."

"You're right, of course." I smiled. "Maybe we should not think so much about what we do, analyze it to death. Sometimes I just want to run on emotion, on fumes, and do something simply because it feels good and not because it makes sense."

"That makes sense," he said, smiling.

He signed the check and put his credit card back into this wallet.

"Thank you again," I said, and got up.

"I really am glad you came," he said as we walked out together. We handed our valet parking tickets to the attendant. "I am, too."

"Really clear out tonight," Sam said, looking up at the night sky. "I'll be able to see Catalina."

"Where do you live?"

"I have an apartment on Ocean Avenue in Santa Monica. Two-bedroom on the top floor facing the ocean."

"That's expensive real estate," I said.

"I know. I solved a murder case that involved the owner of the building, and in appreciation he got me a good deal. It's still up for grabs whether it was a conflict of interest."

"Really?"

"No. I'm just kidding. No one complained about it. Besides, it would have been an insult to turn down his gratitude. He's from the Middle East and takes that sort of thing dead seriously."

"I don't know whether to believe you or not," I said.

My car was approaching.

"Tell you what," Sam said. "It's early. Follow me, and I'll show you the view if you like. I'll even give you something in the way of an expensive after-dinner drink. Another gift from a grateful citizen."

"I don't know." I looked at the time. John wouldn't be home for at least two hours, and I liked the idea of continuing to discuss Mary's abduction.

Or was I just using that as an excuse?

Sam waited, looking at me as if he was holding his breath in anticipation. Whatever caution was spiraling in my chest, I smothered it and nodded.

"Okay."

He smiled, and when his car arrived, I followed him. Almost at every cross street on the way, I thought to turn off and go home, but I held on to the steering wheel as if the car was really in control of itself. When we reached his address, we turned into an underground garage. Most of the buildings in the area had them, and I knew they all had guest parking spaces. He pointed at one when we entered, and I turned into it and parked while he parked in his own space.

"How many units in the building?"

"This one has only eighteen. They tried to get me to be on the homeowners board but gave up when they realized what a workaholic I was. The truth is, I haven't attended one meeting."

"I'm sure they like the fact that a police detective is in the building."

"Not really any benefit unless there's a sign stating that outside," he said, and pushed the button for the elevator.

The moment I stepped in, I felt I should step out. When the door closed, I turned sharply. Sam just stared at me with that soft smile.

"Relax," he said. "You need to take a break, or you won't be any good to anyone, let alone yourself."

I nodded.

When the elevator opened, I followed him to his condo door. He opened it and stepped back.

"Wait," he said. "I should tell you ahead of time that I'm not sloppy, but I'm not exactly Mr. Neat."

"That's a relief," I said.

"What is?"

"A little disorganization."

He laughed and switched on the entryway light, and I entered. The entryway had a tan travertine floor that extended into the small kitchen to the right. The living room was straight ahead and had a wide oval coffee-colored Berber carpet. It looked brand new, as did the soft, dark brown, half-circle leather three-piece sofa. There was a round glass-topped coffee table with two matching side tables. To the right of the sofa was a khaki-cushioned recliner. His wide-screen television was mounted across from the sofa, and to the right of that was a walled bookcase not quite filled. Behind the sofa was a curtained sliding door that opened onto a nice-sized balcony.

Sam rushed into the kitchen and began to put some cups and dishes into the dishwasher. There was an opened box of cereal on the kitchen table. I followed him in and smiled at his effort to tidy up. Through the opposite entrance, I saw his dining room. The cherry-finish formal dining-room table was covered with magazines and newspapers, some paper cups and dishes. There was a vase of silk roses in the center. The table had five chairs, and the dining room had a low-gloss warm honey hardwood floor. A matching buffet stood against the wall on the left. I could see that the dining-room guests would have a magnificent view of the ocean through the two large windows.

"Nice furniture," I said. "You have excellent taste."

"I cannot tell a lie. The place came furnished."

"Well, whoever lived here before had good taste. I guess you don't throw too many dinner parties."

He looked at the table and laughed. "Not yet, but I have high hopes. If you look to the left in the living room, you'll see I have a pretty nice bar set up, too."

"Oh?"

I went through the dining room and entered the living room. He did have a nice bar, and for some reason, it had nothing on it, unlike every other counter or table.

"Don't you use the bar?" I asked.

He came up behind me. "Sitting alone at your own bar is a little depressing," he said, almost in a whisper.

"Well, let's make sure that doesn't happen tonight," I said, and took a seat on a stool. He walked around and put two snifter glasses on the bar.

"Brandy or a good port?"

"Is everything here gifts from the appreciative?"

He put his hand over his heart and pretended to be fatally wounded. I realized I was really laughing, and it felt good.

"Okay, a little port," I said, and he poured some for both of us.

"To Mary's return," he said, holding his glass out for me to touch with mine.

I did it, and we both sipped.

"What are the chances now, really, Sam?"

"Whatever they are, I'll work to improve them," he said.

There was no way to stop the tears. He came around the bar quickly to hold me. I pressed the side of my face against his shoulder, and for a long moment, neither of us moved. I felt his fingers on my hair, and then—maybe I imagined it—I thought he kissed my hair. I didn't move for another moment. Then I caught my breath and sat back.

He smiled. "So, now I have to prove what I said."

"What?"

"The view. C'mon." He moved to the sliding door. He opened it and beckoned for me to follow him out onto the patio.

I did and looked out at the Santa Monica Pier. The Ferris wheel was going and all lit up. We could see a good crowd of people on the pier, going to the restaurants and outdoor games. Most of them were probably tourists. Santa Monica was a big attraction for Europeans. Sam pointed farther out, and I did see Catalina.

"Well?"

"You were telling the truth. It's beautiful, Sam."

"Yeah, trouble is, I don't spend enough time here."

I sipped my port and looked down at the continuous line of traffic, the pedestrians, and the activity below and around us. For all we knew, whoever had taken Mary was down there. Maybe she was, too. A slight chill ran through me despite the port wine. I shuddered, and Sam, out of instinct or just concern, put his arm around me quickly.

"We'll go back in," he whispered.

I started to nod but stopped. I slowly brought my face around. We were inches apart now. Did I truly want it to happen? Was that why I turned and didn't just break out of his embrace and go inside? And if I wanted it, was I rushing toward it out of some desperate need to feel like a woman again, to feel alive again, and to admit to myself that I did have other needs?

Who moved first?

It didn't matter. We kissed, and he held me tightly.

I know I should have pulled away then, but I didn't.

Neither of us moved or tried to kiss again. Finally, he released his embrace, and I turned and walked back inside. It was as if we were both going to behave as though nothing had happened. He followed me in and went behind the bar.

"Do you want some more port?" he asked.

"No. Thank you." I put my glass on the bar. "Maybe this wasn't such a good idea. I think I had better start for home."

He nodded, no argument in him. "Let me come down to the garage with you," he said, coming around quickly.

We went out and to the elevator in silence.

"Sometimes you can have trouble with that gate," he offered as a weak excuse for accompanying me to my car.

I nodded but didn't look at him. As soon as the elevator door opened, I headed for my vehicle. He followed slowly. After I got in, he stood looking at me. I rolled down the window.

"Thanks for the little tour and the after-dinner drink," I said.

He finally smiled. "Grace," he said. I shook my head. "I'll call you," he added when I started the engine.

I nodded and drove to the garage entrance. I didn't look back, but I was sure he was still there looking after me. When the gate opened, I drove out and headed for home.

John had not yet arrived. There were only the small lamps lit in the living room and a hall light. I pulled into the driveway and then into the garage. The silence in my home had the effect of thunder. I could feel myself begin to shake. As quickly as I could, I crossed to the stairway and started up. When I reached Mary's room, I paused and then slowly opened the door. I had my eyes closed, and in my imagination, I saw her lying there, sleeping softly, her golden hair over the pillow, one of her favorite dolls beside her.

When I opened my eyes, the sight of the empty bed felt as if a nail had been driven through my heart. Slowly, embracing myself, I lowered myself to my knees, and there I remained sobbing until my chest and my back ached so much I could no longer stand it.

I rose and went to Mary's bed to stroke her pillow, and then I curled up on her bed as I had done too many times since her abduction. It helped me to feel close to her again, but I was hoping that somehow, wherever she was, she sensed me, too. Perhaps she curled up in whatever bed she had and pretended I was there. I embraced her pillow and closed my eyes.

That was where John found me.

He didn't wake me, nor did he mention it the following morning. It was as if he believed that if he denied what he saw, it would not have happened.

Maybe that was what Sam Abraham and I had done the night before.

For a moment, there was some comfort in thinking so, but that went away when I found myself wanting to remember.

10

Je Ne Regrette Rien

Molly Middleton called me just before noon the following morning. Sam had just finished interviewing her. She sounded surprised that anyone was still looking to solve Mary's disappearance, which annoyed me at first.

"Grace, a Los Angeles detective investigating Mary's disappearance came to see me today to ask questions about Mary and Brad," she began, gasping, her voice straining with excitement as if she had been running in a marathon.

I was surprised but delighted that Sam had gotten right to it.

"Oh, really? What did he want to know?" The calmness in my voice only served to put more tension into hers.

"He asked about Brad's illness and what people thought after his amazing recovery. He wanted to know what I told people about Mary and who I had told, stuff like that. He was polite and all, but he made me feel like I was in court on a witness stand." She lowered her voice as though she didn't want anyone nearby to hear. "He wanted exact times and places. I did my best to remember, but I wasn't exactly keeping a diary." She paused to catch her breath and added, "I hope I didn't do anything wrong. I mean . . . what could I have done wrong?"

I smiled to myself, picturing Sam Abraham standing before her with his little pad opened, his pen poised, and those scrutinizing eyes of his raking over her face and her every gesture. Molly was a nervous person normally. I imagined she always panicked when she didn't have enough milk or bread. I couldn't blame her, however. After all, she had lived through nearly losing her child, only hers was abducted by a disease.

When I was silent, she continued. "I mean, even Brad's oncologist called his recuperation a miracle, so why shouldn't I say that when people at church asked me about Brad and Mary? I'm sure you knew what I thought, right? John was never upset about me talking about it."

"Yes, we both knew what you believed, Molly."

"Right. I don't care what anyone else thinks. I know Brad's recovery is a miracle, and I couldn't think of anything else he had done or we had done with him except visit you and Mary. You know I always thought Mary was special. I hope you're not angry about it. Did I do something wrong? I would just hate myself if I had, especially after what a wonderful thing happened for us. I mean, why would the police come to see me?"

"No, Molly, you didn't do anything wrong. No one is angry. The detective is just trying to find something to help him understand what's happened. No one's blaming you for anything," I said. "How could they?"

"Well, I'm glad of that. I couldn't live with myself if I was in any way—"

"I told you, no one is thinking that."

Now that I had relieved her fear of being accused of anything, she became more indignant. "I mean, why would a police detective come to me, of all people, to talk about Mary's abduction? My goodness, I'm almost as upset about this as you are, Grace. Mary was special to me, too. And I don't mean just because of Brad's recovery. I loved your little girl. We've always dreamed of having a daughter like Mary. Who wouldn't?"

"I know that."

"That detective was so . . . so insistent about the smallest details."

"Well, that's what they do, need to do. I'm sorry he upset you."

"He didn't exactly upset me. He was very nice about it, but shouldn't he be looking elsewhere for some answers?"

"He's looking everywhere, Molly. We should all be grateful someone's still looking," I added, perhaps a little too sharply. I found myself as defensive of Sam as I was of anything.

"Yes, yes, you're right. Of course. I didn't mean to imply anything else."

"Well, thanks for cooperating with him," I said. "How's Bradley?"

"Oh, he's doing great." She paused. "There was something else, something I never told you myself. I'm sure you knew about it, but I thought I should tell the detective since he was asking about it all so intently, and I was afraid if I didn't tell him and someone else did and said I knew that—"

"Oh? What's that?"

"Well, it was during one of those Sundays you didn't

come to church," she began, and then paused like someone who had said too much.

"Yes? So? What?" I felt as if I was pumping a well handle to get it out of her.

"Laurie James's son Samson has type one diabetes. Did you know that?"

"I think so, yes. So? What does that have to do with anything?"

"She knew about Bradley, and she knew what I believed, of course. She had Samson sit with Mary in church. I found out that Laurie told him to hold Mary's hand."

"Hold her hand? I don't understand, Molly. What exactly are you telling me?"

"She was hoping for a miracle similar to Bradley's. You know, that Samson would be cured of his diabetes because of his contact with your Mary. Like what they call the laying on of hands. It's in the Bible, you know."

"My God," I said. "Did John know what Laurie James was doing?"

"I don't think Laurie said it in so many words to him, but I can't be absolutely positive. I know she arranged for Samson to sit next to Mary, and no one objected. I mean, Mary was sitting right beside Margaret. She wouldn't let anything unpleasant happen to her. I thought they were just being nice to humor her. I didn't really expect anything would come of it. Well, I shouldn't say it like that. It makes me sound selfish, but as my husband, Morty, is fond of saying, lightning rarely strikes twice in the same place, and what happened to Bradley was like lightning to us, good lightning."

I almost didn't want to ask, but I knew I had to. "What about Samson James. I mean, since that day?"

"His doctor says it's too early to tell, but he sees big improvement. No one said anything to you about it?"

"No."

"Well, I don't mean to upset you."

"It's all right."

"No, I hear it in your voice. Oh, dear, I don't think I can do anything right when it comes to any of this. I'm just so clumsy with words sometimes." She was fishing for some forgiveness, but if there was one thing I wasn't going to do, it was feel sorry for Molly Middleton now. She had her child, healthy and happy, beside her. I had empty chairs, an empty bed, and clothes hanging in my daughter's closet like flags of surrender.

"I'm not upset," I said in clipped tones. "Thanks for the call, Molly, and thanks for cooperating with the police." I hung up before she could respond.

For a few moments, I sat fuming despite what I had just told her. I wasn't upset; I was enraged. Why had neither John nor Margaret ever mentioned this incident to me? How could they keep such an event from me? What if it had resulted in some emotional or psychological trauma for Mary? Were there other similar incidents being kept from me? Why hadn't Mary said anything about it? She always talked about church and what went on there, especially if I hadn't gone. It was as if she didn't want me to be denied the pleasure. Had John told her not to say anything? Had he told her it would upset me? He was right. It would have.

When I had awoken that morning, I had almost immediately begun sinking into a pool of guilt because of what I had done the night before. The memory of the kiss on Sam's balcony was so vivid that it was as if we had just done it. I battled my way out of the guilt and then lay looking up at the ceiling, luxuriating in the memory of that kiss—defiantly, in fact. John hadn't kissed me that way for some time, not even before Mary's abduction and not even when we were making love because of his determination that we have another child as soon as possible. Whatever guilt I had felt dissipated and was replaced with anger.

John had left for work nearly an hour earlier. He had made no attempt to wake me to join him at breakfast. Perhaps he'd had breakfast out. He did that from time to time when there was some client or associate to meet. I knew that my falling asleep in Mary's room must have annoyed him. I was confident that he'd be at me again about my seeing the therapist. Apparently, he hadn't followed up yet by calling her, but I was more determined than ever not to do it. It was painful and agonizing to face each day without Mary and to worry about where she was and how she was being treated, but I couldn't let go of the feeling that if I did see a therapist and she put me on some medication, resulting in my becoming zombielike, I would be accepting defeat.

What was pain, anyway, both physical and mental, if not a constant reminder that something was wrong? Ironically, if it weren't for pain, we would die from the most minor injuries, traumas, cuts, and internal issues. Pain caused us to seek treatment and cure. I suddenly realized that was why I hated John's religious philosophy. Accepting any tragedy by thinking of it as God's will was essentially denying yourself the emotional and psychological pain. Following that theological logic, how could you seek a cure? It was blasphemy to challenge what God had decided in His wisdom, a wisdom that John was fond of saying was beyond human understanding. Didn't he see the basic contradiction in that?

I wanted to bring his high and mighty logic down to the ridiculous. Why brush your teeth? If God wanted you to have cavities, all the brushing in the world wouldn't matter, not to mention vaccinations to prevent polio, smallpox, typhus, or the flu. *No, I will not accept anything*, I thought. At dinner, I wanted to recite Dylan Thomas's "Do not go gentle into that good night; rage, rage against the dying of the light."

For a while, I walked around the house having this imaginary debate with John and babbling to myself. I was sure that anyone observing me would think I had gone mad. When I opened a drawer, I slammed it closed almost instantly. I practically took the refrigerator door off its hinges going after something inside and nearly shattered a coffee mug when I slapped it down on the table. I welcomed the rage. It seemed to bring relief from my sorrow and make me feel stronger. When the phone rang, I ripped it off the cradle before the first ring had completed.

"What?" I said as if someone had interrupted me.

"Grace, dear, are you all right?" Margaret asked.

"That's a pretty stupid question, Margaret," I replied. My tone took her completely by surprise. She was silent. I could see her standing in her kitchen, holding the phone to her ear with her mouth locked open. "How can I ever be all right?"

"No, no, I didn't mean that. You were gone so long yesterday and didn't come home until the evening, and then, when I saw John this morning, he said you were still asleep so I wondered . . ."

"What do you do, Margaret, sit by the window watching me go to and fro?"

"Oh, you know better than that, Grace." She paused, but I didn't rescue the conversation. "Well, I was heading to the senior center and just wanted to see if you needed anything before I left."

"No, thank you."

"Okay, but don't hesitate to call me if you do need anything. You can call me on my cell phone, and I'll check on you later."

"I don't need anyone to check on me," I snapped back, like someone biting the hand that fed her. Again, she was dead quiet. It had a calming effect on me, and of course, I felt guilty. How could anyone have a better neighbor? "Look, I'm suffering, Margaret," I said in a much softer tone of voice, "but I'm not an invalid, at least not yet."

"Of course you're not. You know I pray for you every day, dear."

"And for Mary."

"Of course. Well . . ."

"Wait, Margaret."

"Yes?"

"Why didn't you ever tell me about Samson James?"

"Who?"

"Samson James, Laurie James's son, the boy who has diabetes and who was placed beside Mary in church one Sunday when I wasn't with you and John."

"Oh . . . oh yes. What a sweet little boy. Why didn't I tell you what, dear?"

"That his mother wanted Mary to touch him so he would have a miraculous cure just like Molly Middleton's son, Bradley. You remember that, Margaret, don't you?"

"Oh, well, John didn't think much about it, so I just assumed you knew. I'm sorry, dear. I didn't mean to keep anything from you. It was a harmless little gesture."

"Right, a gesture."

"Is there any particular reason you're asking about it now?"

I hesitated. I didn't feel like going through my conversation with Molly, and besides, I didn't even know why I was so upset. "No, no reason," I said. "Thanks for calling, Margaret. Enjoy the day." I hung up.

Not long after, John phoned from his office. "Are you all right?" he asked after I had said hello.

"Yes."

"I didn't want to wake you this morning. You looked like you needed to sleep. Did you take a pill?"

"No."

"I'm sorry I wasn't home earlier last night. You know I hate leaving you alone, but . . ."

"I was fine, John."

"What did you have to eat?"

"Why this cross-examination, John?"

"I'm not conducting a cross-examination. I'm just trying to see how you are doing, Grace. Why are you taking this belligerent tone with me?"

"I just spoke with Molly Middleton this morning. She told me about Laurie James asking to have her son Samson sit next to Mary in church one Sunday so she could touch him and cure him. You never said anything about it."

"What's there to say? If she wanted to believe that God might work a miracle for her son through Mary, fine. I never discourage anyone from approaching God, regardless of their beliefs. Besides, Mary wasn't disturbed about it. In fact, she welcomed the attention, as I recall."

"She never said anything to me about it," I said mournfully. "Why not? Did you tell her not to mention it?"

"Of course not. That was our Mary. She had a natural humility, a grace about her."

"Has!" I screamed. "Has, not had!"

"Of course. Whatever grace and beauty God placed in her is always there."

"I don't mean that. I mean she's still alive, and we're getting her back. Tell that to your God, and don't make any appointments with any therapist for me!" I slammed the phone back into its cradle.

My heart was thumping. I gasped and sat, stunned at my own outburst.

Had I gone on the offensive because that was the best defense and I wanted to avoid telling him about where I had gone and where I had eaten the night before? I had a feeling that Margaret had called him right after speaking to me and told him she thought something was wrong. A part of me knew she was just being a good neighbor, acting like part of the family, but a part of me hated being spied on, analyzed, and watched, whether or not the intentions were good.

I still couldn't concentrate on anything all day. I didn't even have the patience to eat lunch. Reading, watching television, cleaning—nothing helped. I even went out to trim some bushes and work on some flowers, but I was unable to do anything for very long. John didn't call back, but that didn't surprise me. His MO for whenever I was upset, even before Mary's abduction, was to ignore me for as long as possible. He treated my emotional reactions almost like a fever. In time, it would go down. Most of the time, he was right. I usually did calm myself by myself, and by the time he returned home or called again, my tantrum was exhausted.

Finally, by three o'clock, I couldn't stand being at home or talking to myself any longer. I dug out Sam's card and called his mobile. He answered quickly. I assumed he could read that the call was coming from my telephone at home.

"Hey," he said. "How are you doing?"

"My friend Molly called first thing this morning to tell me you had visited her. I think it was a bit of a shock for her."

"She didn't seem upset."

"Was she helpful in any way, Sam?"

"I don't know yet, Grace."

"Where are you? What are you doing?"

He laughed. "Sorry," he said. "You just sounded like my mother. Whenever she called me, those were her first two questions. She was always worried that I was in the middle of a shoot-out or something, and for someone who was always involved with law-enforcement officers, you can imagine the anxiety she had. I'm just leaving the FBI office. Called in a few more favors. Nothing concrete to tell you yet."

"I know. If you had something this fast, it would

be one of those so-called miracles we're both hearing about."

"You sound upset. I mean, in a different way."

"Molly told you about the other mother and her son and how they planted him next to my daughter at church, right?"

"Yes."

"I was never told about it."

"Oh. I did wonder why you hadn't mentioned it last night. Samson James. Mother is Laurie James," he said, sounding as if he was reading off something.

"Yes."

"I saw her early this afternoon. Maybe she'll be calling you, too."

"No, I'm not that friendly with her. I don't mean I'm not friendly. She's just not part of what you might call my inner circle, although that circle is growing smaller by the minute. It might be just a dot by now."

He laughed again.

"I'd like to see you," I said. It was as if the words had been regurgitated from somewhere deep inside me. I was surprised to hear myself say them, too.

"Maybe we shouldn't meet again just yet," he said, and then quickly corrected himself. "No. I didn't mean that. I'd like to see you, too, Grace. I'm sure there is some ethical or formal regulation that I'm breaking, but . . ."

"When?"

"I'm sort of off until eight and—"

"I'll meet you at your condo in twenty minutes," I said.

"The code for the garage is one-four-zero-eight and the pound key," he told me. "If you get there before I do."

"I'm sure I will."

I imagined that I was out the door and into the garage before he closed his mobile phone and put it back in the case on his belt. I opened the garage door and got into my car.

The voice I had heard coming out of me seemed like the voice of a stranger. It was as if I had been taken over by someone else, someone far more wicked. I actually laughed aloud imagining John recommending that a priest examine me for a possible exorcism. *Who knows?* I thought. *Maybe that's what I need.*

I was at Sam's condo building first and used the pass code. I parked in the same guest spot and waited until I saw him pull in. He got out of his car and started toward me. Neither of us said a word. We got into the elevator. When the doors closed, he turned to me, and we kissed.

Maybe he was taking advantage of me; maybe I was especially vulnerable. I did feel as though I had been lost somewhere in a desert of sadness, searching desperately for an oasis of love. I wanted to take a long drink of it and revive every part of my body that longed to be touched, but touched with affection and great care. I wanted to be wanted not for the baby potentially waiting to be conceived inside me, but for myself. If adultery could ever be rationalized or justified, it was surely this reason on which it would rely.

Sam held my hand in his while he opened his condo door with the other. Then he turned to kiss me softly again and led me through the entryway and to his bedroom. Our kiss there was longer. He embraced me afterward, and I laid my head against his shoulder for a few moments.

"It's not too late to turn back," he whispered.

"Yes, it is," I said. I kissed him again and folded back the blanket on his bed. He watched me for a moment before he began to loosen his tie.

I undressed with my back to him. My head felt as if it had turned into a beehive, but I also felt as if my body had separated itself from my soul, from who I had been and maybe who I would be. It had a mind of its own. When I turned to him, we gazed at each other like two teenagers who had boldly entered their sexual lives.

He stepped forward, and we kissed and held each other, the rhythms in our bodies beginning to synchronize, heartbeat to heartbeat, blood to blood, lips to lips, until we were lying beside each other and then rushing with a mutual need to be as intimate as possible, soaking ourselves into each other totally but without awkwardness or selfish demand. His gentleness emerged with every caress and with each new kiss. This was making love with concern, tossing aside selfish pleasure to be sure we were first making each other happy and satisfied.

I understood why this would really be called making love and not anything cruder. Love was sharing and caring and sacrificing everything in the moment, your ego and the satiation of your thirst and hunger. We could do this together, reach ecstasy together, cry and moan our pleasure together, and touch something bigger than ourselves together. It was something John and I had once had, and I hungered to enjoy it again.

My body welcomed Sam's touch, his lips moving everywhere, stirring places that had been in hibernation for so long that I had forgotten they existed. When he entered me, I felt we had entered each other. My eyes were in his eyes, my tongue in his mouth, my stomach and my breasts softly entering his. For a few moments, I thought we would never part again.

Making love with passion was truly a form of resurrection. I had been dead inside so long that I had forgotten how to taste, how to touch, how to see, how to smell, and how to hear. I nearly laughed aloud thinking that I was being reborn, that John would appreciate it. I had the prodigal body. My body had been lost and then found. The body that maketh real love shall never die.

When I opened my eyes, I saw Sam smiling down at me.

"What?"

"If you could only see the smile on your face," he said.

"I can. I see it through your eyes."

He brightened even more and kissed me again.

For a long while, we lay side by side silently.

"In the movies," he finally said, "actors usually light a cigarette. It's like a period to a sentence or something."

"I don't want to put a period to this sentence," I said.

He laughed and then sobered. "Look," he said, "we're both going to have some regrets now and—"

I put my fingers on his lips. "*Je ne regrette rien*," I said. "Listen to Edith Piaf. Don't even mention the possibility."

I rose and began to dress. He lay with his hands behind his head, watching me.

"What are you going to do now?" he asked.

"I'm stopping at Whole Foods on the way home to pick up a ready-cooked chicken. For the first time in a long time, I have a real appetite," I said.

I started for the bedroom doorway.

"Grace . . ."

"Don't say anything else, Sam. Sometimes words get in the way."

"I'll call you," he called from the bedroom before I reached the front door. "About the case," he added.

I held the door open a moment, took a deep breath, and called back. "Good."

Then I stepped out like someone who had just been given a good prognosis by her doctor.

"You're going to live," I whispered to myself, and headed for the elevator, my car, the store, and home.

11

A Cursory Prayer

John had set the table. He would often do that. He always did it better than I did, with the silverware, dishes and glasses geometrically perfectly placed, the napkins crisply folded, and the bottle of wine aerating in a carafe. Before Mary's abduction, if she wasn't with me wherever I had gone, she would help him. Everything she did had the same exactness and perfection. She was always looking for her father's approval, no matter how small the task.

John could make the most mundane activities look like works of art, but he had that approach to whatever he did in his life.

"Ah, I wondered where you had gone and what we were going to have tonight," he said when I pulled the chicken out of the grocery bag. "Perfect."

It didn't surprise me, of course, that he wouldn't immediately bring up my angry reaction on the phone.

"I'll warm it up," I said, "and fix up some vegetables and sweet potatoes."

"And I'll do a salad," he said. I saw that he had already begun.

We worked side by side. It was almost as it had been, a

family symphony, the two of us in the kitchen with Mary quietly doing the little she could and looking very serious. Her face, which usually resembled mine, moved from my face to his whenever she concentrated on something intently. Out of habit, I glanced to my right and then to my left, looking to see what she was up to. John caught that and grimaced. Instantly, I replaced his disapproving face with Sam's compassionate one, but my whole body tightened as if I, like Lot's wife, had looked back on Sodom and turned into a pillar of salt.

"Are you all right?" he asked.

"Yes."

"I was worrying about you after that phone call."

"How would I know that?"

"What?"

"That you were worried. Was it on the news I missed?"

"Very funny. So?"

"I'm okay," I insisted.

He nodded and turned back to his salad preparation. "I understand you met the Los Angeles detective who was first on the case," he said nonchalantly as he cut some carrots.

I paused, my heart beating faster. "How did you know that?"

"Right." He raised his right forefinger. "How would I know that? You didn't tell me. The detective certainly didn't tell me. Ah, David Joseph, the FBI agent, told me."

"You spoke to him?"

He turned to me, holding the glittering vegetable knife like a candle in the darkness. "I speak to him periodically, Grace. What do you think? He's even stopped by my office a few times."

"He has? When? You've never said anything about it to me."

"They had nothing to tell us. What would I say? I didn't want to get your hopes up and then have nothing concrete to tell you, did I?"

"Still, I would have liked to have known you were still on the investigation," I said.

"Still? Of course, I would be. I'm just more realistic about it," he added, turning back to the salad preparation.

"Realistic? Is that the way you categorize it?"

"Yes, realistic. Why should I bring more suffering into our home? That's what false hope does."

I returned to what I was doing. "At this point, I'd like to have any hope, false or otherwise," I muttered.

"Don't be foolish. Anyway, David Joseph assured me they're still doing some very vigorous investigating. When he has something significant or new to tell us, he will." He paused and looked at me again. "Why did Molly Middleton bring up the Samson James incident this morning?" he asked. "It happened quite a while ago. Why did she bring it up today?"

I froze for a moment. I hadn't mentioned Sam's interrogating her. "She said Lieutenant Abraham questioned her about it, and she was disturbed. She thought she might have done something wrong talking about Mary and Bradley."

"So, you mentioned that to him? Is that how he knew about Bradley Middleton's recovery? Because I never mentioned it to any of them, nor did Margaret. I asked her."

"I guess," I said. "I can't recall what I did and didn't say. It was very traumatic for me. I actually couldn't get into the department store on my own. I was standing there frozen when he called to me."

He ignored my last statement. "I wonder what he's after there, questioning Molly Middleton about that."

"I don't know, John. We'll have to wait to see," I said. "Maybe you'll hear from the FBI about it soon, and when you do, I hope you'll tell me immediately."

"Yes, of course. How about some blue cheese in the salad tonight? Did you remember to get some? We're out."

"Yes, I did."

I handed it to him. He held the package without taking it for a moment and stared at me. Then he smiled. It was a smile I hadn't seen in quite a while, a smile I recalled winning me over when we were first dating. There was a certain light in his eyes, a look of desire that on anyone else's face I would have called pure lust.

"What?"

"Suddenly, you look better than I expected you would tonight, Grace. Your face has some color."

"Don't be ridiculous. I'm not wearing any makeup," I said, and turned away quickly. I was sure I was turning even more crimson.

John knew how I looked after I made love. I was afraid of his perception. No other man could look at me and come quickly to the conclusion that I had recently had sex with another man, I thought, and then I told myself that I was just being foolish or looking guilty. It was ridiculous to think that he could see such a thing so long after it had occurred. *Get hold of yourself, Grace Clark*, I thought.

"What's ridiculous about it?" he asked. "It was just

an innocent comment. Anyway, you don't have to jump down my throat for giving you a compliment."

"Sorry," I said, turning and softening my smile. "I was more surprised than upset. It's been a while."

"I see. But you know I give out compliments only when I believe they're deserved or justified. That way, they have real meaning, don't you think?"

"Yes, John. You're right."

"I was thinking that we'd take my father to dinner Friday night, drive up to Sherman Oaks and take him to that steak house he likes."

"Fine."

"We should see more of your parents, too. Maybe next weekend, we can spend a day or two in the desert. We haven't been there since . . ."

"I'll see," I said. "It's depressing being around my mother. She doesn't look at me without her eyes tearing up, and my father isn't much better."

"So, it's good for us to buoy them up a bit."

"For us to buoy them up? For us? They didn't lose a child. We did."

"It's charitable, Grace. It's the way you can show your love. You think about the pain other people suffer, too."

I shook my head at him. "Why didn't you go into the clergy, John? Why didn't you become a priest?"

He smiled. "Simple. I wouldn't have had you," he said. "And Mary and the new child we'll have someday. Some of us are meant to be shepherds, and others are meant to be the sheep."

"Excuse me if I don't baaa," I muttered, and we returned to the dinner preparations in silence.

We brought everything to the table and sat. I glanced at the empty place mat at Mary's seat. John had already folded his hands against each other, his fingers forming the temple. He waited for me to fold mine.

After he said his prayers, we began to eat.

"So," he began, "it's rather like divine intervention, your just happening to run into that detective at the mall, don't you think?"

For the first time in a long time, I thought I could agree with him, but for more reason than he would or maybe could imagine.

"Yes."

"What made you finally want to go back there? You told me you were having trouble doing that."

"I wanted to revisit the scene in hopes I might think of something new."

He nodded. "Very logical. It's always when we put something away for a while that we begin to see things we hadn't seen. Did anything come to mind, anything new?"

"I think I realized the exact moment when Mary's hand left mine."

"And that was?"

"Just after we came up the escalator."

He nodded. "You told this to the detective?"

"He went through it with me even though he wasn't there for any investigating. He was off work and doing some personal shopping."

"I see." He continued to eat and then paused as if he had just remembered something. "Margaret was quite upset about her phone conversation with you this morning. She, too, thought she might have done something wrong. She said you practically accused her of spying on you."

"That's the way it felt."

"Worrying over you and spying on you are two different things, Grace," he said.

"Okay."

"Where did you go last night?"

"I didn't feel like staying home alone. And," I quickly added, "I didn't want Margaret's company. Worrying or spying, she still makes me feel like I have a caretaker now."

"I understand. So, where were you?"

"I just . . . had something to eat on Third Street, looked at some shops, and came home."

It occurred to me almost the moment the words were spun out of my mouth that I could probably count on the fingers of one hand how many times I had not told John the truth about something I had done. People lie because they want to deceive for selfish reasons, they want to spare someone something unpleasant, or they are afraid of the person to whom they are speaking. I had so few occasions for any of those three reasons, but at the moment, I was lying for all of them.

From almost the first time I had met John until now, I had idolized and respected his powers and vision. Over time, his super-self-confidence had begun to annoy me, but when we first met, I was drawn to his certainty and self-assurance. How I wanted to be more like him. As he had said earlier, he couldn't even lie to himself. He couldn't give out false compliments. Someone that honest surely had the power to recognize untruth when it came from someone else, especially someone he had loved and been with for so long.

However, if he did see through me, he didn't reveal it.

"Well, I assure you that poor Margaret does agonize over this tragedy and worries, not spies," he said. "Few people have friends like her."

"I'll apologize. I just wasn't in the mood to receive any calls or visitors."

"You can't continue to be a firecracker, Grace. You really should see the therapist. She has an excellent reputation. I did some more checking up."

I slapped my fork down and fumed for a moment. "What?"

"Did you ever consider why it is that you don't need a therapist, John? Isn't the loss of Mary as deep a loss for you as it is for me, regardless of what you think is God's will?"

He thought for a moment, as though I had asked him an excellent question. It struck me that this pensive demeanor of his after something I had asked used to amuse me, if not flatter me. It was as though I had asked something beyond my intellectual capacities, and he would have a better image of me. Right now, however, it was annoying. He looked more like someone humoring someone else.

"Everyone faces crisis differently, I suppose. We come from different backgrounds, different experiences, and simply have different constitutions. It's not unlike why some people can't eat spicy foods and some can."

"I hardly think it's like that."

He shrugged. "It's the best answer I can think of right now," he said, making it seem that I was in desperate need of one.

"I've told you a number of times now. I don't want to see a therapist."

"Well," he said, sighing, "it's not going to be of any value unless you do want to."

"Exactly."

I picked up my fork and ate. In his inimitable fashion, John smoothly segued into describing his company and the changes it was undergoing. If I could close my eyes and rewind time, this dinner would seem no different from dinners before Mary's abduction. Was Sam right? Was John's way of living as if nothing was different the best way to cope? I told myself I didn't care. I didn't want to cope. I wanted to feel the loss of my precious little girl all day and all night. I wanted to reach for her, to listen for her, to smell her hair and kiss her soft cheeks. I ached to do it all, and I would not tolerate any therapy, any psychology, theology, or logic that would keep me from feeling it, from suffering because I didn't have her.

As soon as we had finished eating and I had begun to clear the dishes, the doorbell rang.

"Oh, I expect that's Margaret with another homemade dessert for us. She mentioned she was going to make something," he said, rising. He paused in the doorway and turned back to me. "You can apologize to her now, if you like."

"Yes, teacher," I said, and he laughed.

"Now, that's the Grace I married, the witty and satirical one."

He continued to the front door. I began rinsing off the dishes and putting them into the dishwasher. I sensed that they were both right behind me, watching me, so I spun around.

Margaret was carrying one of her angel-food cakes with chocolate icing. It was absolutely Mary's favorite. She liked it more than Margaret's pies. I simply stared at it. She knew it was Mary's favorite. It was almost cruel of her to have made it and brought it.

"I do want to apologize for upsetting you this morning," she said.

"No, it was my fault. I'm sorry, Margaret. I know you mean well."

"How about some coffee and some of this delicious cake?" John said.

"I'll have some coffee. I don't know if I can eat anything more," I said, and started on the coffee.

Margaret put the cake on the table. "You know," she said, sitting, "it might be a comforting distraction for you to come with me to the senior center one of these days. We're always looking for more volunteers."

"Distraction?" I said.

She glanced at John. "I mean, some respite from your heavy burden, Grace. A soul can stand only so much. We are all being tested all the time, but we can best endure when we take our minds off ourselves and help others. It's better than going to therapy."

"Help others? Better than therapy? What are you two, a team?" I said.

John laughed. "No good trying to fool her, Margaret. She's too smart. We confess that we've put our heads together to come up with something to help you, Grace, since you're so dead set against professional therapy."

"You've got to believe that someday your Mary will be returned to you," Margaret said. "It's important that you be strong and healthy when she does. She would need

someone like that, don'tcha think, dear?" She seemed
ready to burst into tears herself.

"I do believe she'll come home," I said.

"Yes, but someone in your state of mind is so
vulnerable to so many things, and I'm not speaking only
of colds and such. The world is full of predators, as you
know, as we all know. Satan is always just around the
corner," she said, nodding. "Satan appears in all forms to
confuse men so they take their eyes off of God. We must
pray for God's strength and guidance every day."

"Don't turn my house into one of your churches,
Margaret," I said, but not meanly or sullenly.

Even so, John's eyes narrowed. "For where two or
three are gathered together in my name, I am there in the
midst of them," he recited.

"Amen," Margaret said.

"All right, all right. I'll think about it," I said.
"Catering to the elderly might bring me some comforting
distraction. Okay?" I asked John.

He nodded. "We're just trying to help each other," he
said. He put his hand on Margaret's shoulder, and she put
hers over his. "We're all suffering through this together."

I turned to the coffeepot. The two of them were
making me feel even guiltier than I was making myself
feel. I wanted to shoot past them and out the front door,
just run and run forever down the street so I could get
away from my house and them as quickly as I could. But
wasn't I running away from myself more?

"I'll cut the cake," John said when I reached for three
coffee cups and saucers.

Margaret, who knew our house as well as I did, rose to
get the milk and sugar. Moments later, I was sitting at the

table with them and staring down at a piece of cake that John had cut for me despite what I had said.

"I'm getting a visitor tomorrow," Margaret said.

"Oh?" John sipped his coffee. "Relative? Someone from Ireland?"

"No. That Los Angeles detective, Lieutenant Abraham, has made an appointment to see me around nine. I explained that I had to get to the senior center by eleven."

"Did he say why he was returning to speak with you?" John asked.

"No. Just a few questions, he said." She looked at me. "I hope I can tell him something new that will help, although I can't think what."

"He's been inquiring about what occurred between Mary and Bradley Middleton," John said, his eyes on me. "Molly called Grace this morning about it."

"I didn't know the detective had been questioning Mrs. Middleton about Mary and her son. What can this all be about?" Margaret looked to me for an answer.

I simply stared back at her.

"Well, we'll know soon enough," John said. "Just answer his questions as best you can, Margaret."

"Of course, I will. I was wondering if maybe we shouldn't see about getting Mary's picture on milk cartons and such," she said. "I've seen that sort of thing. Don't know if it's of any use, but . . ."

"What do you think, Grace?" John asked. "I could have someone look into things like that, but it will be upsetting to see Mary's picture around. I know how you reacted to *America's Most Wanted*."

"I hardly think what might upset me is the priority."

I nodded at Margaret. "It's probably a very good idea. Thanks."

"Okay, I'll look into it," John said, but not with any enthusiasm.

"You don't really think it will be of any value, do you, John?" I asked.

"I'll do some research on the statistics," he replied. "We don't want—"

"To build up false hopes. I know." I pushed the cake aside. "I'm going for a walk," I announced, and rose.

"Really? Well, what do you say to an evening stroll, Margaret?"

"I'd like to walk alone," I said.

"You spend too much time alone, dear," Margaret said.

"Surely God will be with me. That's not being alone, then, is it?" I smiled at the two of them.

Neither replied.

I walked out of the kitchen, took my light blue leather jacket out of the entryway closet, and left the house. No one followed. I walked down the driveway and turned left, slowing down once I had gone a good thousand yards from the front of our home.

We were familiar with most of our immediate neighbors but not close friends with any of them. All of our friends lived in different places in the city, many in Beverly Hills, some in Westwood, and some in Bel Air. Most of the friends we'd made had been introduced to us by John's business associates. In the beginning, there were planned get-togethers thrown by one wife or another, and gradually a half-dozen or so of us began seeing each other more frequently.

As I walked past the homes in our neighborhood, I

occasionally paused when I saw someone moving past a window, and when I could, I paused to see families seated in their living rooms watching television or even still around their dining-room tables. How insulated and safe they looked to me, and how envious I was. Surely families who watched old television shows in which parents and children went through relatively minor crises but always in the end found security and love felt the way I longed to feel again. How could I become like them? Could I, too, crawl into the glow of that world and never face fatal or serious emotional losses? What was the secret? What had I done to be standing alone out there looking in at them and feeling my insides crumble and shatter?

I looked up at the sky. City lights made it almost impossible to see any stars, but I knew they were there. I closed my eyes and kept my head back as I whispered a prayer to John's God.

"Spare us, oh Lord. Whatever mysterious purpose you have, please reconsider. Bring my baby back to me."

The sound of a car horn followed by some shouting around the corner shook me out of my meditation. I lowered my head and walked on. At the end of the street, I turned right and walked to San Vicente Avenue, where there was lots of traffic, people walking, and restaurants buzzing. The world went on, despite the pain and loss of anyone in it. Other people might pause to sympathize and shake their heads, but moments later, just as they had to avoid thinking of their own inevitable deaths, people embraced the comfort in socializing, working, or simply playing at anything that was strong enough to be a distraction. Who could fault them? There was no place for anger, only envy, I thought.

I sat on the patio of a juice bar and took out my cell phone. For a few moments, I just stared at it, and then I tapped in Sam Abraham's number.

"Hey," he said. "What's up?"

"I just felt like calling you. I needed to hear your voice."

Was it wrong for me to load all of my hope on him now? Was that too much pressure?

"Where are you?"

"I left the house and took a walk."

"By yourself?"

"Yes. I left John and Margaret at the kitchen table. She announced that you were coming to see her tomorrow."

"I thought she might."

"What are you doing, Sam? Where is this leading? I don't care whether it will take me to another disappointment. I need something, some hope. Please."

He was silent for so long I thought I had lost the connection.

"Sam?"

"Where are you, exactly?" he asked.

I gave him the cross street.

"I'm ten minutes away. Stay there."

I went inside and ordered a juice, then returned to my table on the patio. Looking around, I saw many coeds who were probably attending UCLA. There were many apartments in the area that catered to college students. I told myself I was too young to covet their carefree demeanor, the excitement in their laughter, and their flirtations. They had everything to live for, every dream still a possibility, and every romantic adventure yet to be lived. Of course, some of them would suffer great disappointment, probably even great tragedy, but surely none of that seemed even remotely possible tonight.

How depressing I am, I thought. It did me no good to think that no one would blame me for it. I hated it. I recalled being at the movies not long ago with John, and him looking around and telling me how statistically at least half of the patrons would experience some kind of cancer, how another percentage would have fatal heart failure at an age younger than expected, and how another percentage would die or be maimed in an automobile accident.

"Thanks," I'd told him. "Glad we're going to see a comedy, at least."

He had smiled. He could live with all this depressing information because he didn't connect real people to it, put faces and biographies with the numbers, and he had that damned tolerance for the inevitable and the real.

Sam pulled up at the curb. I practically leaped out of my chair and got into his car. He started away.

"I was just in West L.A. looking for a pimp who is a person of interest in a particularly brutal murder of a prostitute."

"I'm sorry I interrupted."

He looked at me and smiled. "He's not going anywhere. I'll find him tonight, I'm sure."

"What do you have, Sam? Why are you interrogating Margaret Sullivan again tomorrow?"

"Look, this might not go anywhere. I know you said you don't care, but I want to be sure to make you understand that."

"I understand. I understand."

"Remember when I told you the FBI was combing

its files for anything similar in the way of an MO in the state?"

"Yes."

"Well, when you mentioned that story with the Bradley Middleton boy and then I learned about this Laurie James and her child, I put something else into the mix with the FBI search."

"What?"

"Children who were thought to have some miraculous power like the laying on of hands, that sort of thing."

"And?"

"Two came up in Southern California, both girls," he said.

I shook my head. "What does that mean?"

"Someone is out there listening for these stories. You know, like Santa listens to see who's naughty and nice."

If my heart hadn't actually stopped, it had fooled me.

12

Alone

I didn't like slinking around, but I asked Sam to drop me off at the beginning of our street. He pulled to the side, and for a few moments, neither of us spoke. I stared ahead at the cul-de-sac and my house. If Margaret was still there keeping John company, I was confident that they were talking about me, about how to handle me. I had gone from a competent and intelligent, caring wife and mother to someone who had to be guided and controlled. Of course, as always, that was for my own good, when in reality, people who were handled were handled so that the people close to them could be more comfortable in their presence.

I had no doubt that John was very disappointed in me and in almost everything I did these days, not that I did much. Since I continued to avoid socializing whenever possible, I was sure he hated our friends pecking at him with questions about how I was, what my state of mind was, and what they could do to help. A man as self-confident and opinionated as John abhorred being dependent on anyone for anything. Once again, something for which I had first admired him had now lost its polish and glitter. His self-confidence had become arrogance, and his opinions were more bigoted, narrow, and uncompromising.

As I sat beside Sam, both of us silhouetted by the streetlights and looking more like dark shadows of ourselves, I wished I had the strength to tell him to put his car into drive and take me away. My home was cradled in misery and depression. I could almost see the sadness leaking out of the windows and under the front door, merging with the pockets of darkness to make them deeper and thicker. I had little interest in cleaning or caring for anything in the house. I didn't even make our bed these days, something that John passionately hated. He threatened to bring back a maid, but then he would go right to the bedroom when he returned home from work and make the bed himself. Sometimes he would rip it down and put on fresh sheets and pillowcases. He would do it all silently, but I was sure he was feeling as if he were Sisyphus in the Greek myth, condemned to push a boulder up a hill just to have it always roll back down.

Our lovemaking to conceive a new child surely had to seem pointless to him. We didn't speak or whisper sweet nothings. The foreplay was practically nonexistent, yet he didn't complain about my lack of enthusiasm and emotion. He simply rolled over and went to sleep like someone who expected everything to be different in the morning.

Where did that come from, that idea that if you could just pass through another dark night, all your troubles would be gone? There was that old adage doctors were supposed to use, "Take two aspirins and call me in the morning," because in the morning, you'd be better. I would be the first to admit that any drug right now was tempting. How I wished I could sedate myself and not wake up until Mary was returned. It would seem as if only hours had gone by and not days, weeks, and months. For once, I understood John's unyielding faith in death being nothing but a sleep, an escape from the cares and woes of our lives, and then a joyful awakening. Was that what I was wishing for, an easeful death?

"Look," Sam said, breaking the silence, "I didn't sleep much at all last night agonizing over what we had done. Don't misunderstand me. I wanted to make love to you very much. The truth is, I was attracted to you from the moment I first saw you, and I condemned myself for that. I wasn't supposed to be thinking about anything but what might have happened to your child, but there I was, infatuated like some teenager. I hated leaving the case because I was leaving you. I don't know how many times I replayed that conversation we had in your bedroom. I'd go to sleep with you on the inside of my eyelids, listening to your voice. But I know, or rather, I fear, that you were with me only because I'm trying to solve this abduction. It's a horrible case of taking advantage of someone victimized, and I woke up this morning hating myself almost as much as you hate whoever took your Mary."

"That's not completely true," I said. "In fact, I'd be a liar, lying to make myself seem the better person, if I agreed with you."

"I don't understand."

"I felt guilty, too, but not because I was committing adultery. I felt guilty because I wanted to enjoy myself, feel like a woman again, and for the time being put aside my sorrow over the loss of my daughter. It was selfish.

The fact is, I feel I took advantage of you, used you, and not vice versa."

He smiled and shook his head. "You're saying all that to make me feel better."

"No." I turned to him. "I have no doubt that if we had met under different circumstances and you had flirted with me, I would have responded. I have a hole in my heart a mile wide right now, but let's just say there was a gap forming already. I mean it, Sam."

"You must have been in love with him when you married him, right?"

"Yes." His question brought an old smile to my face, one I used to wear knowing that it made me look softer and, dare I say, more beautiful. "John is a very interesting man. Few men look as much like Cary Grant or George Clooney these days, and any young woman out there on the dating scene will tell you that finding a substantial man, someone who really knows what he wants but is also competent, self-reliant, and well balanced, is practically an impossibility. It's the age of Me. Look at Me. Want Me. Do what Me wants to do. John knew how to build a family, a home, a life, quietly, without the Me overriding every aspect. Everything is carefully constructed, sensible, and logical."

I looked at my house and continued, "How many couples our age do you know who already have their final arrangements signed and sealed? A man like John brings great comfort. I guess I always liked being taken care of, always craved the security, but something more than just the loss of my daughter occurred when she was abducted. There was the loss of the illusion that you can be safe. No one has arms that protective."

"Superman has his kryptonite," Sam said.

"Yes, but I'm just as much to blame. I led him on to believe that I would or could fit neatly into his world, especially his faith. Now I find myself intolerant of his damn refusal to rage at God over what has happened to us. It seems more natural to do so. Everyone blames God for something one time or another, don't you think?"

"Yes, I've heard that many times. Of course, most eventually regret it and go on following whatever spiritual path they had been on."

"I can't imagine doing that."

"I'm sorry, Grace."

"Yes, I know. I know that when you say that, you really mean it, Sam."

"This might come off stupid for me to say," he began, with his head down like someone about to pray, "but are you absolutely sure that John doesn't rage in private or question it all? Maybe it's something he doesn't want you to see. Maybe he thinks it will cause you more pain."

"You're right. That is something stupid for you to say. Are you trying to drive me away?"

He shrugged. "Just trying to be—"

"Don't say 'fair,' Sam. This isn't a game."

"I know. Maybe just trying to be sure." He nodded toward my house. "You'd better get back."

"Yes."

"I'll call you tomorrow," he whispered.

"You'd better," I said, and got out of the car. He didn't move away from the curb, but I didn't look back until I reached the driveway and saw him make a U-turn and drive off.

Margaret was gone. John was in the living room reading. He looked up when I entered.

"Barb Locken just called. She wants you to meet with her and Netty for lunch tomorrow. I told her you would call her back."

I grimaced.

"You can't keep driving them away, Grace. If you don't want to see a therapist, at least try to work yourself back a little yourself. Margaret was right, you know. If, God willing, we ever do get Mary back, you don't want to be some mental invalid. She'd need you more than ever. Get stronger, for all of us."

"Okay, John. I'll call her back."

He set his book down. "I've been trying to avoid something, but I really can't," he said.

"What?"

"There's a three-day software convention in Vegas that I have to attend on Saturday. I'll be back Tuesday. I could bring you along, but . . ."

"No, I wouldn't go. You go. You do whatever you have to do."

"Margaret could stay with you."

"Please, John. You can see how she gets under my skin right now. Why did she make us Mary's favorite cake, of all things?"

"She thought it was yours, too. It's one of mine."

"It was insensitive. I won't say anything," I quickly added. "Don't worry, but I don't need her hovering."

"Whatever you think," he said, his voice sounding defeated. "We're still on for taking my father to dinner tomorrow night, right?"

"Yes."

"And maybe when I return from Vegas, we can talk about visiting your parents, at least one night."

"Okay."

"Good," he said, and raised his book to return to his reading.

"I'm going to bed."

"I'll be up in a while," he said.

"I'm tired," I emphasized so he wouldn't expect me to make love.

He simply nodded, keeping his eyes on the pages of his book.

Sam's words hovered around me, echoing in my ears. It occurred to me that I had been avoiding John whenever I could, and therefore he had much more time alone. Mary wasn't there for him to talk to and keep him company while I was attending to something. He, just like me, was condemned to more solitary hours than either of us would want, I'm sure.

What did he do when he was alone? Could Sam be right? Was my rage so great that it covered innocent things and blinded me to what was really happening? Did I want to push John away? Was this half my fault, if not more? What he had said earlier about different people reacting to disappointments and tragedy in different ways wasn't untrue. Did I hate him, hate everyone, for not being me? How would I even begin to come back from this?

Maybe John was right and I did have a need to return to some semblance of socializing, not only for him but also for myself and, believing that Mary would return, for her. I called Barb and agreed to meet her and Netty for lunch. What's more, I rose before John did in the morning and started our breakfast. He looked surprised and happy about it when he came down. He was more talkative than usual and said he'd make our dinner reservation when he was at the office.

"I could call that maid service and get someone to help you with the house again," he said, this time sounding more as if he was making a concerned offer and not a threat.

"No, I'm fine. Don't worry."

He nodded and finished his breakfast.

"No one expects our lives to return to what they were when we had Mary," he told me just before he left for work. He stood in the doorway looking back at me. "But we have to hold ourselves together and be strong for whatever the good Lord has in store for us."

I said nothing. He waited a moment and then went out to the garage. I heard him start the car and back out. When the garage door closed, I got up. In about an hour, Sam would be interviewing Margaret. I didn't know exactly what he was looking for by talking with her, but I hoped that whatever it was, he would hear it.

After I made the bed and cleaned up a little in the kitchen, I sat by the front window and looked out to see if I could catch Sam leaving Margaret's house. I didn't think he would just come over and ring my doorbell. I was right. I saw him drive off. I felt very nervous, hoping for a phone call from him. I tried to calm myself by doing more housework, washing clothes, vacuuming, and giving our en suite bathroom a good going over. When Sam didn't call, it took every bit of self-control for me not to call Margaret and interrogate her about Sam's interrogation, but I didn't want to do or say anything that might cause a new problem. She knew I was waiting to hear something about it, however, so I was surprised when I saw her drive off for the senior center. I couldn't help wondering if Sam had told her not to say anything to anyone, especially me.

I really didn't want to meet my friends for lunch. Barb Locken could be more curious than a kitten. She was one of those people who saw no subject as being off the table, no matter how intimate and private it might be. If she asked something about our sex lives and others complained about how nosy she was being, she would just make that silly little baby rattle of a giggle of hers and say, "What's the problem? You could ask me, and I wouldn't be embarrassed."

Netty Goldstein could be like Barb's private little Greek chorus, seconding anything she said and repeating any defense she offered. But it was also true that both of them would drop anything and everything they were doing if you called on them for any help or any favor. We all made these little compromises to keep a safety net of friends, I thought. Compromise was so much a part of life. I smiled, thinking of one of my father's favorite sayings: "A branch that won't bend breaks."

I was surprised at myself when I started to dress for lunch. Not just looking presentable but looking very good was back on my mind. Surely, my friends were expecting me to look vacant, depressed, and very plain. It had been my MO ever since Mary was abducted, despite where I had gone with John or with them and their husbands. I hadn't had my hair done since. Most of the time, I tied or pinned it up. I cut my own bangs. I knew it was too dry, and the ends were splitting, but taking a shower and washing my hair had become something to do as mindlessly as brushing my teeth, which reminded me that I had missed my semiannual dental checkup. Postcard reminders about that and other regular appointments were raining down on me.

Barb wanted us to meet at the Ivy in Santa Monica. She was always on the lookout for Hollywood celebrities and chose restaurants where this one or that one had been seen. Driving toward the ocean, of course, brought back my assignations with Sam. I even took a street that would cause me to pass by his apartment building. He had told me that when he was with me, he was reminded of feelings and excitement that he had experienced as a teenager. I was feeling the same way. It titillated me to approach that building and look up at his patio, where we had first kissed.

The two women were waiting at a table when I arrived. I had the sense that they had been there a good fifteen minutes before me so they could plan how they would behave, what they would say, and what they would tell me about their lives. They expected me to be unstable. I could see the anticipation and anxiety in their faces.

Barb never looked older than a teenager herself because of her diminutive facial features and small frame. She bought her clothes often in the teenage sections of department stores. It helped that she had nearly perfect skin and thick light brown hair that she kept in the new pixie style.

Netty, on the other hand, was like one of those girlfriends you have in order to draw a strong contrast and bring more attention to yourself. She was at least fifteen pounds overweight, never seemed to wear the right shade of lipstick for her complexion, and, despite the heaviness in her face, always cut her hair too short, which highlighted her plumpness.

I could see the surprise on Barb's face when she set eyes on me. "You look great," she burst out when I approached the table.

"Yes, you do," Netty said.

"Thank you." I sat across from the two of them.

"I know you're doing your own hair. It's fine, but you've got to try this new hairdresser I found," Barb said. "She has the magic touch or something. I'm not talking about just me, but everyone I see who uses her."

"You didn't tell me about her," Netty said.

"Oh, I didn't?" Barb dug into her purse and produced a card, which she handed to me. "When you call, mention my name. She'll be more accommodating."

"You never gave me that card," Netty said.

"That was my last one. I'll get another one for you."

The waiter took our drink orders.

"You know who I think I just saw? Charlize Theron," Barb said, nodding toward some tables on our right.

"No, that woman was too short," Netty said. "Although, I will admit she looked like her."

Barb shook her head. "It was Charlize. So, tell us what you've been doing, Grace. We haven't seen you in so long. How do you spend your nights? I know it has to be so difficult for you. We want you to know we've been thinking about you almost every day."

"We do," Netty said.

"I do what I have to do to get through the day," I said, and looked at the menu. Neither spoke, but I saw them glance at each other.

When the waiter brought our drinks, I ordered the Chinese chicken salad, and then, as if they wanted to make me feel good about everything at the table, the two of them ordered the same thing. Barb continued to talk about hair, makeup, and clothes she had recently bought. She spoke quickly, like someone who was afraid to hear the other person speak but especially afraid to have any long moments of silence. She went on to talk about new restaurants she and her husband, Bob, had found or had recommended to them. Netty parroted everything she praised.

"Molly Middleton called to tell me about that detective interviewing her recently," Barb went on without skipping a beat.

The waiter brought our food.

"Yes, she called me, too," I said.

"I'm glad they are still putting in the time to find Mary," she added, and started eating.

I did, too. It didn't surprise me that Molly would call to tell our friends about Sam's interviewing her.

"What's the connection? Why interview Molly about her son and Mary?"

"I don't know, Barb. They run down leads. That's what they do."

She nodded and then brought up another restaurant she and her husband and Netty and her husband had gone to last weekend.

"I ate so much," Netty said. "It was a feast."

"I told you not to choose the buffet. You never know when to stop," Barb told her.

I smiled to myself. These two were no different from how they had ever been. For a while, at least, I thought it had been smart of me to meet them for lunch. This was a good distraction.

"I know you and John haven't gotten out that much," Barb continued. "I think it's a good idea that you're taking your father-in-law out tonight. It must be difficult for him, too. I mean, having lost his wife after so many years together."

"John told you we were going to take his father out tonight?" I asked, surprised. John was not one to talk with any of my girlfriends on the phone for a second more than he had to, and he certainly wouldn't have introduced new topics of conversation.

"Yes, he mentioned it."

"Why?" I said, smiling, still finding it out of character for him.

"Why? He wants you to get out more, do more socializing. He's naturally worried about you, as are we all," Barb said.

"Absolutely," Netty echoed. "We've always talked about getting you out to lunch with us and maybe do some shopping afterward. We didn't need him to suggest it."

Barb looked at her sharply.

"Excuse me?" I said. "What do you mean, him to suggest it? When did you see John, Netty?"

"Oh, I didn't see him."

"Barb?"

"I didn't exactly see him, Grace."

"He called you? John called you and told you to go to lunch with me?" I asked, lowering my fork.

Barb gave Netty another sharp look. She had obviously gone off the script. "Netty's right. We've been talking about going out to lunch with you all the time, but we didn't know when we should call, when you were ready, when—"

"Ready? You mean, when I could put my daughter far enough out of mind to be able to sit and talk about hair and makeup and gape at movie stars?"

"No, no, of course not," Barb said, biting down on her lower lip.

"When did John call you?"

Both were silent.

"When?" I demanded, raising my voice.

"Last night. He said you had gotten to the point where you were going out by yourself, and he thought that you would be more apt to accept an invitation to lunch and—"

"I see." I stared down at my food. The little appetite I had worked up dissolved.

"Where do you go by yourself?" Netty asked.

I looked up at her and at the way she had emphasized "yourself." Was I being paranoid? Were the two of them on a fishing expedition, one that John had ordered? "Where do *you* go by yourself, Netty?"

"Me? Nowhere. I mean, I go to the grocery store. I get my nails done. I . . . I don't go out at night by myself." She looked to Barb for some help.

"We don't want you to be by yourself, especially these days, Grace," Barb said. "It's been so long since we were all together to do anything. We want you to know that's not because of us. Don't be angry at John. He's only looking out for you. You have a wonderful husband. I mean, other husbands . . ." She stopped herself.

I smiled. "Would have blamed me for everything and deserted me by now?"

Neither spoke. I reached for my light sweater.

"Grace, please," Barb said. "I didn't mean to imply something bad."

"I don't blame you for anything, either of you. I know how hard it must be to say the right things, do the right things. I'd be just as flustered, probably. I want you both to know I'm okay. I'm going to get Mary back. I don't need to be handled. I'm fine. I'm stronger."

I started to take out some money.

"Oh, no, this is on us," Barb said.

"No, it's not," I said, throwing down a hundred-dollar bill. "It's on John. Be sure to give the waiter no more than a fifteen-percent tip. That's John's standard tip."

I smiled at their shocked faces and then turned and left the restaurant. I slowed down once I was outside but continued toward the parking garage. Why was I so sensitive? What would they think? Would I have reacted like a paranoid if I hadn't been with Sam? I almost stopped and turned back. But I didn't. All I wanted now was to get away from them.

And talk to Sam.

13

There Are Lies, and There Are Lies

He didn't answer when I called his cell phone. I left a message: "Call me as soon as you can."

Then I drove out of the parking lot. It was often overcast until one or two o'clock in Santa Monica. It added to the bleakness inside me. Following San Vicente into Brentwood, I crossed into blue sky and felt as if I had popped up in a pool or in the ocean and could breathe.

Sam didn't call back for nearly three hours. I was home trying everything I could to calm myself, from redoing my clothes closet to washing some windows. Eventually, I had to succumb to taking one of my tranquilizers. Then I sat in the living room and stared out the front window at the manicured properties on our street, the perfectly trimmed palm trees, the cropped hedges, the rich bougainvillea that in some places looked dabbed onto a Matisse canvas, the occasional vehicle, and the even more occasional pedestrian. At times, with no activity and barely a breeze moving the oleander, eucalyptus, maple, and oak leaves, it seemed I was staring at a photograph. Even the birds barely flitted and looked as if they had been artistically placed. I didn't know if the deep silence was floating out of my house to the street or from the street into my house.

Finally, Sam called. I lifted the receiver so slowly I was sure he thought no one was going to respond. My "Hello" seemed to come from a place I had never known inside me.

"Hey," he said. "What's up?"

"I'm not having a good day. Did anything come of the interview with Margaret? What are you looking for specifically now, Sam? Please, tell me something," I begged.

"Listen. David Joseph is doing me some big favors here. He's been treating me as if I was part of the FBI team. I have to follow their protocol. We have to work with unsubstantiated theories. There are a few going, all of which could be dead ends. I know it's practically impossible for you, but try to be a little more patient. Trust me."

"John's leaving for Vegas tomorrow. He'll be gone for three days."

"Really?"

"I want to see you," I said.

He was silent a moment. "I've got to go someplace tomorrow, out of town."

"Overnight?"

"No."

"Can I go with you?"

"Grace, this isn't smart."

"It is for me," I said. "I want to see you, and it's not just to talk about the case."

I could practically feel his mind working. "How can you work this out, going with me?"

"John leaves early, before eight. What time are you going?"

"I was planning on leaving about then," he said. There was another pause. I sensed that he was trying to come up with another excuse.

"John lied to me for the first time," I said, practically in tears. "He told me two of my girlfriends called last night to invite me to lunch. Only they didn't call. He called them to get it set up."

"That's not so bad a lie. He wants you out and about for your own good."

"You're defending him, defending his deception?"

Sam laughed. "It's not a mean deception, is it, Grace? What do you want me to say?"

"Nothing. That's what you're good at saying," I said, and hung up.

Seconds later, the phone rang.

"Okay," he said. "I'll leave at nine. Drive over to my place to park your car."

"Good."

"I've got to get back to work," he said. "You all right?"

"No, but I'll be better."

"Sure you will," he said. "Tomorrow," he added, and hung up.

Having something to look forward to buoyed my spirit. I rose and directed my energies to things I had neglected cleaning for so long. John was home from work earlier than usual. He said he wanted to get his packing done for Vegas so he wouldn't have to do it when we returned from dinner with his father, but the next thing out of his mouth was, "How did the lunch go with the girls?"

"You mean, you didn't get a report?" I asked. He paused on the stairway.

"Excuse me?"

"Why did you tell me they called to ask me to lunch when you had called them to arrange it?"

He came down a step. "They said that?"

"Not voluntarily. Netty has a loose tongue, and Barb had to confess to the conspiracy."

"There's no conspiracy, Grace. I met Bill Locken at Rudy's Deli, and he mentioned that Barb wanted to call you to have lunch, but she was afraid of being turned down again or upsetting you. I said I would let her know when she should try. That's all. Instead of resenting the effort people are making to help you, you should show some appreciation."

"I don't like being lied to," I said. It was a weak comeback because he was right. Even Sam had said so. John was the reasonable one, and now that I heard him say what would be the simple truth to anyone who heard it, I felt guilty about blowing off Barb and Netty.

"There are lies, and there are lies," he said, fixing those dark blue eyes on me so intently I had to look away.

I knew I shifted my eyes the way anyone who was guilty of some indiscretion might. It made me feel smaller still.

"Nobody was out to hurt you, Grace. Nobody wanted to bring you any more pain, least of all me," he said in a softer tone.

I looked up at him. "I'm sorry," I said. "I should have understood all that."

He came down the stairs and surprised me by hugging me and kissing my forehead and then stroking my hair lovingly. I looked into the smile that had once captured my female imagination entirely.

"That's my girl," he said, and brought his lips to mine. It felt like our first kiss. It was as if he truly had the power to send me sailing back through time to our early days together, when infatuation matured into love and a world of wonderful promise. "You will be restored," he said. "My prayers will be answered."

He hugged me again and then turned and headed back to the stairway, pausing midway.

"Dad's really looking forward to tonight," he said. "Let's show him he doesn't have to worry about us." He flashed his smile again and hurried up to do his packing.

I stood there staring after him, stunned. What was really happening here? What had I done? Was it me? Had I been driving him away? Was I the one destroying this marriage? Was I turning on him as a way to avoid turning on myself, keeping my blame and my guilt over what had happened to Mary subdued, if not completely buried?

Would I have been happier if my husband had collapsed and become a blubbering idiot, unable to function? What was I blaming him for anyway—his strength, his reasonableness, his clear logic, and his clear vision of what was real and what was not?

I should have let Barb finish her sentence at lunch, I thought. She was right. It was something I thought about all the time but refused to credit John with doing. Was it only because of his faith that he did not turn on me, blame me for the loss of our daughter, or was his love for me that strong after all? Was I angry because he had the strength to forgive? It struck me that many hated Christ for the very same reason. They wanted to hate, to fight, and to get their revenge, and Christ stood in their way with his damned turning the other cheek and letting he who was without sin cast the first stone.

I felt so confused, so lost. I looked up the stairway after John. Once I had rushed to him whenever I had fears or doubts, and he was always there with his calmness, his clear thinking, and his careful logic. His religious devotion kept him centered, and although I refused to accept it as deeply as he did, I didn't hesitate to draw comfort from him. Maybe I was a hypocrite. *You go pray. You attend church, and you say the prayers at dinner, but I don't mind enjoying God's graces thanks to you.* Was that who I was?

I started up the stairway, determined to do what John had asked, be solid and comforting for his father. I worked harder and with more interest on my hair and my makeup. I chose a bright pantsuit and put on earrings and the matching necklace John had bought me for my last birthday. He had finished packing for his Vegas trip, showered, and dressed and sat waiting for me in the living room.

"Wow," he said when he saw me coming down the stairway. "Dad won't have any trouble understanding why I fell in love with you."

I started to respond with typical feminine humility and then stopped, smiled, and said, "You're only saying that because it's true."

He laughed and gave me another hug and a kiss. Later, in the car on our way up to Sherman Oaks to pick up his dad, he asked me if Margaret had called or stopped by.

"To fill you in on the interview she had with the detective," he said when I didn't respond.

"No, I haven't heard from her. You didn't speak with her?"

He shook his head. "When would I speak with her?"

"I thought you might have called her from work."

"No, I figured if she had anything to say, she would have said it to you."

"Sometimes people are told not to say anything," I offered.

He looked at me as if that idea had never occurred to him. Then he nodded. "Well, if there's anything to tell us, they'll tell us," he concluded.

His father was so happy to see us looking brighter and wanting to enjoy ourselves that he didn't mention or ask a thing about the investigation. We all skirted around any references to Mary, and even to John's mother. Before we dropped him off after dinner, he did say, "I'm confident things are going to turn out all right for you."

"For all of us," John corrected.

"Yes, for all of us."

He kissed me good night, then looked at John and said, "No doubt as to why you fell in love with this one."

Both of us looked at each other and laughed.

"What?" his father asked.

"Like father, like son," I said, and he nodded, understanding.

I realized it was a good laugh, a full laugh, the sort of laugh that makes you feel warm and hopeful. As we drove home, I looked to the stars, and for the first time in a long, long time, I prayed silently that God would look down upon Mary and comfort her wherever she was. I felt confident that He would.

Later, John made love differently from the way he had

been making love. It wasn't solely mechanical. He was more tender and did whisper his love for me. I fell asleep more easily than I had for some time and woke only when I heard him moving around the bedroom. He was already dressed.

"Oh, I'll get up to make you breakfast," I said, moving quickly.

"No, no. Rest, Grace. I'm having breakfast with some of my associates at the airport." He glanced at his watch. "Perfect. Okay, I'll call you tonight."

"Have a good trip," I said.

He kissed me good-bye and left. I did lie there for quite a while, thinking, analyzing everything John had done and I had done. Somehow I had constructed a wall between us, but not where I intended that wall to be. It was a wall closing out any expression of affection. How many times had John offered it before and I had refused to recognize or acknowledge it? Did he turn from me because I had turned from him? Was he afraid, tiptoeing around me with his love because he was afraid of rejection? I lay there thinking about all of this for so long that when I looked at the clock, I realized I would never be able to meet Sam at nine. I wasn't sure what I was going to say, but I reached for the phone and called.

"I think it's better I don't go," I said when he answered. "You were right. I'm sorry if I held you up."

"It's okay. You okay?"

"Yes, I'm good."

"You sound good. I'll call you later."

"Sam," I said quickly before he could hang up.

"Yes?"

I hesitated. Did I want to risk losing his interest,

which might sabotage his renewed determination to solve Mary's abduction? And if I was holding on to him for solely that reason, wasn't I using him just the way he thought he might be using me?

"Wherever you're going today, does it have to do with Mary's abduction?"

"Yes, it does," he said. "I'm going to visit one of those mothers whose daughters were said to have done something miraculous."

"What are you looking for?"

"A connection. A reason to believe there's a well-organized plan to this madness."

"Now I feel guilty about not going with you."

He laughed. "Don't worry. If there's anything to come of it, I'll find it."

"Okay," I said.

"Maybe we can meet tomorrow," he suggested.

"Maybe," I said.

After he hung up, I got out of bed and went down to get some breakfast. While I sipped my coffee, I thought about yesterday and picked up the phone to call Barb. I apologized for how I had behaved. Of course, she kept saying I needn't, that both she and Netty understood. I had no doubt, however, that they had both told and retold the story about what had happened at lunch, pollinating the phone lines with their increasingly exaggerated descriptions of this unbalanced, close-to-a-nervous-breakdown friend they had tried to help. It would become a game of Telephone during which one listener would tell another, and that one would tell another, until the original story would be so expanded that the last one hearing it might expect to see me on the nightly news after being arrested for running wildly through a mall stabbing people with a pair of scissors or something.

We made a vague agreement to try it again in the near future, which sounded more like an oxymoron than ever. I told her to pass my apology on to Netty, who, if I had called her, would surely have told me the same things anyway. Still, I felt better about it.

The sound of the doorbell surprised me. It was Margaret. I had assumed that she would avoid me for a while, following Sam's admonition. She looked upset when I opened the door.

"I'm sorry I didn't come to see you yesterday or call you after I had come home from the senior center," she began.

"Come in," I said, stepping back. "I was just finishing breakfast. Do you want a cup of coffee?"

"Yes."

She followed me to the kitchen and sat at the kitchenette. The disturbed expression on her face at the door hadn't left her. I glanced at her while I took out another cup and saucer.

"What is it, Margaret? Why are you so upset?"

"The detective did request that I not talk to anyone about his interview, but his questioning brought up something else I had neglected to tell you, and that bothers me. I can't imagine why it would matter if I told you now. I was troubled about it all night. I knew you had gone to have dinner with your father-in-law."

I poured her some coffee. "Yes, we did."

"And I didn't want to come over or call you late."

"What is it, Margaret?" I asked, sitting across from her.

"I know you were angry about my not telling you about Laurie James's boy."

"It's all right, Margaret. I'm over it."

"No, there was more. You're bound to hear about it eventually, I'm sure."

"More? What more?"

"There was this woman who came to church one Sunday after what happened with the James boy. She wasn't a member of our church. I guess John never told you about her, either?"

"No. Told me what?"

"The detective interviewed Laurie James before he came to interview me. She mentioned the woman to him. She was a friend of a friend sort of thing, don'tcha know. Anyway, I didn't find out until later, really, but she was being treated for lung cancer. A smoker, I imagine."

"She wanted to sit next to Mary, too?"

"No, all she wanted to do was meet her, touch her, hold her hand for a moment. It all happened so fast I barely knew it had occurred at all. In fact, I was in a conversation with Sarah Conklin, and you know how Sarah can be. She practically swallows you whole when she corners you."

"What did you see?"

"Just John talking to her and then her talking to Mary and holding Mary's hand. When she let her go, Mary reached up for her, and the woman brought her face to Mary's hand. I stopped dead in my tracks to watch it. Mary held her hand on her cheek for a few seconds. The woman had her eyes closed and seemed . . ."

"What?"

"Brighter. Then she turned and left. She didn't come into the church, you know."

"What did John say about it?"

"He didn't say anything much. I asked him who she was, and he said she was Laurie James's friend. I asked him what that was about, and he just shrugged. Then we went inside and I didn't think much more of it, until the detective asked yesterday, that is." She sipped her coffee.

"What about the woman? Why even mention her now?"

"As I said, I had forgotten all about her, but Sheila Bracken . . . you know Sheila. She's been over my house. Her husband died five years ago. She helps at the center?"

"Yes, yes, I know who she is. So?"

"Sheila told me she had met Laurie James, and Laurie told her that her friend had gone into a remarkable remission."

"Because of Mary? She said because of Mary?" I asked, perhaps with a little too much animation. Margaret actually sat back.

"Well, she didn't say for certain, but she mentioned her, and Sheila knows how close I am to you, Mary, and John, so she told me about it. Sheila told some other people at the center. But I never told anyone there stories about Mary to make her out to be something other than a normal but beautiful and intelligent little girl. It's certainly not any of their business. Even so, I had the feeling from the way that detective was questioning me that either I or someone I spoke to had done something wrong. Is that why he came to see me?" she asked.

How would she know I knew any more than she did? Was she fishing?

"He's a detective. He has to follow evidence, information. I have nothing more to tell you," I said as casually as I could manage.

She studied me as if she was looking to see if I was telling the truth. "I'm just beside myself thinking about it, Grace. I couldn't live with myself if I in any way—"

"Don't think like that. Let's wait to see what the detective makes of it. They work on theories, fantasy police work," I said, parroting Sam. "It might very well end up being nothing."

"Well, I do hope they come up with something, of course. I miss her very much."

"I know you do, Margaret. Thank you."

She finished her coffee. "I know John has gone to Las Vegas."

"He told you to keep an eye on me?"

"Yes," she confessed. "If you like, you could come with me to the center today. We're making a little lunch party for them."

"Does Sheila help out at the center, too?"

"Yes."

"Maybe I will go along," I said.

"Oh, how nice. I'll pick you up in, say, an hour," she said, rising. "We've got to make some salads, coleslaw, and potato salad, and Sheila makes this macaroni and cheese they love, just like kids."

"What? Oh, yes. Should I bring anything?"

"Just yourself, dear," she said. She smiled. "I feel so much better having told you all that. I hope I didn't upset you."

"Not in the least," I said.

I smiled, but my insides felt like a ball of rubber bands,

each beginning to snap. I cleaned up the breakfast dishes and went upstairs and changed to go with Margaret. Afterward, I checked my purse and saw that I had only a five-dollar bill. The hundred I had thrown on the table in the Ivy and the money I used to pay for parking had nearly cleaned me out. Even though the world revolved around credit cards these days, I hated going out with so little cash on me. I didn't want to have to stop at the bank, so I went down to John's office and workshop.

It wasn't often that I went in there alone. I never cleaned it, and when we had a maid, John was adamant about her not going in there. He was the only one who would dust, vacuum, and wash the floors of his office. He was afraid for his remarkable collection of ships in bottles and whatever project he had on the worktable at the time. There was one there now; there was always one, it seemed.

I stood there for a moment, recalling how proud John could be of a completed project. Even before Mary could really appreciate what he was saying, he would give us a little lecture about the one he had just done. Some of the ships were based on paintings, and he would have pictures of the paintings along with the bottles. He knew the artists, and he knew when the paintings were done. Not only that, but he also prided himself on knowing the history either of the ship or of what was happening around that ship wherever it had been sailed. I realized that his hobby was really quite educational, and I imagined he expected that when Mary was older and in school, he would leap at the chance to show her his model of one of the ships built and sailed during the period she might be studying in her history class.

He had two dozen shelves filled with ships in bottles. Fearful of what an earthquake might do since we lived in California, he was careful to use the tape patches that kept the bottles from being shaken off a shelf. The variety of ships impressed everyone he permitted to view them. I knew there were schooners and freighters, pirate ships, and individually famous ships such as the HMS *Victory*, which he explained was the most famous ship in the history of the Royal Navy, Horatio Nelson's flagship at the Battle of Trafalgar in 1805.

I had bought him the kits for some of the ships. There was a hobby shop on Melrose in West Hollywood run by an elderly Englishman who was probably as knowledgeable as John, if not more so. I always felt safe taking his suggestion for John's birthday, Christmas, and even our anniversary.

Now that I stood in the workshop and looked around at the craftsmanship, I felt as if I had entered a cathedral. These were John's icons. Judging by the way he respected them, the high esteem in which he held them, they did hold an almost religious significance for him. I moved as softly and devoutly to his desk as I would walk down the aisle in church. I didn't want to disturb a thing, not nudge a chair or move a pencil.

We kept some cash in a metal box in the bottom left drawer of his desk. Usually, I would ask him for some money, and he would get it. It wasn't locked, but we didn't keep all that much in it. The only way John attempted to hide it from a burglar was to put it between some files in the drawer.

I knelt down and carefully opened the drawer. Then I parted the files and reached in for the metal box. It wasn't very big, about twice the length of a dollar bill and twice the width. I plucked out four twenties and closed the box. When I went to put it back, I saw a slip of paper at the bottom of the drawer. The box had been lying over it. That surprised me, because when it came to any of his papers, whether they were receipts or letters, no one was more meticulous about organization and filing. John hated a messy desk or sloppy bookkeeping. Something must have fallen out of a folder, I thought. I'd just put it on his desk so that when he was there next time, he would find it and file it.

I turned it over, lifted it out, and put the metal box back. When I put the slip on his desk, something written on it caught my eye. I lifted it and read it. It was a receipt from a shop in Pomona, which was east of Los Angeles.

It was a costume rental store.

It was for a Santa outfit.

14

The Receipt

My legs were actually trembling. I gazed around the room for a moment and then hurried out to the kitchen to get a glass of cold water. I stared at the receipt on the kitchen counter. The date on it was two days before Mary's abduction. That day, that month, and even those hours were branded on my brain.

When I reached for the phone, I could see my fingers were trembling worse than my legs. I think what upset me the most was not knowing what the receipt meant. If a man dressed as Santa hadn't been the subject of some interest for both Sam and the FBI, it would mean nothing, of course. It was simply that anything and everything that had to do with Mary's disappearance loomed larger than life for me. Slowly, taking a breath practically after each number I pressed on the key pad, I called Sam's cell phone.

"Abraham," he answered. I could tell that he was in his car speaking through his Bluetooth connection.

"Sam . . ." My throat closed.

"Grace? What's up?"

I rushed it out before I choked up again. "Sam, I was

looking in a drawer in John's desk for some spare cash we keep in a metal box, and I found a receipt under the box."

"Yeah? So?"

I nearly laughed. Sometimes when you're very excited and you're on the phone, you forget that the person you're speaking to hasn't seen what you've seen or isn't looking at what you're looking at. It's not unusual. People talk with their hands while they speak on the phone all the time, and what is sillier than that? Italians were supposedly the most known for it, and the joke was that they didn't even need the phone. It got in the way.

"The receipt is from a costume store. It's for a Santa outfit." He didn't respond. "Sam!"

"Take it easy," he said.

"I don't know what it means," I said, fighting back the tears.

"Grace, all it means right now is that a Santa costume was rented. Calm down. Who is listed on the receipt as the customer?"

"The customer?" I looked at it. "John signed it."

He was silent for a few moments, and those few moments intensified the fire burning under my breasts.

"Okay. Did his company have a Christmas party?"

"What?"

"Most companies throw a party for their employees. Does John's? Did you ever attend one?"

I felt my body soften. It was as if I was a balloon version of myself and air was seeping out as I settled in my clothes.

"Yes, yes, they do, and I've been to a few, actually, all of them except for the one the Christmas after Mary's abduction."

"Okay. Did someone play Santa at the party?"

"Yes," I said. "But never John," I quickly added.

"That doesn't matter. John's their business manager. It's his job to keep track of receipts. The party was a company expense, I'm sure."

"Maybe," I said. "He just doesn't . . . I mean, I don't think he ever brings company receipts home."

"Maybe he picked this one up and forgot about it. Where was the shop? I know the agency checked every damn one in Los Angeles."

"Pomona," I said.

"Um . . . maybe someone at the company lives near there or something. The agency couldn't check every costume shop in the state. Anyway, I'm beginning to believe that whoever is involved here is not just operating in California, Grace. The costume, if indeed it was part of the abduction MO, could have come from anywhere in the country."

"Oh."

"Look, Grace, don't create more static at home for yourself and John. Put the receipt back where you found it, and forget it."

"Yes, of course, you're right. Sam?" I added before he could sign off.

"Yes?"

"I can't wait until tomorrow. Please. Let's see each other when you get back."

"I won't be free until about nine, nine-thirty, Grace. Thanks to David, I'm having dinner with some FBI agents to continue to talk about Mary's disappearance."

"It's okay. I'll meet you at your apartment. Call me when you're close to getting home."

There was that clear moment of hesitation, but then he agreed, and I hung up. I didn't care if I was forcing myself on him. I had to know what he and the FBI were doing on Mary's case.

Margaret was sounding her horn. She was in my driveway. I sucked in some air and counted to ten. That, plus Sam's calm and logical analysis of the receipt, calmed me. I hurried back into John's office, put the receipt back where I had found it, and hurried out to get into Margaret's car.

"Oh, how nice you look," she said.

"For me, the bar has been quite lowered when it comes to looking nice, Margaret."

"And what does that mean?" she asked as she backed out of our driveway.

"Considering what people expect me to look like, it's not hard to invite compliments when I brush my hair and wash my face."

"Oh, away with ye, dear. You're one of those women who can't look bad no matter how hard they try," Margaret said.

As Margaret navigated through the Brentwood streets and then into West Los Angeles, it occurred to me that I had never been driven by her anywhere. It was always the other way around. Right now, she looked so cool and confident to me, and as always, modestly elegant. I say modestly because Margaret rarely wore much jewelry other than her cross and her wedding ring. She didn't spend a great deal of money on her clothes and her shoes. Somehow, because of the way she took care of her things and the way she wore them, they didn't look terribly out of style or worn.

There was never any question in my mind that Margaret had lived a harder life than I had. I knew it broke her heart that she had never had children, but being a practicing Catholic, she would never even contemplate divorcing her husband. I think she never agreed to adopting because she had lived with the hope that something miraculous would occur and that one day, even in her forties, she would get pregnant. After that, she had thought herself too old to adopt a young child anyway, and then her husband had his heart attack, and in her way of thinking, she was to be forever a widow. She was very critical of single parents and never in a million years would become one.

That was all why Margaret grew so attached to Mary and had become a part of our family. I had to admit that sometimes I was jealous of Mary's affection for Margaret. I was afraid that she would have a bigger influence on her than I would. Even at two, Mary was repeating some of Margaret's adages, and sometimes I thought she sounded as Irish as Margaret. However, if I made any comment that was even slightly critical of Margaret's relationship with Mary, John would pounce. He always came quickly to her defense, just as he did now.

And yet as I watched and listened to her on our way to the senior center, I couldn't help but still be somewhat envious of her. She always had a glow about her, a wonderful emotional balance that gave her an innocent beauty, the kind of beauty usually found only in the young, the virginal young. I would never deny that she took Mary's abduction almost as hard as I did, but almost immediately afterward, she could handle it. She could live with it mainly because of her faith. It did the same thing for her that it did for John. I was envious of them both now for having it, but I was still afraid of it, afraid of the acceptance.

"I know that when you see these people, you're going to be reminded of a room full of young children, even though some of them will be dressed to the nines," Margaret warned. "They'll complain if they see that someone else has more or something better, mark my word. Some of them can be terribly impatient, and some of them might be terribly demanding. They might forget to say please and thank you, just like some unschooled tykes. But it doesn't take much to depress them, either, and get them narky. Then they'll start on the litany of their complaints and rabbit on, talking about their illnesses, the cost of their medications, the usual food they have to eat, and their ungrateful families."

"It doesn't sound like something you can come away from feeling invigorated, Margaret."

"Oh, but you do," she insisted. "Despite all that, you'll feel their appreciation. Everyone needs someone to love and appreciate."

"What about you?" I asked, the question coming out before I had time to reconsider how cruel it might sound.

Naturally, Margaret did not take it that way. "Well, I have you and John, and someday, I hope to have Mary again and . . ." She turned to me and smiled. "Perhaps her little sister or brother? I know she wants one."

"What do you really think of Mary?"

"Pardon?"

"Do you think she has the miraculous power to help people? Did she cure the Middleton boy, help Laurie James's son, and put that woman into remission simply by touching them? Is that what you told people, Margaret?"

"Oh, I never said it like that to any of these people, dear."

"What did you say, Margaret?"

She looked at me. We were about to pull into the senior center's parking lot. "What I believe," she replied.

"What exactly is that, Margaret?"

"That God can work miracles through any of us if He so chooses." She pulled into a parking space.

"Is that what's happening here?" I asked, nodding toward the building. "God is working miracles through you and the other volunteers, too?"

"Oh, no, dear," she said, smiling. "Everyone in there still has his or her backaches, high blood pressure, diabetes, and arthritis, believe me. No one has regained a breath of youth. There's been no laying on of hands here, except to do something mercifully charitable. It makes you feel better, even better than they do," she added. "Give it a try."

She opened her door. I hesitated.

"I hope I'm not going to hear a lot of consoling, Margaret. I'll feel trapped in there."

"Don'tcha think I know that, dear? Everyone knows what you've suffered, but no one is going to dwell on it. I can guarantee that."

"What did you do, warn them I was coming and tell them to mind their p's and q's?"

"Of course," she said.

I had to laugh, and then I stepped out into the bright sunshine. It was funny how more often than not these past months, I was unaware of whether it was overcast or sunny when I stepped out of the house. The joke about people in Southern California was that they were oblivious about the weather because, except for the June gloom at the beaches, it was always the same. The weatherman could tape his report a week before sometimes.

"When days are as glorious as this," Margaret said, seeing me squint, "you can't help but believe there's good about."

She reached toward me as if I were adrift and she could pull me to safety. I took her hand.

"Try to have faith, dear," she said. "No matter how long the day, the evening will come."

"Not my day," I said. "And I don't look forward much to evenings anymore."

She ignored that, kept her smile, and led me to the entrance. The senior center had a small lobby brightened by a skylight window, but the center itself was really just one big room with long tables now covered with white paper tablecloths. There was a kitchen behind it. The settings on the tables consisted of paper plates, paper cups, and plastic forks, spoons, and knives. To take away from the austere appearance, vases of fake colorful flowers were spaced along the tables. The walls had clean light brown paneling, and the floor was a dark brown Spanish title. The walls held plaques given out at senior events, pictures of presidents and governors, and pictures of philanthropic benefactors. Two women were putting jugs of water on the tables. They waved to Margaret and waited for us to enter.

"This is my neighbor, Grace Clark," Margaret said. "Grace, this is Sheila Bracken and Delores McMann."

Both wiped their hands on their aprons and held them

out at once. I greeted them both but kept my gaze on Sheila. I was expecting them to look uncomfortable, not knowing what to say, but neither lost her smile. Margaret apparently had given them firm orders that included "not a drop of sadness splashed on your face." I could hear her say it.

"Welcome to the feed," Delores said. "Just watch your hand if you put something on the table in front of one of our guests. Some of them are downright cannibals."

"Oh, it's not that bad," Margaret said. "Don't go turning her into a Nervous Nelly. She'll move so much on her toes that she'll look like she's in a ballet."

They both laughed.

"Irma and Mr. Packwood are in the kitchen," Delores said. She widened her big brown eyes and lifted her eyebrows, deepening the furrows in her forehead. "Someone forgot the napkins." She swung her eyes toward Sheila.

"No one told me in so many words," Sheila said in her defense.

"How many words does it take?" Delores retorted. "You know how we go through them. Anyway, I sent Mr. Huber out for a couple of cases. Mr. Huber looks after the building," she told me. "We do lunches five times a week, and every other weekend, we hold a dance with refreshments."

"A dance?"

"Slow," Sheila said. "Five steps a minute."

The two of them laughed.

"Blarney. I've seen a few of them tear up a rug," Margaret said. "How about Mr. Martin and that Mrs. Stern? She taught ballroom dancing, you know."

"I thought she might have done that," Sheila said.

"Well, let's get to it," Margaret said. "They'll be on us like locusts in two shakes of a rabbit's tail." She turned to me. "Whoever said older people have small appetites was either a hog himself or dumber than a doornail."

The other two women laughed, and then we all headed for the kitchen.

After I was introduced to Irma Kaplan and Simon Packwood, the head cook, Margaret announced that I made the best potato salad she had ever eaten, and that was quickly my assignment. Neither of them had much of a reaction to the mention of my name. I glanced at Margaret. She kept her *Mona Lisa* smile, but I could see that she was proud of the way everyone was heeding her warnings.

I was ambivalent about it. Even though it made things easier for me, I couldn't help being a little upset that anyone could put aside my tragedy as easily as they might a flat tire or a broken appliance. To stop thinking about it, I got busy quickly. Less than a half-hour later, the seniors began arriving. I could hear the chatter and the laughter, but I kept to working in the kitchen. I was hoping for an opportunity to speak with Sheila alone.

But that didn't come easily. Margaret had been right about how demanding the seniors were. As soon as we had the luncheon prepared, we were all out there serving and rushing around to get this or that. Someone wanted colder water, someone else asked for more macaroni and cheese, others wanted the bread that was on another table, someone else complained about her chair and needed another. I found most of them cheerful and appreciative, however, all the men giving me compliments when I was introduced to them. When there was a pause before dessert, the head of the center, a man named Carl Souter, began to speak, introducing officers and some benefactors who had attended.

Sheila retreated to the kitchen with Irma to prepare the desserts. I followed, and when I had the chance, I asked Sheila to tell me exactly what Laurie James had told her about her friend.

"Oh, you heard that story?" she asked in return.

"Of course. Where were you when Laurie told it to you?"

"We were at lunch in Century City, that fusion place."

She described the incident on the steps of the church exactly the way Margaret had described it to me.

"Who else heard the story?"

She listed the names of the other women. I knew one of them, Carla Shanley, but only because of her infamous sister, Alice Francis, a Sister of Mercy who had received an automatic excommunication because of her role in an abortion for a critically ill pregnant woman at the hospital in Nevada where she had worked for nearly twenty years. Sister Alice claimed that a nurse had merely laid her hands on the woman's stomach and she went into a spontaneous abortion. The church did not accept her story. It was the subject of debates at our church for a long time. John supported the church's decision, of course. Margaret felt sorry for Sister Alice.

"I imagine your daughter was bothered a lot by people looking for miracles," Sheila said. "That's what everyone at the table predicted, and everyone felt sorry for her. It can be quite traumatizing for a little girl like yours, although I must say, she didn't seem at all disturbed when I saw her."

"If any more of that was happening, I didn't know of it," I said. "I didn't even know about that time you've described."

She looked at me oddly. "We all feel so sorry for you and your husband. I know it's been so long. Is it hopeless?"

Suddenly, I felt a wave of nausea and was a little dizzy.

"I'll never accept that it is," I said, and walked out of the kitchen.

The speeches had just ended. Not everyone was staying for dessert. Margaret was helping a woman to her walker. I tapped her on the arm as soon as she was finished.

"I've got to go home," I said. "I'm sorry. I'm not feeling well."

"Oh. Well . . ." Helplessly, she looked around at all the work left to do.

"Don't worry. I can call a cab," I said. I took out my cell phone and started for the lobby.

"Oh, no, Grace. I'll take you home."

"It's not a problem, Margaret. Finish what you have to do here, please."

I kept walking. Less than ten minutes later, a taxi arrived at the front of the center, and I got in and gave the driver my address. When I got home, I went up to the bedroom to lie down. I thought about taking one of my pills, but thankfully, I fell asleep on my own and was awoken when the phone rang. It was nearly five.

"How are you doing?" John asked.

"Oh." I sat up, scrubbed my cheeks with my palms, looked at the clock, and said, "I fell asleep."

John laughed. "The seniors exhausted you? Margaret said that might happen."

"I guess," I said. "What are you doing?"

"Just getting a little rest and preparing to go to a dinner meeting. What are your plans for tonight?"

"Tonight? I have no plans, John. I'll just make something simple for myself. I have that new novel I want to start. It will be an early night."

"Okay. I'll call you sometime late in the morning tomorrow," he said. "You know how to reach me if you need me for anything."

"Yes."

"Oh, someone's buzzing. These guys are exhausting me with their questions. I swear, I don't know what they're teaching them in business schools these days. Call you tomorrow," he repeated, and hung up before I could respond.

I rose, soaked my face in cold water, and then went down to think about what I actually would eat. I hadn't had any lunch and did have an appetite. Almost everything I could think to prepare would be too much for one person. I ended up doing some eggs and cheese and onions in an omelet. Just as I sat down to eat, Margaret called to see how I was.

"I just needed some rest," I said. "I'm fine."

"Sheila told me what she told you. She was quite worried that she caused you to be upset."

"It had nothing to do with her. Please tell her so."

"Would you like me to come over and prepare something for you? I have a casserole that's way too much for me. That's the burden of being a widow and a good cook," she added.

"I've already made something for myself, thanks. Please, don't worry about me, and thank you for taking me today. I did enjoy doing something at the center. Most of the people were delightful."

"Good. Maybe you can go again."

"Maybe," I said with enough drift in my voice to indicate that I didn't want to commit to any specific day or date.

"Call me if you need anything, anytime."

"I will. Thanks, Margaret."

My parents called a few minutes later. It seemed that getting some food into myself was going to be a real task after all. My mother went on and on, telling me one insignificant little detail after another about her and my father's day, just to fill a phone conversation and avoid asking or saying anything that would bring up Mary. When she was finished, my father got on. He did get me to laugh by describing an argument he'd had on the golf course with one of his regular foursome, a man name Charles Branson, whom he had caught cheating twice before.

"I told him he moves his balls better than any stud I know."

I could feel how my laugh comforted him. He asked about John and then became a little concerned when he learned that I was home alone for nearly three days.

"We could come to L.A.," he said.

"I'm fine. I'll call you if I need anything," I promised.

Especially since Mary's abduction, whenever I spoke to my parents, I found myself becoming a little girl not much older than Mary was. A child never really grows out of thinking of his or her parents as Mommy and Daddy. They might be more formal and think of them as Mother and Father or even a little less formal and think of them as Mom and Pop. When you're older and your friends hear you refer to your parents as Mommy and Daddy, they either smile because they do the same thing or ask, "Do you always call your parents that now?" Referring to your mother as Mommy if you're in your thirties, forties, and fifties might seem odd, I suppose, but I found some comfort in doing so. It was as if they were really still able to protect and care for me, when, in fact, it was becoming clearer and clearer that I was or soon would be protecting and caring for them.

Maybe I was wishing I was back to being a little girl at an age when the biggest worry I had was whether I could play with my dolls or my friends a little longer. Why do we want so much to get out of that warm and comfortable world of innocence in which responsibilities are so simple and world events so unimportant?

I once mentioned this thought to John, and he sat for a moment and thought seriously about it and then said that what I was asking was exactly the point of the story of Adam and Eve. "God originally created us to be children," he said. "We ruined it, and so we have the burden of adulthood and responsibility. We have the burden of winning back God's favor."

"I'd rather be Eve," I said.

He laughed. "Be careful what you wish for. She suffered from vanity and screwed it up."

I called him a chauvinist, and we both laughed, but that was back then. Now I wondered if I had screwed it up, if what was driving me toward Sam was not my need to feel like a woman but my vanity, my need to have someone else look upon me again as beautiful and desirable. I was full of contradictions. As I told Sam, John would quote Walt Whitman.

I finally finished eating and even had some coffee and a piece of a pie that Margaret had recently brought. Then I did try to start a novel, but my gaze would float off the page like the movable indicator on a Ouija board, leading me to the clock and the hour when Sam might call. Finally, just after nine, he did. I had been really afraid that he wouldn't call at all, so I practically lunged at the telephone.

"I could see you in the morning," he began after I said hello. "Do you really want to come over now?"

"I'm half out the door," I told him.

"All right. I'll wait for you in front. I'm almost there."

"You weren't going to call me, were you?"

"No," he said, "but I thought of . . ."

"What?"

"The desperation in your voice and the pure lust in my heart."

"Sounds like the perfect combination."

"For what?" he asked with a little laugh.

"The strength to face another day," I told him.

And I was off.

15

Transience

I followed Sam into the garage and took what was becoming my personal parking space.

The first words out of my mouth when he and I met at the elevator should have been, "What have you learned to help find Mary?"

Instead, neither of us spoke. We kissed, he took my hand, and in silence we got into the elevator. He put his arm around my shoulders and held me close to him as we rode up, and then, still without either of us speaking, he opened his condo front door and we entered together.

"I need a little after-dinner drink," he said, heading for the bar. "You?"

"Whatever you're having."

I took off my light blue leather jacket and dropped it on the sofa. Then I watched him prepare our drinks. He remained behind the bar. I sat on a bar stool and looked at him. He seemed to be avoiding looking at me and went right at his drink. I sipped mine.

"What is it, Sam?"

"This is going to bite us both in the ass," he said,

swinging his left arm as if the apartment was all he had meant.

"If that happens, I won't feel it. I don't feel much these days."

"Yeah, well, for now, at least, neither David nor any of his agents knows we're seeing each other like this."

"You're telling me the FBI is that oblivious? Not a good thing to tell someone who is so dependent on them to save her little girl." I finished my drink.

"Maybe I'm just good at hiding things."

I stared at him. He looked down and twirled his drink.

"Are you going to tell me anything about today, anything more?"

He looked at me as if he was making that decision right at the moment. Then he nodded. "The only reason I'm still in on what they're doing," he began, "is that my instincts about Mary's abduction were right in line with what they have been investigating. Over the past three years, five children, all about Mary's age, have been abducted in three Southwestern states—two in California, one in Arizona, and two in New Mexico. One of the children was a boy, so it's not just a girl thing."

He came around the bar to sit beside me, continuing, "As you can imagine, missing children are a major concern for the Bureau and local law-enforcement agencies everywhere because of how dramatic and traumatic it is not only for the parents who've lost these kids but also for parents who fear losing their own. Most of the abductions that occur every year are family abductions for a variety of reasons. Some are runaways, of course. The least number of missing children are classified as not family abductions. Statistically, that falls somewhere between three thousand and five thousand a year, which is still a big number. A serial abductor is always a fear." He reached for my hand.

"What happens to them? Are they the children being sold into Mexico?" I asked.

"Some for sure. Something like forty percent of these kids are sexually abused."

I gasped.

"I have no evidence, nor does the FBI, that sexual abuse is taking place in Mary's case or that it was the motivation for her abduction," he quickly added.

"But it could be?"

"Anything could be, but I told you that because I'm confident that where I've been heading in Mary's case— and apparently, along with what I've got and what I've done, not where they are heading—involves a different motivation."

"Where are we heading, then?"

He sat back. "A lightbulb went off when you mentioned that boy, Bradley Middleton, who suffered from acute lymphoblastic leukemia."

"Mary's supposedly miraculous cure of him," I said, nodding. "And the two others you now know about."

"Exactly. I keep up with all of our bulletins, maybe better than most, and I recalled reading about one of those other missing children in California. There was just a one-line reference to a story in the local newspaper about how she was thought to have miraculously cured a little boy who was suffering from the same illness. They had met only once at a playground, and immediately thereafter, the sick boy went into an unexplainable full recovery. Apparently, she had been involved in three other so-called miracle recoveries, one involving an older man with lung cancer, whom she again had met only once, another involving a teenage boy who had a brain tumor, and another with a teenage girl who had a serious ovarian tumor. In all of those cases, the disease and the tumors appeared to have evaporated soon after contact with her."

"Was that whom you saw today, the mother of that child?"

"And the father, yes. They told me about a woman who visited them after the fourth story had appeared in the newspaper. She wanted to see their daughter and speak with her. The parents saw no harm in it. I think they were basking in the glow of such a story about their child, maybe wanted it all to be true."

"The fools."

"Can't blame them. Most people are innocent and naïve when it comes to the evil that lurks around them."

"Adam and Eve."

"Pardon?"

"Nothing. Forget it. What about this woman?"

"I know she was not who she claimed to be. She claimed to be a reporter for a national religious newspaper. After I interviewed these parents and got a description of the woman, I called the newspaper, and they had no one by that name on their staff now or back then, ever, in fact."

I waited, my heart thumping. "What does that mean, Sam?"

"Well, I brought everything I had to our dinner meeting tonight. In three of the other missing-child cases, a woman fitting the same description and claiming similar credentials had appeared to see and speak with the children. They have cast a wide net, hoping to pick up on this woman, but she hasn't surfaced anywhere else. It's a little more difficult for a woman to disguise herself. No beards or mustaches, but hair color, different styles of clothing, maybe different makeup could go a long way. Of course, we can't discount that it might not have been a woman at all. That's happened, too. There are great female impersonators out there."

"No such woman came to see me or John. At least, not that I know of," I said.

"You hadn't mentioned her, so I assumed not."

"So, there's nothing concrete yet?"

"Nothing pointing us to a specific person or place, but we have concluded—and when I say we, I mean the FBI, of course, with me tagging along—that this, Mary's abduction, is part of a serial abduction narrowed down by the characteristics I described. I'm sorry," he said, taking my hand again. "We're not there, but we're closer."

"What if you get there too late?"

"We don't know exactly why they've been taken, Grace. We can't speculate on it ever being too late. It would make no sense for them to have taken such children and then to harm them, would it?"

"Yes, if my neighbor is right about what's out there."

"Margaret?"

I nodded.

"Meaning what?"

"Satan and his followers . . . they wouldn't want to see God working miracles through little angels."

"Somehow I don't think it's that," he said.

"Police instincts?"

"It's gotten me this far."

I took a deep breath. "I don't know how much longer I can go on like this. Today I decided to go with Margaret to the senior center to help with the luncheon. She thought I was going to distract myself and do a good deed."

"Why were you really going, then?"

"I knew that woman, Sheila Bracken, was a volunteer, too, and I wanted to hear from her directly about my Mary and this woman who had come to the church one Sunday, wanting Mary to touch her. John had never mentioned it. I'm sure he thought that it would be disturbing for me. If I had been there, I wouldn't have permitted it. Who knows what sort of emotional turmoil it could cause in a child?"

"Did Sheila tell you anything that you hadn't heard before?"

"No. Well, she told me that she'd talked about it at a luncheon."

"So, other people heard it and could spread the story?"

"Yes. She said they all predicted that people looking for miracles might bother us, bother Mary. One of the women, Carla Shanley, has a sister, a nun who was excommunicated for claiming that she didn't assist in an abortion but that the abortion was miraculously spontaneous. It was a well-publicized case, a national story."

"I don't recall it."

"Alice Francis. She was a Sister of Mercy nun. She worked in a Nevada hospital. Claimed the nurse she was with merely laid her hands on the woman. John and Margaret had a bit of a tiff over it. Margaret expressed some sympathy for Alice Francis, but John is relentless when it comes to his support of the church. Anyway, that's what I got from Sheila. It didn't make me happy to hear that they all predicted that Mary would be some sort of hope to desperate people."

Sam narrowed his eyes. "But from what you've been telling me, Mary didn't seem to be bothered. She was close to you, of course, but she never told you about the other little boy and the woman?"

"No. I suspect my husband told her not to tell me, even though he says he didn't. Now I wish he had not treated me as if I was so damn fragile."

He sat back thoughtfully.

"What?" I asked. Suddenly, it was more difficult to get words out of him.

"Yesterday, when you phoned, I had the sense that things were better between you two."

"I'm so confused," I said. I felt my throat closing, my eyes starting to soak in tears, tears that had always been hovering under my lids, threatening to appear. "I don't know what's right or wrong anymore. Yesterday John seemed like the sensible and caring person, and I came off like the insensitive, unappreciative, irrational one. It's difficult enough living with the guilt around Mary's abduction. I can't carry anything additional." I took another deep breath. My lungs felt as if they were filled with water, not air.

He nodded. "I understand."

"Good. I don't. For a while, I thought that maybe I could be more like John and assume my life again, sort of be seventy-five percent instead of zero. I tried and still try, but every time I do, I shudder, wake up, and have this heavy panic that it will lead to giving up on Mary. Does that make any sense to you?"

"Perfect sense. It's too soon to live like you've lost her for good anyway, Grace. Some of these missing children have been found after years."

"Years," I repeated. It was like trying to swallow a cup of sour milk.

Sam looked at his watch. "Isn't John going to call you tonight?"

"He did already. John doesn't call more than once when he's away. He's probably already asleep or preparing for his meetings tomorrow. Besides, if he didn't find me at home, he'd call my cell phone."

Sam shook his head.

"I know," I said. "It's going to bite us in the ass."

We looked at each other. Neither of us smiled.

"I don't want to be alone tonight," I said practically in a whisper.

"You're seducing me, Mrs. Clark," he kidded.

"I guess I'm not bad for someone out of practice."

"No, you're not bad at all," he said, and leaned forward to kiss me.

We slipped off the bar stools together and walked hand-in-hand into his bedroom. "I hope I'm not just any port in a storm," he said.

"Don't mention ships," I told him, and kissed him again.

Minutes later, both of us naked, I embraced him under his blanket and buried my face in his chest. He kissed my hair, stroked my shoulders, and kissed my neck, slowly moving down to my breasts and my stomach. I moaned softly and leaned back on the pillow.

Sex was rapidly becoming a respite, a time-out from my sorrow, my anxiety, and my anger. When he entered me, it was truly as if I could step out of not only my body but my entire life. The past and the present, even the future, evaporated. I was nameless, floating on the rhythm of the ecstasy being created between us. I didn't see him or hear him. It was like making love to a ghost, my orgasm sending me farther and farther away from myself, until I had drifted too far and cried out with a mixture of grand pleasure and fear. He tightened his embrace around me and whispered my name as if he knew I needed to hear it. Moments later, luxuriating in our comfortable exhaustion, we lay still and silent, as if we were both afraid that a single vowel or consonant, even too heavy a breath, would shatter the glow.

He brought my hand to his lips and kissed it. Then he put his arm around my shoulders and closed his eyes. I curled up against him. His body was harder than John's, more muscular and, dare I think, more manly. Strangely, I didn't feel guilty until I thought that. That, even more than my lovemaking, seemed to be more of a betrayal. It was as though I hadn't really committed adultery until I admitted to myself that I enjoyed Sam's body more than I enjoyed John's.

As I lay there drifting, I was struggling with the thought that I was really drawn to Sam for one reason. He was more determined than John to find our daughter. He was my hope, and for that, I would gladly sell my soul, which I knew was something John would truly believe I had already done. Every other reason for my being there was probably a rationalization, but I could live with that. In fact, it amazed me now how much I could live with after Mary's abduction. Nothing was off the table. The mother in me was that strong.

Of course, I knew that Sam had these thoughts, too. For a few moments, I considered all of this from his point of view. He was a good man, and a good man by definition couldn't help but feel guilty, feel he was simply taking advantage of me for his own pleasure. It struck me that neither he nor I would completely get over this possibility, ever.

We both fell asleep, but I knew that I had to get up very early and get back to my house. Sam knew it, too, and was up ahead of me. He was half dressed when I opened my eyes.

"I've got some coffee on. You want to shower?"

I looked at the clock and sat up quickly.

"No, I'll shower at home," I said. I reached for my clothes. "Margaret will be calling me in an hour or so to see how I am, and she'll go into a panic of some sort if I don't answer."

"And John?"

"He won't call early. He'll squeeze me in between a breakfast meeting and something else."

"I'll put some coffee in a hot cup. You can take it along. I don't want you driving in your sleep."

"Oh, I'm awake," I said, smiling. It took me only a minute to get my clothes on, but he was standing in the entryway with a cup of coffee anyway.

"You sure you're all right?"

"I'll be fine. Don't worry," I said. I took the coffee, kissed him on the cheek, and went to the door.

"Grace."

I turned and waited. I could see that whatever it was,

it was something he had agonized about. There was that look on his face, the look of someone who was struggling with his own tongue to formulate the words.

"What is it, Sam?"

"Can I ask you to do something without you asking me any questions why?"

"Probably not, but I'll make every effort."

"I'll promise to explain as soon as I can. Will that be good enough?"

"I guess it will have to be, otherwise I'll be on social security before I open this door."

He smiled. "Okay. I want you to call me when you get home. I want you to give me the address of that costume shop in Pomona and the numbers on that receipt you found."

"But what—"

He held up his hand. "Something occurred to me last night, and I want to follow up on it today. Trust me?"

I nodded.

"And when you call, no questions. Just give me the information."

"All right, Sam."

I walked out to the elevator. My heart was racing so hard and fast I thought I might faint in the hallway before the elevator door opened. I went down to my car, finished what I wanted of the coffee, and dropped it into a garbage bin in the garage. Then I got in and drove out.

The city was just coming to life, so the traffic was very light. It took me half the time to get home, and the first thing I did was go into John's office and get the receipt. Then I picked up the phone and called Sam. I gave him the information.

"When will I hear from you?" I asked.

"Soon. I promise," he said.

After I hung up, I went upstairs to shower and change. As I was on my way down, the phone rang. I rushed to it, thinking it might be Sam already with some information, but it was John.

"So," he began, "how was your night?"

It was always difficult for me to tell from the tone of John's voice what he really meant or what he was really thinking. He was like that with most people, however. It was a power he enjoyed, the power to keep from revealing himself unless he wanted to. Sometimes, when he was having fun at the expense of one of his friends at a dinner party or elsewhere, he would deliberately take a contrary position on an argument and seem perfectly believable. It wasn't until he had driven whoever it was to frustration that he would break a smile and admit that he was just teasing. Some believed him; some didn't. Everyone agreed that he would be a terrific poker player, although he hated gambling of any kind and wouldn't even play church bingo.

"Tired," I said.

"So, you didn't take a pill?"

"If I do, I still wake up tired, John."

"Okay. I might cut things short here and come home earlier than I expected tomorrow."

"Really?"

"I thought that would make you happy."

"Of course it does," I said.

"Right. I'll phone from the airport if that's what occurs. What are you doing today?"

"A little grocery shopping," I said. "Not much more."

"I gotta go. I see someone waving to me. The meeting's starting. Call you later," he said.

John was never one to say "I love you" at the end of a phone call, so I wasn't surprised not to hear it this morning. When he told me that he thought things said routinely lost their meaning because they were like words without passion, I hit back, reminding him of prayers recited mechanically in church.

"Not me," he countered. "I don't recite what I don't feel."

Maybe he was telling the truth. Who was I to deny that he always brought a devout passion to his church and his Bible? When he read his favorite psalm or any psalm, he read it so dramatically that anyone listening would hear how much he believed in the words he spoke.

Even though I, like any woman, needed and wanted to be cherished on an almost daily basis, I saw merit in what he was saying. Precious things lose their value when they become too abundant, too common. So be it with "I love you," I thought, and let it go. Now, however, it was something I desperately needed to hear. Why didn't he see that? Was it me, keeping that wall up between us?

I made some breakfast for myself and sat thinking about how I might spend the day.

The phone rang, and again I thought it might be Sam. It was Margaret. I tried not to sound disappointed, knowing that might bring her right over to mother me.

"How are you, dear?" she asked.

"I'm okay, Margaret. John might come home earlier tomorrow."

"That's good," she said. "Do you need anything? I'm going to the supermarket."

"I'm fine."

She hesitated and then asked, "Did I see you drive in this morning?"

"What are you doing, sitting by your living-room window all morning? You really are watching over me, Margaret. I asked you not to do that."

"I wasn't there to watch your comings and goings, dear. You know I like to look out at the street. Were you visiting your parents?"

"No, Margaret." I didn't add anything, and there was a brief silence.

"Oh, well, is there anything new about Mary?"

"Not yet."

She was obviously waiting to hear more.

"Thanks for calling, Margaret," I said. "I'll speak to you later."

"Yes." Her voice seemed to drift off before I hung up.

I did have to do some grocery shopping myself, but most of what Sam had told me the night before about missing children lingered in my thoughts. I went to my computer and sat reading up on various missing-children cases and then read about reported incidents of miraculous healing. It went from the ridiculous to the sublime, stories about people who were healed over the telephone, even over the Internet. There were people advertising their pamphlets guaranteed to teach someone how to heal through prayer, and of course, there were those selling miraculous objects, stones, jewels, and pieces of cloth worn by prophets. I realized that there was an entire industry for miracles out there, obviously a very profitable one.

If people were willing to pay so much for something

their every instinct should tell them was phony, what would they pay if they had evidence that it was not? There were pages and pages of testimonials made by people who were supposedly healed of their cancers, addictions, diseases, and even inherited malfunctions. Nothing was off the table when it came to miracles.

Something occurred to me, so I shut down my computer and went into John's office and turned on his. I knew how to check to see what he had in his bookmarks, the sites he had gone to and wanted to remember. Because of his penchant for facts and information, John was an expert when it came to surfing the Net. Almost everything I knew about computers I knew because of John's instruction.

He had so many sites bookmarked. Most of them had to do with business and Internet software, but not far down the list, there they were: some of the same sites I had gone to in order to read about miraculous healing. I tried to convince myself that this really shouldn't surprise me. Once a topic was raised in his presence, John ravished any information about it, whether it was political, social, or religious. He would never argue without detailed facts and references, which was why most people avoided arguing with him, especially if they wanted to hold on to their beliefs. It did them no good to try to attack the source of his information, either. He always had cross-references. In college, after all, he was a champion debater.

I shut down his computer and sat there thinking.

What was Sam pursuing now? What had come to his mind last night? Why was he so confident Mary wasn't in any physical danger?

The only way to keep myself from obsessing about it constantly was to busy myself with something else. I went grocery shopping and decided to go to a Whole Foods on Montana because I could prolong the day by walking the avenue first and looking in at the boutiques. I bought myself a frozen yogurt with fruit and cereal for lunch and then finally went into the grocery store and accumulated three full bags of groceries. After I got home and put everything away, I watched television to keep myself from agonizing about the investigation.

I didn't hear from Margaret all day. I think my tone of voice had shut her down for a while, and I was grateful for that. I knew she meant well, but I thought my dependence on other people was actually doing more to weaken me at a time when I needed to find new strength. I had no idea how I would go about it, but somehow, I told myself, I was going to get more active in the investigation and the search for Mary.

Then, as if the devil himself could listen in on my thoughts, the phone rang. I knew almost the instant I heard his voice that Sam was going to say something that would bring thunder and lightning right into my house.

"David Joseph has decided to call John in for a formal interrogation," he said.

"What? Why?"

"Because of what I've told him."

"What did you tell him?"

"What bothered me last night and has been troubling me ever since we met that day in the mall and went through how Mary disappeared from your side was why would a little girl so bright and so devoted to you let go of your hand and let herself be led away from you so easily? Why wouldn't she call to you?"

"And?"

"Not only from what you told me but from what I learned from others, she seemed too smart to be fooled by just someone dressed as Santa. Besides, why wouldn't she call to you to tell you Santa wanted her?"

"Yes. I suppose that was why I didn't put much credence in the idea, either, when it first surfaced."

"You were right not to," he said. "That was why we were thinking Santa might just be a diversion, but what if Mary recognized who the Santa was, and what if whoever it was put his fingers to his lips, indicating that she should be silent so they could both surprise you?"

"What are you telling me, Sam?"

"John wasn't just keeping a record for the company. He was the one who picked up the costume."

"But it could still have been for the company party. You said so yourself, right?" I asked with a note of desperation.

"No," he said. "The man who played Santa at the party already had his own costume. He's had it for years. This was the fourth time he played that role, because he's the president of John's company. That's when he gives out the Christmas bonuses."

"But then, why would John . . . why would he do that? She's our daughter."

"I'm working on that. It's why I have to speak to him."

"Oh."

"Look, there might very well be a perfectly innocent reason for it, but I'm not calling you just to tell you this."

"What else do you have, Sam?"

"That Sister Alice Francis you told me about, that so-called miraculous abortion that saved the woman's life . . ."

"Yes?"

"I looked up the story. Her picture in the papers . . ."

"Yes, what?"

"I faxed it to those people I interviewed yesterday. They said they think it was the same woman."

"Well, does the FBI know? Are they looking for her?"

"Yes, but so far, no result. She left the hospital and the area without any forwarding address."

"What about her sister, Carla Shanley? She might know where she is."

"I visited her about an hour ago. She hasn't heard from her in years. She said it was as if she disappeared off the face of the earth." He paused and then asked, "Did John ever mention her again or recently . . . anything?"

"No."

"You're sure?"

"Yes. Neither he nor Margaret ever discussed her or that case again."

"Okay, but there's another reason I called, Grace."

"What?

"What did you do with the receipt?"

"I put it back where it was."

"Good."

"Why?"

"For now, it might be better if John doesn't suspect that you gave me the information on that receipt."

16

Trust

What Sam was implying left me so cold that I felt as if I was moving into rigor mortis. I stood there for almost a full minute after he hung up and clung to the receiver like someone who was afraid to let go of a strap on a subway. The earth did seem to tremble under my feet, and I thought the room swayed. Shadows born out of the descending late-afternoon sun shoved the sunlight away from the windows, and the darkness unfurled like a shroud being cast over me. I heard a small gasp and realized it had come from me. Then I returned the phone to its cradle and stepped back, as if I thought it might leap off the wall and attack me.

It rang again, the sound slicing through my breasts and across my heart. Frozen, I let it ring and ring until the answering machine went on and I heard John's voice.

"Grace, where are you? I'll try your cell phone, but just in case, I'm on my way to the FBI office in L.A. I had to come home earlier than expected. I've been asked to answer some questions. You haven't been asked, or I'd have heard from you, right? Or would I? Bob Mercurio is meeting me there in about five minutes. Innocent people need lawyers more than guilty people these days. On second thought, I'm not going to call your cell phone, Grace. Why be repetitive? I think you already know all this. I think you have what we call insider information, don't you?"

I heard the click and then the dial tone before the answering machine went off. The panic that stung me exploded and fanned out through my body the way a crack in a windshield would fan out into a glass spider web. What did John know? More important, what had John done?

My first instinct was to call Sam, but what would I say, and how would I sound? I could feel that I was losing myself, falling into a frenzy. I fought it back and tried to think rationally—ironically, to think the way John would think. What was it Sam had asked? Had John ever spoken again about Sister Alice Francis? Not to me, I thought, but he certainly could have discussed her with Margaret. I would ask her, but first I thought I would look in John's office. This time, when I entered, I didn't feel any awe. It might be his temple, but it wasn't mine, not now. I went to his file cabinet and began to search. I didn't know what I was looking for, exactly, but John was so organized that it took me less than a minute to place my fingers on a file labeled "Sister Alice Francis." He had never told me he was keeping this file.

I took it out slowly and sat at his desk to open it. Inside were more news clippings, a theological debate printed in a religious newspaper, and more stories on so-called miraculous healing, some of which I had seen on the Internet. Almost lost between the pages of these documents was a slip of paper with what looked like a telephone number. I recognized the area code. It was outside of Phoenix. Whose number was it? Could it be hers?

I sat there for nearly an hour, reading all the information John had collected, hoping that something would provide a concrete lead about Mary's abduction and what exactly John was searching for. I kept returning to the Arizona phone number. Why was it here with these papers? Was this how to reach Sister Alice Francis? If I called her, would I spook her and drive Mary even further underground? But maybe if I did speak to her, I would learn something specific that would end this agony.

Before I could reach for the phone, it rang. This time, I wouldn't pretend not to be home. If it was John calling from the FBI office, I was determined to ask him why he kept the file and whose number it was.

It was Sam. He sounded like someone who had lost all he owned and loved. "Grace, I'm afraid I have some bad news."

"What is it?"

My whole body tightened like the body of someone who was about to be hit and hit hard with a belt or a whip. I could feel myself closing, my whole body turning into a fist. *Mary*, I thought. *Something terrible has happened to her*. Margaret was right. Satan was out there walking the earth.

"I just came out of a meeting with my chief. I have to leave the case. I'm on suspension," Sam said.

I felt both relief and terrible disappointment. "Why?"

"John's lawyer made a formal complaint about me and you. David Joseph at the FBI is very upset. My chief almost exploded in front of me. He was that angry. Everyone knows about us, and now it looks like I am deliberately trying to implicate John to further my relationship with you. It's a bite on the ass, all right. I'm sorry. This is all my fault. I should have known better."

"I had the feeling John knew about us. I could hear it in his voice when he left a message on the answering machine just a short while ago, telling me he was going into the FBI office. If he knew about us, why would he keep that to himself until now? How did he find out?"

"I don't know, Grace. I'm sorry. I don't know what to tell you. I'm not even supposed to make this phone call. I'm making it from the only pay phone I know nearby. That's how paranoid I've got to be and you've go to be. Maybe you should go visit your parents for a few days. It's a crazy world. People do crazy things. I'm not there to protect you."

"I can't believe John would be violent," I said.

"Everyone who is ever questioned about neighbors who went on a rampage says the same damn thing, Grace. If anything happened to you, I'd . . . I don't know what I'd do."

"I'm not thinking about myself right now, Sam. I searched John's office. He has a file on this Sister Alice Francis," I said. "News clippings, articles in religious digests, articles about miraculous healing. I've been sitting here reading it all, trying to find some clue. I did find a slip of paper with an Arizona phone number. Maybe it's hers. Maybe if you—"

"I can't do anything about it now. You'll have to call David Joseph. Any evidence I hand over or even mention could be discredited. There's a pretty obvious conflict of interest here. I mean, everything is now on the table, even that you . . ."

"Even that I what? Say it!"

"Even that you or you and I might have arranged your own daughter's kidnapping."

"What?"

"Maybe you're trying to frame John. Maybe I'm part of it. Don't you see?"

"This is insane."

"Of course it is, but I don't doubt some idiot will propose it as a possibility. I'm so sorry. I still think you should go stay with your parents for a while."

"I can't go to my parents'," I said. "I couldn't deal with their hysteria about it, and I would feel I was letting Mary down if I just went into hiding, Sam. I'm going to go over to see Margaret. She's been a rock of support for me. She'll be just as upset about all this."

"Just call David."

"You just said I could even be a suspect in my own daughter's kidnapping."

"No one has anything but conjecture."

"Conjecture? Tell me something, Sam. If they think everything you say and do is tainted because of our affair, why won't they think the same of me?"

"There's a better chance they'll believe you because you're her mother."

"So I go and have an affair with the detective investigating her disappearance and corrupt all the evidence? Some mother," I said dryly. "At the least, I'm sure they have a very bad impression of me."

"Grace, please."

"Okay. I'll get Margaret, and we'll call David Joseph.

She can explain more about this Sister Alice Francis thing."

"I wish I could be there with you. I'm sorry."

"Sam, if you say that one more time, I'll clobber you with the phone."

I thought he laughed. It might have been a sob, but I didn't wait to find out. I hung up and glanced at the slip of paper with the Arizona telephone number on it. Without hesitation now, I lifted the receiver and tapped it out. Almost immediately, the voice of a recorded operator came on stating that the number was no longer in service. No forwarding number had been left.

Frustrated and with the file in hand, I went out of the house and over to Margaret's. There was only a single lamp on in the living room, but I could see that the kitchen was well lit. I pressed the door buzzer and waited. She didn't come, but when I reached to press it again, I listened first. I could hear the recording of Latin hymns sung by monks. She loved playing them in the evening. I recognized one of her favorites, *Gloria in Excelsis Deo*. It begins with words that the angels sang when the birth of Christ was announced to shepherds in Luke 2:14. Margaret had explained it to both me and Mary so many times we could recognize and recite it at the drop of a hat.

I thought she was playing it rather loudly tonight and that was why she didn't hear the door buzzer, which wasn't very loud anyway. Her house was actually fifteen years older than ours, and as John was fond of telling her, it desperately needed to be renovated. Margaret would just laugh and say, "Just like you Americans. You want to renovate everything, especially your faces."

I recalled how that brought a particularly crimson blush to John's face. He was not a fan of any plastic surgery except for reconstruction after an accident or operation. Margaret was the only one he permitted to tease him, however.

I tried knocking and then walked around to see if I could get her attention through a window. She wasn't in the living room, and from what I could see, she wasn't in the kitchen, either. I saw that she had a pot on the stove and a setting on the table, but it didn't look as if the range was lit under the pot. I went directly to her back door. I didn't expect it to be unlocked, but to my surprise, it was. Margaret was too damn trusting, I thought, and then immediately thought, who was I to say that about anyone now?

"Margaret?" I called from the opened door. There was no response. Now that I was in the opened doorway, I realized that the music was very, very loud. I entered and closed the door behind me. "Margaret?"

The back door was right behind the kitchen. I realized that I hadn't been in Margaret's two-story house for some time now. She had tried to have John and me over for dinner a few times, but John always had some conflict, or I wasn't up to it. Relentless, she would simply bring her home-cooked meals over to us.

As I passed through her kitchen and into the short hallway that went by her small dining room to the living room and the stairway, I thought that John had been right about the house. It had a very tired, worn look. The rugs were thin, the molding nicked and stained, the wallpaper faded. Maybe with it in that condition, Margaret was reminded of her old home in Ireland.

"We don't fear old things and age like you Americans do," she would say. "A modern cooker isn't going to make your food taste better if the cook doesn't have a well-tried recipe, you know. How many Colonial homes get ripped down to make way for the chicken coops you call condos or what's that other word, projects?"

John would shake his head at her but usually not disagree too strongly.

I started up the stairway. The steps creaked, and I remembered her telling us that she liked them creaking so she could hear the devil if he dared to come up while she was asleep.

"Margaret?" I called as I ascended. *Damn, that music is loud.*

I paused in the hallway. Other than the flickering light that appeared to be coming from candles lit in the last room down, the hall and the other rooms were dark.

"Margaret?"

I stepped forward slowly.

Where was she?

When I reached the last room and turned in the doorway, I felt my heart bob under my breast like a yo-yo. Around a nine-by-twelve photograph of Mary in a gilded frame was a semicircle of burning white votive candles, the sort usually placed before statues of saints. But the large framed photograph at the center wasn't the only picture of Mary. There were a half-dozen on either side of the semicircle, all in frames and hung on the walls. Over a maple rocking chair lay Mary's dress, the light blue one she had worn the day she was abducted. It had a fringed white collar. Beside it was the ribbon she had worn in her hair, and at the foot of the chair was her pair of blue thong sandal shoes. I stood there mesmerized for a few moments and didn't even realize that the recording of the singing of the hymn had been turned off. Very slowly, I turned to look back down the hallway toward the stairs. Margaret stood there gazing at me.

"Margaret," I said, stepping forward, "where were you?"

"I was only in my bathroom, Grace, fixing my hair. It's time to pray."

"Pray?" I looked back into the room with the candles and Mary's pictures and clothes. "Why do you have Mary's things, the things she wore the day she disappeared? How could you have those? And all her pictures on the walls, the candles? You have it set up like a shrine."

"It is a shrine, Grace." She stepped toward me slowly. "I'm sorry. I told a little white lie when you asked me what I believed about our Mary. The miraculous work she's done was not just an episode or two of God's grace, Grace." She smiled. "You're so lucky to have that name, Grace."

"What white lie?"

"Mary *is* special. Mary's an angel, Grace. She has God's blessing to do good work on earth. She will heal many more people, bring health and happiness to so many more people. You shouldn't worry. She's safe."

"You have her clothes. You know where she is," I said, just realizing what she was saying and what it meant.

"She's in the lap and embrace of the Lord," Margaret replied, and stopped to look up. "Blessed be His name."

"It was you," I said, approaching her faster now. "You

were the one who beckoned to her at the mall that day. That's why she walked away without any fear. You pretended you were going to surprise me or something, didn't you? You led her down that escalator and . . . and to what, to whom?"

"To where she belongs, Grace. To where she can pray comfortably and be nurtured and protected like the blessed others."

Her angelically peaceful smile vanished and was quickly replaced by an expression of anger and disdain.

"She wouldn't reach her God-given powers in a home where her mother challenged the Word and her father tolerated it."

"John doesn't know what you've done," I said, coming to my second realization. I held up the file. "It's this woman, isn't it? But then, why . . . why did he research Sister Alice Francis?"

"Oh, I told him to do that. I tried to get him to see, but your John is such an analyst. He prays and believes in scripture, but he's skeptical, too. He doesn't think anything wonderful has happened since the crucifixion. His damn facts. I told him more than once that he was turning his back on God's good work." She nodded at the file. "Sister Alice knows. She brought that angelic woman to that poor young girl's bed that day and saved her. She has a gift, our Sister Alice. She can see who has the angelic light inside him or her. She knew Mary had it and needed her love and guidance so she could grow into the angel she was meant to be."

"How did she know? You told her about those other children?"

"Of course I did, and one day, she came to see her, too.

I arranged it, just a walk on the street with Sister Alice passing by, just a few words, a touch, and she knew. She knew I was right about Mary."

"Then you arranged for the kidnapping."

"Kidnapping isn't the right word. I delivered Mary to her. She was waiting for her in the mall parking lot. It was like Jesus finding his disciples. Remember? 'Come with me and be a fisher of men.' Only Sister Alice would softly say, 'Come with me and be a healer of men.'"

"Where did she take her?"

"To sanctuary, of course," Margaret said. "Come with me now, and we'll pray together." She nodded at the shrine of Mary that she had created. "You still might be saved, Grace."

She reached out for me. I pulled my arm away from her.

"What sanctuary? Where?"

She stood back, looking surprised at my outrage.

"You're out of your mind, Margaret. You've done a terrible thing, and you'll burn in hell for it."

"He sows weeds among the wheat," she said, now glaring at me angrily. "Matthew Thirteen."

"You're insane. Where is my daughter? Where is Mary?" I screamed and charged at her, seizing her by the shoulders and shaking her as hard as I could. She just smiled back at me. I threw her against the wall.

"You can't bring down the angelic."

"I'm calling the police, Margaret." I started away.

"You mean your lover?" she said. "No whoremonger, no unclean person hath an inheritance in the Kingdom of Christ and of God. Ephesians Five: Five."

I turned on her. "You told John this, didn't you? You've

not only been watching me constantly, you've been following me."

"I knew you didn't deserve Mary," she said. "And you want to have an angel returned to you to live within your home? We would never allow it."

"Mary is not an angel. She's a living, normal little girl. You can quote all the biblical text you want, but you're still nothing more than a kidnapper. You and . . ." I waved the file in her face. "This madwoman. We'll soon put an end to all the misery you've caused in God's name."

I started for the stairway again. There was just a slight turn, but out of the corner of my eye, I saw her start toward me and stepped to the side just as she lunged, her hands clenched. Her left fist struck my right shoulder but glanced off, and the force of her assault continued to carry her forward. I heard her scream as she tumbled head over heels, snapping her back sharply when she hit the bottom steps. For a moment, I just stood looking down at her in shock. Then I descended slowly. I heard her groan. She opened her eyes and looked up at me.

"Why didn't the God you serve stop your fall?" I asked.

Her eyelids fluttered and then closed.

"What's the matter? No biblical retort?"

I studied her for a moment. She didn't look as if she was breathing. I knelt down and felt for a pulse, but I couldn't find any. She looked as if she was still smiling. I pulled back in horror and then turned and hurried to the phone in the living room. My first phone call was to 911.

"There has been a very bad accident," I said, and gave the operator Margaret's address. I started to call Sam next but stopped. Instead, I dug into my purse and came up with David Joseph's card. As soon as someone answered, I gave my name and asked for him. I was told he was in the field and that they would contact him and he would get back to me.

"You've got to have him get back to me immediately!" I shouted into the phone. "I know who took my daughter!"

"Okay, Mrs. Clark," the agent said in placating tones. "I'll get to him as soon as I can. Are you home?"

He sounded so unimpressed. What, did the FBI think I was still trying to implicate my husband as part of a conspiracy with Sam?

"No, I'm . . . I'm next door. My neighbor, Margaret Sullivan, was part of this. She's had an accident on the stairway. I've called nine-one-one."

"An accident? Did you call the police?"

"I just said I called nine-one-one."

"Fine. Stay there. Someone will be there soon, I'm sure."

I went back to the stairway and looked at Margaret. Did she think she had died with the secret of Mary's whereabouts? Was that why she looked as if she was smiling? Maybe she had reason for her confidence. Sam was inaccessible, and the FBI would take their own good time about it because my affair with Sam had poisoned the well. All this while Mary was in the hands of some religious fanatic doing who knew what to her. I felt like pounding on Margaret's body until she was resurrected long enough to give me the information I needed to rescue my daughter.

Instead, I went mad in her house, tearing open drawers in the kitchen and sifting through anything and everything, looking for some clue. Then I went through everything I could find in the living room that might hold some answer—books, armoire drawers. There was nothing.

I heard the sirens and went to the front door just as the ambulance followed by two patrol cars pulled into the driveway and in front. The paramedics opened the ambulance and got out their gurney, and the policemen hurried to greet me.

"What do we have?"

"Margaret Sullivan. She took a bad tumble on her stairway. I think she's dead," I said as the paramedics rushed by me and gingerly approached Margaret's body. The first patrolman whipped out a notepad.

"What happened?"

"I'm Grace Clark. My daughter was kidnapped nearly a year ago—Mary Clark."

"Out of a mall," the second patrolman said. "I remember that case."

"Yes." I nodded toward Margaret. "She was part of it."

"This woman helped kidnap your daughter?" the first patrolman asked.

"Yes."

"Did you push her down the stairs?" the second patrolman asked quickly.

"No. She fell trying to push me down. Go on up. You'll see the insanity in the shrine she built to my daughter."

They looked at each other. Other patrolmen stepped up but didn't enter.

The paramedics looked toward us, and one shook his head while the other tried some CPR.

"This could be a murder scene," the second patrolman whispered to his companion.

"Get on the horn," he said. "Where do you live?" he asked me.

"Right next door. She babysat for my daughter often."

"Okay. Why don't we find a place for you to calm down?" he said, nodding toward the hallway. "An investigator will be here soon."

"The FBI will be here soon," I said. "I called them."

"Oh. Good."

"We have to search this house to see if we can find any address, someplace where they're keeping my Mary."

"Absolutely. Let's just take it a step at a time."

"Maybe if we go upstairs . . ."

"No, we don't want to disturb anything yet, ma'am."

"I didn't kill her. She tried to stop me from calling you. I was upstairs . . ."

"All right, all right. Let's just get you settled. Maybe a glass of water."

He guided me somewhat forcefully away from the scene at the stairway and toward the living room. The sight of it gave him pause. I had tossed everything, pillows, books, magazines.

"What happened here?"

"I was looking for anything that would tell me where my daughter is being held captive," I said.

He nodded. "Maybe we will sit in the kitchen, then," he said. When he looked at how I had torn apart the counter drawers, the papers, he paused again.

"Let's just wait outside," he said. He took me out of the house, past the other patrolmen who had arrived, and opened the rear door of his patrol car. "You can sit here in the meanwhile."

"No," I said. "I want to wait for Agent Joseph."

"I'll bring him right to you."

"I live right there," I said, nodding toward my house. "I can wait there."

"Afraid not, ma'am. Please," he said, nodding toward the inside of the patrol car. He tightened his grip on my upper arm.

"You don't understand what's happening here," I said, but I got into the car, and he closed the door. I sat for a moment watching them all, and then I dug into my purse and took out my cell phone.

"Sam," I said when he answered. "You've got to help me. I know who kidnapped Mary. It was Margaret. She was working with that Sister Alice Francis. Oh, you should see what she did in one of her rooms, the shrine she built to Mary. She has the dress and her shoes and the ribbon Mary wore that day."

"What?"

"She said terrible things to me, Sam. She is the one who told John about us. She had been following me, watching me. She said Mary was with Sister Alice Francis in some sanctuary."

"Okay. They'll get it out of her, then."

"No, they won't. Margaret's dead."

"Dead?"

"She tried to kill me on the stairway and fell herself."

"Jesus, Grace. I begged you just to call David."

I started to cry.

"They won't let me do anything there," he said. "If I came, it would only make matters worse. Did you ever call David?"

"Yes. They said they would give him the message."

"He'll be there."

"But as soon as Sister Alice Francis finds out about Margaret, she'll go on the run again."

"David will handle it right. He's aware of all that. You've got one of the most experienced agents on the case. Trust him."

I though about Margaret.

"I don't care about his experience. I don't trust anyone anymore, Sam," I said, feeling my tears harden on my cheeks. I took a deep breath and finished with something I regretted saying instantly after I had said it. "Even you."

I closed my cell phone and stared out at the scene being played before me. It looked like a Shakespearean dumb show, the mute mimicking of a tragedy, with me as the tragic character trying to keep the curtain from closing.

17

Harmony

There was a preliminary argument between David Joseph and his agents and the Los Angeles police department about who had jurisdiction of the crime scene. I had to wait on the sidelines for them to determine who would be the lead investigators and conduct the first interview with me. When I saw a vehicle pull up front with a photographer stepping out and a woman rushing around to join him, I went into a small panic. Margaret's death would make the late-night news.

"Easy," David Joseph told me. "We're on it."

He intercepted them and pulled them aside. Whatever he told them kept them back. The police photographers and the medical examiner were already inside. David Joseph had seen the shrine to Mary and wanted to be sure no one from the media would. The house itself was being roped off, yellow tape placed around the stairway and even the doorways of the kitchen and living room.

Now that David Joseph was able to tie what they saw to the kidnapping investigation, he established himself and the FBI as lead investigators and decided to take me over to my house.

"Where's my husband?" I asked.

"He was with his lawyer when I got the call."

"Did you tell him what has happened?"

"I rushed out. Someone in my office probably told them something about it by now. Let's go inside, Mrs. Clark."

An L.A. detective accompanied us, however. I sat on the sofa in the living room and recognized Special Agent Tracey Dickinson. For a few moments, it seemed as if no time had passed at all. I was right there again at the initial stakeout after Mary's abduction. Tracey brought me a glass of cold water, and just as I lifted it to my lips, John came into the house.

I looked up at him, my lips trembling so hard I didn't think I could utter a word. He looked from me to the FBI agents and the L.A. detective, and then, without any hesitation, he rushed to me, kneeling down in front of me to take my hand.

"It's all right," he said. "I'm here."

If there was really such a thing as a miracle, I felt it then. I could feel John's strength entering my body. The sense of protection and security I had enjoyed with him before Mary's abduction returned and with it that wall that had stood between us and all that had threatened our happiness and health.

My tears broke free. He dipped into his jacket and produced his handkerchief to wipe my cheeks, then rose to sit beside me.

"You don't have to say anything to anyone," John said. "We can wait for Bob or have him meet us wherever they decide to take us."

"No, it's all right. I have nothing to hide about it. I

don't want to waste any more time than necessary on this," I said after drinking some more water. "As soon as she finds out about Margaret's death, she'll pick up and disappear with my daughter."

"All right. Then just tell us exactly what happened, Mrs. Clark," David Joseph said.

"Did you strike her on the back of her head?" the L.A. detective asked instantly. David Joseph gave him a dirty look.

"What? No, of course not."

"The medical examiner found trauma at the back of her head. It could have happened from the fall, of course," David Joseph explained softly.

"I did grab her and shake her before she came at me on the stairway, and I threw her against the wall. Maybe she hit her head then. I can't remember. I was trying to get her to tell me where my daughter was."

"Why don't you listen to her first before you come to any stupid conclusions?" John told the detective.

"Take it easy," David Joseph said. He glared at the detective, who stepped back. "Please, go on, Mrs. Clark."

"When I entered that shrine she had built for Mary, I saw the dress, the shoes, and the ribbon Mary was wearing the day she was abducted. You all saw that room, all the pictures, the candles. What else do you need to know that Margaret was involved in the abduction?"

I looked from David Joseph to the L.A. detective. To an outsider, especially a professionally skeptical police detective, I supposed it could appear to be a case of a woman gone mad and, at the least, a case of manslaughter if that trauma on Margaret's head could in any way be tied to her fall on the stairs. I imagined they might consider that I pushed her anyway. Maybe they thought I was simply outraged by the sight of the shrine and the clothes.

David Joseph nodded. "Don't worry. They'll determine pretty quickly if the blow to the back of her head was from the fall or whatever and if it contributed at all to her death."

Was that supposed to make me feel better, or was it a veiled threat?

"Her death? Her fall? Why aren't we concentrating on Mary?"

"We will. We'll comb the house and see what we can find, and we'll keep this out of the news for as long as we can. Let's go back over how you came to go over there. What exactly happened?"

I looked up at them all again. The prospect of relating the events seemed suddenly daunting. A great and deep fatigue gripped my body. I could feel the room start to rock.

"Are we having an earthquake?" I asked with my eyes closed.

"What?"

"Maybe we should give her a chance to rest for a while," Tracey Dickinson said. "She's been through a helluva lot."

"You get your best information as close to the incident as possible," the L.A. detective said.

I opened my eyes to look at him. I could see no compassion in his face, no concern whatsoever about Mary. He looked annoyed, as a matter of fact. Perhaps his dinner had been interrupted.

"Are you a practicing idiot, or did you just naturally

become one?" John asked him. His face turned rosy. "Go search Margaret's house. Stop wasting time on her. Our daughter is with a mad religious fanatic, and other missing children might very well be, too. Do your job," he added sternly.

"I need to lie down," I said.

I started to get up. John rose first and took my arm. I paused when I stood and looked at the rest of them. No one looked very sympathetic.

"And she won't have anything else to say until she speaks with our attorney," John said.

The L.A. detective smirked.

David Joseph nodded. "Why don't we wait until morning, then?" he said. "We'll do what we can over at the other house in the meantime."

He nodded at the others, and they started out.

For a moment, the two of us stood there. John seemed to be wearing the same dazed expression I could feel on my own face.

"C'mon. Go up and lie down. It's a good idea. You've been through a horrible time," he said. He walked behind me up the stairway to our bedroom. When I sat on the bed, he asked if I wanted something.

"Tea? Maybe something stronger?"

"No. Thank you."

I stared up at him. Suddenly, as if he were a snowman caught in blazing sunshine, he started to crumble before my eyes. All of his face trembled, not just his lips. He sank softly to his knees and buried his head in my lap. The movement was so fast and so unexpected that I couldn't speak. I held my breath. I could feel his sobbing begin, and I placed my hand softly on his head.

"I'm sorry," he mumbled. He raised his teary eyes toward me. "It's all my fault, Grace. All my fault."

"No."

"Yes, it is. I missed so much that was happening because I didn't want to believe it, and when I realized it, I threw up a wall between us. I used my religious beliefs to keep from blaming myself. I drove you away from me by refusing to . . . to feel like a man, to cry like a man has to cry, to shake my fist at the sky and demand to know why us? I thought if I was my usual stone self, my efficient, tight-lipped, arrogant ass, I could somehow get you to stop mourning. It was wrong to ask you to do that. I know that now. I know it too late."

"It's not all your fault, John."

"Yes, it is. First, I should have seen through Margaret. I should have realized from some of the conversations we had that she had a fanatic streak running under her religious façade. I missed all the clues and put you in that dangerous place all by yourself. I should have been at your side."

"I'm sorry, John. I should have been stronger. I know how disappointed you must be."

"More in myself than in you. I know that other men might not think like this. Other men might just think of their own pride and how they have been hurt, but I know I had a lot to do with the path you chose. Is that where you want to go now?"

"No," I said. "I want to have Mary back and us back."

He nodded, took a deep breath, and rose.

"I'm not going to ask you to forgive me, John. I know you will. I have to forgive myself. Do you understand?"

He nodded. "Get some rest. I'm going to see what Bob

can do about helping us get through this quickly. I'll be in my office."

He walked out, not as firm and confident as always. He looked beaten, and I hated myself for seeing him that way. I lay back and closed my eyes. I was tired, emotionally exhausted, but I had to gather my wits. Everything had happened so quickly. I felt as if the very ground had been lifted from under my feet. Margaret Sullivan, of all people. I had thought she really loved us. It was too great a shock. The last few hours were a blur.

I fought back against sleep at first. What if some determined reporter got into the story despite David Joseph's assurances? I don't think I slept fifteen minutes. All I could think was that they were out there, worrying more about Margaret's death and whether it was an accident or manslaughter. They had already wasted too much time on me.

I rose and rinsed my face in cold water.

We have to do something, I thought. *We have to find some way to be part of this, to make things happen.* Without Sam's personal concern anymore, I was afraid we would fall through the cracks, that something else would come up. The search for Sister Alice Francis would end up on some lower agent's desk or, God forbid, in the hands of that L.A. detective.

I started down the stairs. Halfway down, I thought I heard John talking and moved to the doorway of his office. He was sitting there, holding one of his ships in a bottle and talking about it as if Mary was sitting on the floor beside him, listening in her inimitable patient and curious way that did make her very, very special. Watching and listening to him, I could feel myself softening, the love for him I had always had rising like blood pressure. He looked up when I entered.

"We'll get her back, John," I said. "I know we will."

He embraced me, and we stood there holding on to each other like two people about to say good-bye forever and ever. The ringing of the door buzzer sent us both out.

David Joseph was standing there alone.

"What?" I asked. I seized John's hand. I felt the ultimate fear rising to capture my heart and hold it hostage. They surely had learned that Mary was dead. He wore a funereal expression on his face.

"We've just been through a thorough review of Margaret Sullivan's telephone calls," he began. "She called a number in San Bernardino five times this past week alone. We tracked the address. I gave it to the local police, but no one is going to do anything until we get there."

"Where?" John asked.

David Joseph was silent.

"Look," John said. "We need to be there for her."

"I don't know. We're—"

"I lost her!" I screamed at him. "I've got to be there when she's found. Please!"

"It could be dangerous. We don't know what we'll find, even if she's there, and—"

"We're not worrying about ourselves right now."

"My God," John said. "You know what she's just been through. She practically solved the case herself, but you don't involve yourself in someone's death and not come out of it shattered, especially someone who was supposed to be like another grandmother to our daughter."

"I know. I know. That's precisely why I suggest you just wait here for us."

"We won't wait. The moment you leave, we'll follow you," I swore.

He paused, studied my face.

"I'm getting into our car, Grace," John said. "Meet me in the driveway."

"Okay," David Joseph said. "It's against my better judgment, but okay. I'll stop in front in a few moments."

I breathed relief.

John squeezed my hand softly and put his arm around my shoulders. "I'll get your jacket," he whispered.

I stood watching the cars in front of Margaret's house, still not trusting anyone, even the FBI.

John returned with my leather jacket and helped me get it on before putting on his own jacket. We stepped out and closed the door, then walked down the driveway.

"What if this is a wild-goose chase?" I asked.

"I think we'd both rather be on it than here. We've been here enough," he said, "waiting, hoping, and, yes, praying. It's time we were out there."

I smiled. *Why can't we hope still?*

David Joseph lived up to his promise and pulled up in front of our house. He had Agent Tracey Dickinson with him. I was glad there was another woman in the car. We got into the rear and started off into the night, two other cars behind us.

As we drove, David Joseph talked. "Now, listen. If we're lucky and this is where she is," he began, "you should understand that when missing children are found after this length of time, they're not necessarily happy about it."

"What are you talking about?" I demanded.

"We don't know how she's been brainwashed, Mrs.

Clark. You know about Stockholm syndrome, the most famous case I can recall being Patty Hearst."

"Something about liking your captors?" John said.

"Exactly."

"Hostages feel adulation, have positive feelings toward the captors. It's irrational," John explained, taking over in his usual manner, right now a manner I really appreciated. "I read where the statistic is as high as twenty-seven percent of victims show some evidence of Stockholm syndrome."

"That's correct, Mr. Clark. It could really be a factor for someone as young as Mary, especially since she's been brought up with strong church influence, and this is all about religion. Also, look who delivered her to this situation, someone she had trusted and probably even loved. My guess is that some of those phone calls Margaret Sullivan made might have been to speak with her, comfort her, assure her that you and your husband were fine with the idea of her being with someone as holy as Sister Alice Francis. Who knows, right?"

I put my hands over my eyes to block out the thoughts he was putting in my head.

"That's why I am reluctant to see you confront her too soon. She probably has to go into some psychological counseling, even someone as young as she is."

"Her mental age is way above her chronological age," John said. "Mary won't have the usual reactions," he added confidently.

"Which might be all the worse, Mr. Clark. These aren't stupid people. People confuse fanatics with stupidity, but some of the smartest propaganda was created by Nazis. They'll use logic and reason, as well as faith, on her once they see how smart she is. Your daughter might seem like a stranger to you for a while. It will take time."

"We're quite aware of all that," John said. He held my hand to reassure me. "What do you think I've been doing this whole time? I've been reading up and studying and talking to people who are experts about this sort of situation. We'll be fine, Agent Joseph. Don't worry about us."

"Well, I worry about the child, too," David Joseph said.

"That's exactly why we insisted we go along," John countered.

It felt so good to have him at my side, my defender, our defender. I used to believe there was no problem, no difficulty, that John couldn't solve and overcome. I had lost that faith for a while, but it was coming back in spades.

"Okay, okay," David Joseph said, accelerating.

"If she is indeed there, Agent Joseph, do we have any idea how long she's been in this location?"

"No."

I looked ahead at the taillights of cars and the headlights of others. The darkness seemed to be unfolding as if God Himself was peeling it back for us.

"She was so close, really," I muttered loudly enough for everyone to hear.

"People, children, have been kidnapped and kept literally next door," Tracey Dickinson said. "Seriously. We had a case like that only two months ago."

"Well, I've got to hand it to you people for getting Margaret's phone records and sifting through them so quickly," John said.

"This case has never been relegated to some back burner, Mr. Clark."

"I can't say I was equally impressed with that L.A. detective you had alongside you in the house."

David Joseph laughed. "Sticky Bogner. I know him well. He got the nickname from the way he attaches himself to anyone else's investigation and somehow winds up with some credit, if not all of it. He's relentless, so if you need to solve something, he's good to have on the case."

"Someone must have told him he wasn't good enough to be a criminal investigator or something when he was a kid," Tracey added.

If I could have laughed, I would have, but every part of me was twisted tight in anticipation. Even my lungs hurt.

We drove on, speeding through the night like some missile homing in on its target. David Joseph used his GPS when we arrived in San Bernardino. Before he made another turn, he tried calling ahead.

"Anything?" he asked. He listened and then flipped the phone closed.

"They're just approaching the house," he said.

The turns he took following the GPS instructions eventually brought us to a side road that had no street lights. Looking ahead, we could see a half-dozen vehicles, two local San Bernardino police, and one ambulance.

"That's just a precaution," Tracey said quickly. We pulled behind the last vehicle.

The house itself was well off the road and built at the crest of a small rise. It looked like a very large Queen Anne, with spindle porch posts. It appeared to have three floors, the top floor perhaps a loft or an attic. There were lights on in practically every window. A half-dozen police officers and another half-dozen FBI agents from the San Bernardino area were in front and on the long porch.

We stopped and got out of the car.

"All right. You've got to stay back for now, Mr. and Mrs. Clark. I'll let you know as soon as I can. I promise," he said.

John and I got out of the car and watched them walk up the drive. What struck me and frightened me was the silence. Suddenly, we heard an engine start behind us and saw the ambulance move toward the driveway.

"Oh, my God," I said.

"Easy," John said. "We don't know if anyone was really hurt and, if anyone was, whether it was the people keeping the children or one of the children."

The paramedics got out of the ambulance and moved quickly into the house with a stretcher.

"I'm not waiting way out here, John," I said, and started up the driveway. John followed on my heels.

A figure stepped out of the shadows. It took me a moment to recognize and remember Special Agent Frommer, one of those who had been the first at our home after Mary's disappearance.

"Hold on, please," he said, putting up his hands.

"What's going on?" John demanded.

We all turned as the paramedics carried out a bald, stout man who seemed to be was dressed in a monk's robe. They brought him to the rear of the ambulance.

"Took four of our guys to bring that bastard down. Someone apparently broke his arm in the process. He was sort of the security."

"What about the children?" John asked.

"They're all inside. David's trying to make sense of it."

"We're going in," I said.

We continued toward the house.

"Whoa, horse," Frommer said, running ahead of us. "You can't go in there yet. It's not all clear."

John stepped up to him.

"It'll take more than all you have here to stop us," he said. He reached for my arm and continued walking toward the porch steps.

Every officer and agent turned as we started up. Tracey Dickinson stepped out.

"Our daughter," I said, moving forward. "Is our daughter one of the children in there?"

She took one look at me and stepped to the side without speaking. John followed me into the house. My heart wasn't just pounding. It was as if I had a closed fist under my breast trying to break out of my chest.

David Joseph was standing in the doorway of what looked like a small chapel. He turned when someone indicated that we were there and then came over quickly.

"Mary?" John asked.

"She's here; she's safe," he said. "There are four others. I've called social services and therapists."

"There is no therapist more important for my daughter than I am," I said.

"It's been a long time, Mrs. Clark."

"I don't need you to remind me," I said. I could feel John's body pressed against mine. We were like conjoined twins now, moving forward together, both of one heart, one determined purpose.

David Joseph looked at us as if he knew something we didn't and then took my hand. I glanced at John, who nodded toward the chapel doorway, and then we walked with David Joseph and entered.

There were two rows of five wooden folding chairs facing a large framed print of Christ on the cross. Just to the right of that was a lectern and what looked like a large Bible. The front of the lectern was draped in red velvet.

All five children sitting in the first row before the altar turned when we entered. For a moment, I didn't recognize Mary. Her hair was cut very short. She wore what looked like a cassock, as did all of the children. All of them had short hair. She rose slowly, but she didn't cry out for either of us, nor did she smile with any sign of relief. I held my breath. Were the warnings David Joseph had given us about to show their ugly faces? Would Mary resent that we had come?

"Mary!" I cried. I held out my open arms. I looked at John. He smiled.

"Mary!" he cried.

She stepped into the aisle and smiled as if she had finally recognized us. "Hello," she said. "We pray for people to visit us, people who need us."

People? Visit?

I couldn't speak. I just rushed forward and embraced her, covering her hair, her face, with kisses. When I paused, I looked over her shoulder and saw the four other children, three girls and a boy, staring at me. They looked desperate for a mother's kisses, the memory of something they had nearly lost. Without anyone telling them to do so, they approached and gathered around us. I had the urge to embrace them all, but suddenly, they began to recite what I knew to be the Miracle Prayer.

"Lord Jesus, I come before you just as I am. I am sorry

for all my sins. I repent of my sins. Please forgive me. In your name, I forgive all others for what they have done against me. I renounce Satan, the evil spirits, and all their works . . ."

Mary began to recite it, too.

"I give you my entire self, Lord Jesus, now and forever. I invite you into my life, Jesus. I accept you as my Lord, God, and Savior. Heal me, change me, strengthen me in body, soul, and spirit. Come . . ."

None of the police or agents near us said a word or tried to stop them. I held on to Mary and looked up at John. He saw the worry and desperation on my face. It was as if I thought these children could pull her away from me through their devotion.

He knelt down beside me and reached for Mary. Then he lifted her into his arms and stood. He nodded at me. We weren't going to wait for them to finish. They all sounded as if they were under hypnosis. In any other place, in any church, at any other time, people listening would smile and commend them, but to me and, I was sure now, to John, they all, including my Mary, sounded like a Greek chorus reciting over the dead.

When he turned her away from them, she continued to recite the prayer, even as he carried her out of the chapel. I was right behind them. We seemed to be fleeing with her in John's arms. Once we were out of the room, he lowered her to her feet and knelt to brush her short hair and touch her face. She didn't look at all frightened, and that frightened me.

"Do something!" I told him, cried to him.

"Mary, don't you know who we are? We've come to take you home. Do you understand? You should never have been brought here. Margaret did a very bad thing."

She looked as if she was sorry for us. I looked at John and then at David Joseph.

"You've really got to let us take her to be checked out physically first, Mrs. Clark, and give some time for her to visit with a therapist. Remember how long she's been in that woman's control."

"John!"

"He's right, Grace," John said.

Suddenly, as if she finally really realized who was holding her and who was with her, Mary screamed, "Daddy!"

John nodded. "Yes, honey. Yes. It's Mommy and Daddy. We're here now. You're safe again." He brushed her hair. The tears were streaming down his cheeks, cheeks that I once thought couldn't stand the touch of tears and would evaporate them on the spot.

I knelt beside them, and we huddled, both of us surrounding Mary with our arms and our very souls. It seemed we would never let go, but I turned when I heard other people hurrying up the front steps and into the house. David Joseph began directing them into the chapel. An African-American woman who looked to be in her late thirties stopped next to us.

"This is Mr. and Mrs. Clark, one set of parents," David Joseph told her. "And their daughter, Mary."

John and I stood, each of us holding one of Mary's hands.

"Hi. I'm Lois Western from Child Protection," she told us, and looked at Mary. "Hello, Mary."

"Hello," Mary said.

"I'm here to help you and the other children."

"No," Mary said without any tone of resistance. "We're here to help you."

I brought my closed fist to my mouth.

John reached for me. "It's all right," he said. "It will be all right. She just needs time to adjust."

There was that strength again, that wonderful damn self-confidence and self-assurance. I wanted to drown in it.

I looked at Mary, who was still holding my left hand. She smiled up at me.

"You'll have to go with this nice lady first, Mary, but we'll be right with you."

"It's all right, Mommy. I don't mind." She looked toward the doorway and then at John, as if she knew far more than anyone, especially us, anticipated. "Will you and Daddy be coming along?"

"Yes," I said. "We'll be coming along."

The other children began coming out of the chapel, escorted by other people from Child Protection.

"We have a vehicle right outside," Lois Western said.

I turned when I heard more activity in the direction of the stairway. Two police officers were bringing Sister Alice Francis down. She was dressed in a nun's frock, but she was in handcuffs. I felt like lunging at her and ripping out her throat to wipe away that damn arrogant smile she tossed at everyone as she descended. John sensed it and gripped my forearm a little tighter.

"Relax, Grace. She won't get off, no matter how good the lawyer," he said. "Don't worry."

"Yes, but wherever she's put, she'll see it as just another chapel. You can't punish someone like that."

"Then leave it to God," he said. He smiled. "I remember some other things from the Bible and recall something about Him not being happy about impersonators."

I nodded and thought, *Yes, yes.* John's eyes were opened wider, too.

Then I let go of Mary's hand so Lois Western could take her out of the house.

"C'mon," John said. "We have a lot to do yet to get her home."

We followed everyone out and paused on the porch. Out there beyond the freeway and the city lights, the stars were far more visible. I know it was just because of that, but I still told myself that they were far brighter than usual. Either the God that John claimed we could never fully understand had changed his mind, or He had nothing to do with any of this. I wasn't going to ask Him. I was going to wait for Him to tell me.

In the end, what difference did it make anyway, as long as the result was the same and you could find goodness and mercy, hope and happiness, still out there waiting like ripe fruit to be plucked and enjoyed?

As we descended the steps to follow our daughter in the direction of her own restoration and resurrection, I sensed that I was having one of my own. I did feel reborn, and, like someone saved, I looked back at the shell of myself that I was leaving behind. I was glad to leave it, not only because it was stained with sin and sorrow but also because it was really not me.

How many different ways do we follow to find our true selves, and how often do we take the time to rejoice once we do?

"We'll be fine, Grace," John whispered. "It's going to be fine. Don't worry."

I tightened my grip on his hand.

Maybe all Jesus meant when he said "I am the light of the world" was "Through me, you will see yourself, and you will know that if you make the effort, you will see that you're worth every beat of your heart. Maybe then you won't hurt the ones you love."

And really, what else was left for anyone, be he preacher or pope, rabbi or imam, to say?

Epilogue

～⚬～

If I were to be honest with myself, I would have to admit that for most of our time together and our marriage, I wanted to see John's faith shaken. I had a love/hate relationship with his strength and confidence. For most of our marriage, I was dependent on it, but I resented the dependence and so, perhaps unfairly, resented him. At least, that was one of the conclusions we reached in marriage counseling.

Despite everything, it still surprised me that John agreed to go to counseling, even though I knew he had problems with the concept of divorce. Many theological experts had real disagreements over what Jesus had said about it. My husband held with the strict interpretation that when Jesus responded to the Pharisees about divorce, he clearly stated, "What God hath joined together, let not man put asunder." In Matthew 19:9, it appears that sexual immorality is a reason for divorce, but John always held that it didn't mean that the marriage could be dissolved; it meant that the husband and wife could be separated but could never marry anyone else. Marriage was a holy sacrament, and that was that.

However, I could see that what he witnessed now in Margaret's betrayal of our daughter and Sister Alice

Francis's fanatic belief that God created angels not just out of the dead but also out of the living gave him pause. He had never accepted the idea that anyone but Christ could perform a miracle. He wasn't even that keen on saints, but accepted a saintly miracle with the understanding that it was usually a one-time event.

We learned later that Sister Alice Francis saw herself as being on a divine mission to ensure that whoever God had determined had the power to be angelic, especially to heal, should be protected and, essentially, trained. She saw herself as running a parochial school for angels. It was too risky to leave these chosen children with sinful parents who, first, would be skeptical of their divine powers and, second, would not nurture them as they should be nurtured.

All of this gave him great pause. I could almost feel his recalculations, his new doubts. It was as if he suddenly saw religion brought down by man and not vice versa. He had new eyes, and with them came fresh skepticism and, in a real sense, a deeper faith.

Of course, there was so much about this that I still didn't fully understand. Before John and I reconciled, I had coffee with Sam at a café in Brentwood. The FBI was wrapping up the details of the kidnappings, and one thing hovered out there and haunted me: the Santa Claus costume. I was afraid to ask John about it immediately, because that would bring my affair with Sam right to the forefront of our discussion.

Sam admitted that he had no explanation. "In our pursuit of the kidnapper, it was sort of what storytellers call a MacGuffin, something Alfred Hitchcock often employed in his films."

I shook my head. "I never heard of it."

"Yeah, well, I'm a big reader of detective stories and thrillers. Characters in the story get obsessed with something that might be a central focus in the beginning of a story but often is completely forgotten by the end."

"Like a red herring?"

"Yeah, something like that. There's some explanation for the Santa outfit, but whatever it is, it won't have anything to do with Mary's abduction."

Actually, I didn't have to ask John about it. He brought it up because his boss at work told him that Sam had asked about the Christmas party. He went into his office and opened one of his large file-cabinet drawers and showed me the costume.

"I was going to wear it on Christmas Eve," he said. "Just to do something fun with Mary."

I nearly broke out in tears. He shrugged and put it on his desk. "I had been out in Pomona with Tommy Marshall for a meeting and saw it in the window of this costume shop. He was going to return it for me. After her abduction, I forgot about it. I guess I'd better get it to him. Probably some fine is attached like for an overdue library book."

Whoever was wearing a Santa Claus outfit in the mall that day remained a mystery, or what Sam had called a MacGuffin. There was never any evidence to the contrary, and as Sam had learned by going through the other cases, even cases that were completely different, a Santa Claus outfit did not play a role in any.

Sam had been reinstated, but he was looking to move to San Diego.

"I think I need a fresh start," he said.

We were both silent, each nearly drowning in our own thoughts. When he looked up at me again, I knew that whatever he was going to say was going to sound like a permanent good-bye.

"You should know that I blame myself for what happened between us," he began.

"Don't treat me like your confessor," I said. It was cold, and I immediately regretted it. "Sorry. I guess I don't want to hear you say it. I don't want to feel that I brought unhappiness to someone else."

"You didn't bring unhappiness. You're a very special woman, Grace. The fact is, most, if not all, of my comrades in law enforcement would admit to wanting to do what I did. A few actually told me they were jealous and even congratulated me on having the balls to do it."

"It would take that," I said to lighten the moment.

He laughed but grew serious again quickly. "The bottom line is that I should have known better. I took advantage of you, and I'm sorry, but I'm not a hypocrite enough to tell you I didn't enjoy our time together. That's a half-ass apology."

"Works for me," I said. "And I'll never believe it was all your fault, Sam."

"Can your marriage survive?"

"Theologically speaking, it cannot die," I said, and he laughed again. "I don't know yet. I feel a lot of guilt myself when it comes to that. I tried to find anything and everything I could about John that would mitigate my own guilt, and I'm not going to be satisfied with just his forgiveness. As I told him, I've got to find a way to forgive myself."

"Yeah, well, don't be too hard on yourself. You were

betrayed by someone you had trusted with your daughter. That's a lot of trust to invest in anyone."

"What frightens me now and makes me wonder if I'll ever trust anyone again is the fact that Margaret was so good at hiding her religious insanity."

He shrugged. "There are a lot of religious fanatics hiding among us. Shall I remind you about terrorists? She was just a different kind. Anyway, don't think about all that now. Just give your time and your thoughts to your daughter."

"No worries there," I said. I looked at my watch. "In fact, I have to go. We have an appointment with her therapist."

He nodded. I stood up. There was no doubt that this was the final good-bye.

"Thanks, Sam. If your extra effort came about because of your attraction to me, I'm grateful it happened."

"I'd better get good and married," he said, smiling, "so if I'm helping someone as pretty and as nice as you in the future, I won't lose my perspective."

"They keep saying marriage is a sacrament," I replied, leaned over to kiss his cheek. Then I walked out without looking back once. As I drove away, I could feel him falling back into a memory that I would someday have trouble believing ever happened. At least, that was what I hoped.

Twenty minutes later, I joined John at Mary's therapist's office. Meg Thornton was an interesting woman in her early thirties who had studied in England and the States. I liked her, but I was also a bit put off by her professional excitement. I foresaw articles, if not a book, in her near future concerning Mary's case and the dramatic psychological effect of religious fanaticism on children. John wasn't concerned about it. In fact, he was quite intrigued with the whole thing.

"I think it's going to be a while, maybe years, before Mary will come to accept that what was done with her and to you and your husband was wrong," Meg said. "I hate to use the tired term *brainwashed*, but there are so many similarities to how other kidnapped victims and prisoners of war are treated. You'll have to have great patience. Certain words and actions will trigger automatic responses in her for some time."

"A child's version of *The Manchurian Candidate*?" John offered.

"Well." Meg smiled. She had striking gray-blue eyes and a very comforting smile that sat in her soft, plump cheeks. I liked the way she kept her apricot-brown hair pinned back and free-flowing down her neck at shoulder length. "I guess we can put it that way for simplicity's sake, but it's not that bad. At least, she wasn't being programmed to cause anyone any pain or harm. On the contrary, it was diametrically opposite. It's the view of herself that we have to adjust. As you know, she bonded with the other children, too, which was very clever. That way, they found companionship and were never permitted to see themselves as somehow too odd or freakish. There were others like them, special, chosen others."

"What about the way she acts and talks about Margaret Sullivan?" I asked.

"That won't change dramatically until her realizations about the entire affair change, Mrs. Clark. For now, it's difficult to get her to see beyond Margaret being called to be with God. Assignment of blame, guilt, and sin all will come in time."

"How can you be so sure of that?" John asked.

"You and your wife have provided her with a very stable environment. She loves and respects you both. After a while, you'll return to being the authority she most trusts and believes."

John looked at me. Neither of us had told Meg much about our own problems. I knew that John was wondering, as I was, if we could return Mary to that stable environment Meg had referred to. Perhaps more to ensure that it would happen than for any other reasons, we were both motivated to make our reconciliation successful.

At family dinners now, with my parents and John's father fawning over Mary and the two of us standing aside to watch, I felt more of the sorrow that I should have felt at John's mother's passing. She should have lived to see the reunion. When I told John that later, he nodded and turned away quickly. I knew he was fighting back tears, and I reached out for him.

"Even Superman cries," I said.

He turned back and smiled.

Days and weeks passed into months. Meg Thornton's predictions seemed to be coming true. We could both feel Mary's slow but sure return to herself as she was before the abduction. Once again, the two of us joined John in his office when he had finished a new ship and sat to listen to his passionate historical explanation of the ship. We smiled and clapped and hugged.

And then I saw a very interesting thing happening to John whenever he began to recite Psalm 23 before dinner.

Mary was just as attentive, but there was a little hesitation in John's voice, in his entire demeanor. It was as if he was afraid that returning to anything biblical, talking about God and religion, even attending church, might damage Mary's recovery.

I asked him about it eventually, and he said I was right. He was kind of gun-shy. "It's like anything. You love horseback riding or rowing, swimming, anything, but one day something nearly fatal happens when you're doing it, and you're always extra-cautious, extra-fearful. That woman poisoned those children with the Bible and prayer," he said bitterly.

"I guess we're all in some form of therapy, then," I said.

He studied me for a moment as if he was seeing me again for the first time. "I know you're waiting for it every day, Grace. We dance around it, but I'm not going to say anything about forgiveness," he said. "We both hurt each other in different ways. It comes with the territory. The main thing is, we're going through it together, I hope." He smiled. "I don't say it often. I don't say it enough. I'm a tight-ass sometimes."

"Sometimes?" I kidded.

"Yeah, well, I love you, Grace. I know I love you as much as any man can love any woman. I might even love you more than God intended a man to love a woman, and if that's sinful, then so be it."

There were no other words necessary.

We kissed and held each other. And then, one day, I awoke in the morning and realized with the instincts of a woman and a mother that I was pregnant. Later, my doctor confirmed it. Both John and I thought Mary was happier about it than we were. When she found out that I was having a boy, she began her make-believe conversations with him. She helped me set up the nursery and sat with John and me as we went through possible names. She surprised us both by suggesting Stuart.

"From *Stuart Little!*" she exclaimed.

John and I looked at each other, both thinking the same thing. She wasn't going to the Bible for a name. She was going to one of her favorite children's books. It was as if we were witnessing some sort of breakthrough.

"Absolutely," John said. "He'll be Stuart Clark." He looked at me. "We'll use your mother's maiden name for his middle name. Stuart Robinson Clark."

Mary clapped.

Was she really completely ours again?

Months later, we decided to have a Saturday afternoon at one of our favorite beach towns, Laguna Beach. After lunch, we walked along the beach. It was a magnificent day, not a cloud in the sky, with a calm breeze. There were young people everywhere, surfing, playing volleyball and racquetball games, and a few games of basketball on a nearby court.

But off to the right, almost hidden in a far corner, sat a mother and a young boy. They were having a little picnic. As we drew closer, we saw that the boy's right leg was in a metal brace. He was a thin, dark-brown-haired boy. Strands of hair danced around his forehead in the breeze, but he didn't brush them back. He stared ahead at the other young people frolicking and laughing. I could feel Mary's hand tighten around mine, and then, suddenly, she broke free and ran ahead.

"Mary!" I called.

She ignored me. John and I looked at each other and watched her.

She ran up to the boy in the leg brace and started to talk to him, and then she reached for his hand, and he, hesitant at first, gave his to her. She held it for a moment and then let go, turned, and ran back to us. I saw the boy's mother smiling at us.

"What did you do, Mary?" I asked. "What did you say to that little boy?"

"I told him not to be afraid. I told him he would be well again soon."

"Are you sure of that?" I asked her.

"Oh, yes," she said. "I'm very sure."

She saw another little boy lose his grip on his kite string. It started to drift off. His father rushed ahead and grasped it before the kite sank into the ocean. Mary turned to us and smiled.

"See?" she said.

In her eyes, fathers and mothers would always be there, would always save the moment somehow.

John and I looked at each other, and I'm sure we both thought the same thing.

Why not let her believe?

Forbidden Sister

Virginia Andrews

Now available from
Simon & Schuster

Turn the page for a preview
of the thrilling first installment
in a brand new series

Prologue

My mother wasn't supposed to have me. She wasn't supposed to get pregnant again.

Nearly nine years before I was born, she gave birth to my sister, Roxy. Her pregnancy with Roxy was very difficult, and when my mother's water broke and she was rushed to the hospital, Roxy resisted coming into the world. My mother says she fought being born. An emergency cesarean was conducted, and my mother nearly died. She fell into a coma for almost three days, and after she regained consciousness, the first thing her doctor told her was to never get pregnant again.

When I first heard and understood this story, I immediately thought that I must have been an accident. Why else would they have had another child after so many years had passed? She and Papa surely had agreed with the doctor that it was dangerous for her to get pregnant again. Mama could see that thought and concern in my face whenever we talked about it, and she always assured me that I wasn't a mistake.

"Your father wanted you even more than I did," she told me, but just thinking about it made me wonder about children who are planned and those who are not. Do parents treat children they didn't plan any differently from the way they treat the planned ones? Do they love them any less?

I know there are single mothers who give away their children immediately because they can't manage them or they don't want to begin a loving relationship they know will not last. Some don't want to set eyes on them. When their children find out that they were given away, do they think about the fact that their mothers really didn't want them to be born? How could they help but think about it? That certainly can't be helpful to their self-confidence.

Despite my mother's assurances, I couldn't help wondering. If I weren't planned, was my soul floating around somewhere minding its own business and then suddenly plucked out of a cloud of souls and ordered to get into my body as it was forming in Mama's womb? Was birth an even bigger surprise for unplanned babies? Maybe that was what really happened in Roxy's case. Maybe she wasn't planned, and that was why she resisted.

Wondering about myself always led me to wonder about Roxy. What sort of a shock was it for her when she first heard she was going to have a sister, after having been an only child all those years? She must have known Mama wasn't supposed to have me. Did she feel very special because of that? Did she see herself as their precious golden child, the only one Mama and Papa could have? And then, when Mama told her about her new pregnancy, did Roxy pout and sulk, thinking she would have to share our parents' attention and love?

Share her throne? Was she worried that she would have to help take care of me and that it would cut into her fun time? Although I didn't know how she felt about me for some time, from the little I remember about her, I had the impression that I was at least an inconvenience to her. Maybe my being born was the real reason Roxy became so rebellious.

My mother told me that my father believed her complications in giving birth to Roxy were God's first warning about her. However, despite her difficult birth, there was nothing physically wrong with Roxy. She began exceptionally beautiful and is to this day, but according to Mama, even when Roxy was an infant, she was headstrong and rebellious. She ate when she wanted to eat, no matter what my mother prepared for her or how she tried to get her to eat, and she slept when she wanted to sleep. Rocking her or singing to her didn't work. My mother told me my father would get into a rage about it. Finally, he insisted she take Roxy to the doctor. She did, but the doctor concluded that there was absolutely nothing wrong with Roxy. My father ordered her to find another doctor. The result was the same.

Roxy's tantrums continued until my mother finally gave in and slept when Roxy wanted to sleep. She even ate when Roxy wanted to eat, leaving my father to eat alone often.

"If I didn't eat with her, she wouldn't eat, or she'd take hours to do so," my mother said. "Your father thought she was being spiteful even when she was an infant."

According to how my mother described all this to me, Roxy's tantrums spread to everything she did and everything that was done with her or for her. My father complained to my mother that he couldn't pick Roxy up or kiss her unless she wanted him to do so at that moment. If he tried to do otherwise, she wailed and flailed about "like a fish out of water." My mother didn't disagree with that description. She said Roxy would even hold her breath and stiffen her body into stone until she got her way. Her face would turn pink and then crimson.

"As red as a polished apple! I had no doubt that she would die before she would give in or get what she wanted."

I was always told that fathers and daughters could have a special relationship, because daughters often see their fathers as perfect, and fathers see their daughters as little princesses. My mother assured me that nothing was farther from the truth when it came to Roxy and my father.

"*Mon dieu.* I swear sometimes your father would look at Roxy with such fire in his eyes that I thought he'd burn down the house," my mother said.

Although she was French, my mother was fluent in English as a child, and after years and years of living in America, she usually reverted to French with my father and me only when she became emotional or wanted to stress something. Of course, I learned to speak French because of her. She knew that teaching it to me when I was young was the best way to get me fluent in the language.

"Your sister would look right back at him defiantly and never flinch. He was always the first to give up, to look away. And if he ever spanked her or slapped her, she would never cry.

"Once, when she was fourteen and came home

after two o'clock in the morning when she wasn't even supposed to go out, he took his belt to her," my mother continued. "I had to pull him off her, practically claw his arm to get him to stop. You know how big your father's hands are and how powerful he can be, especially when he's very angry. Roxy didn't cry and never said a word. She simply went to her room as if she had walked right through him.

"She defied him continually, breaking every rule he set down, until he gave up and threw her out of the house. You were just six and really the ideal child in his eyes, *une enfant parfait*. Why waste his time on a hopeless cause, he would say, when he could spend his time and energy on you instead? He was always afraid she'd be a bad influence on you, contaminate you with her nasty and stubborn ways.

"Your sister didn't cry or beg to stay. She packed her bags, took the little savings she had, and went out into the world as if she had never expected to do anything different. She didn't even look to me to intercede on her behalf. I don't think she ever respected me as a woman or as her mother, because I wouldn't stand up to your father the way she would. Sometimes she wouldn't even let me touch her. The moment I put my hand out to stroke her hair or caress her face, she recoiled like a frightened bird.

"Maybe your father hoped she would finally learn a good lesson and return, begging him to let her back into our home and family and promising to behave. But if he did have that expectation, he was very good at keeping it secret. After she left, he avoided mentioning her name to me, and if I talked about her, he would get up and leave the room. If I did so at dinner, he would get up and go out to eat, and if I mentioned her when we were in bed, he would go out to the living room to sleep.

"So I gave up trying to change his mind. Sometimes I went out looking for her, taking you with me, but this is a very big city. Paris is a bigger city, but more people live here in New York. It was probably as difficult as looking for a needle in a haystack."

"Didn't you call the police, try to get her face on milk cartons or something?"

"Your father wouldn't hear of it for the first few months. Later, there were newspaper stories and a magazine article about lost girls, and your sister was featured. Nothing came of it. I used to go to other neighborhoods and walk and walk, hoping to come upon her, especially on her birthday, but it wasn't until five years later that your father revealed that he had seen her. He told me only because he thought it proved he was right to throw her out.

"He was at a dinner meeting with some of his associates at the investment bank. After it had ended, one of them told him he had a special after-dinner date. They walked out together, and a stretch limousine pulled up. The man winked at your father and went to the limousine. The chauffeur opened the door, and your father saw a very attractive and expensively dressed young woman inside the limousine. At first, he didn't recognize her, but after a few moments, he realized it was Roxy. He said she looked years older than she was and that she glared out at him with the same defiance he had seen in her face when she was only five.

"Later, he found out she was a high-priced call girl.

She even had a fancy name, Fleur du Coeur, which you know means 'Flower of the Heart.' That's how rich men would ask for her when they called the escort service.

"*Mon dieu, mon dieu!* It broke my heart to hear all of that, but I didn't cry in front of him."

Even now, talking about it brought tears to her eyes, however.

My mother told me more about Roxy after my father had passed away. I was devastated by my father's death, but now that he was no longer there to stop it, I wanted to hear as much as I could about my forbidden sister, the sister whose existence I could never acknowledge.

I had no trouble pretending I was an only child. Since the day Roxy had left, I was living that way anyway. My father had taken all of her pictures off the walls and shelves and dressers. He had burned most of them. Mama was able to hide a few, but anything else Roxy had left behind was dumped down the garbage chute. It was truly as if he thought he could erase all traces of her existence. He never even acknowledged her birthday. Looking at the calendar, he would do little more than blink.

He didn't know it, but I still had a charm bracelet Roxy had given me. It had a wonderful variety of charms that included the Eiffel Tower, a fan, a pair of dancing shoes, and a dream catcher. My mother's brother had given it to her when my parents and she were in France visiting, and she gave it to me. I never wore it in front of my father for fear that he would seize it and throw it away, too.

Of course, I could never mention her name in front of my father when he was alive, and I didn't dare ask him any questions about her. My mother was the one who told me almost all I knew about Roxy after she had left. She said that once my father had seen Roxy in the limousine, he had tried to learn more about her, despite himself. He found out that she lived in a fancy hotel on the East Side, the Hotel Beaux-Arts. I had overheard them talking about it. The Beaux-Arts was small but very expensive. Most of the rooms were suites and some were full apartments. My mother said that my father was impressed with how expensive it was.

"The way he spoke about her back then made me think that he was impressed with how much money she was making. Before I could even think he had softened his attitude about her, he added that she was nothing more than a high-priced prostitute," she said.

She didn't want to tell me all of this, but it was as if it had all been boiling inside her and she finally had the chance to get it out. I knew that she went off afterward to cry in private. I was conflicted about asking her questions because I saw how painful it was for her to tell these things to me. I rarely heard my parents speak about Roxy, and I knew I couldn't ask my mother any questions about her in front of Papa. If I did ask when he wasn't home, my mother would avoid answering or answer quickly, as if she expected the very walls would betray her and whisper to my father.

However, the questions were there like weeds, undaunted, invulnerable, and as defiant as Roxy.

What did she look like now?

What was her life really like?

Was she happy? Did she have everything she wanted?

Was she sad about losing her family?

Mostly, I wanted to know if she ever thought about me. It suddenly occurred to me one day that Roxy might have believed that my father risked my mother's life to have me just so he could ignore her. He was that disgusted with her. Surely, if Roxy thought that, she could have come to hate me.

Did she still hate me?

The answers were out there, just waiting for me. They taunted me and haunted me.

I had no doubt, however, that I would eventually get to know them.

What I wondered was, would I be sorry when I did get to know them?

Would they change my life?

And maybe most important of all, would I hate my sister as much as my father had?